Call it Fête

Lowri Charles

you're da best! ♡

lauri ♡

CONTENTS

To the people who step up when it isn't the plan. The step-parents, the god-parents, the uncles, aunts, and friends.

CONTENT WARNING

Although this is a light-hearted, cosy read, this book does touch upon content that might not be suitable for some readers. This includes off-page deaths, difficult family dynamics, homophobia, and fatphobia.

ONE

IT'S ALWAYS EASY TO find a parking space until you desperately need one.

I drive up and down the street three times before I give up and dump my lime-green rustbucket on the double yellow lines at the end of the road. A Chelsea tractor sneers at me from the edge of the dedicated parking bay. Judgey bastard. I stick two fingers up at it as I run across the road and into the playground, aiming for the red brick building of Beechmill Primary School.

The blue doors haven't seen a lick of paint since I last attended, and they slam into the walls when I fling them open. Of course, I'm late. I'm always fucking late. Ever since Rory was thrust, unexpectedly and completely against Mum's wishes, into my life, I've never made it to an appointment on time. I'm the worst parent ever. This meeting is important to him, and I've failed.

The school's old caretaker grumbles as I zip past him, muttering something about having just mopped there. I ignore him. Just like I ignore the smell of lunchtime's potato smileys and those slices of pizza that only school chefs can cook – thick and cardboard-like, but ambrosia to a small child.

In my desperation to leave work and get here, I've forgotten where to go. Each classroom I peer into is empty and dark, filled only with the ghosts of my childhood. My curses grow louder until I skid to a stop in front of the last room at the end of the longest corridor known to man.

The cold metal of the door handle bites into my hand as if to warn me off. Of course, it had to be this room. It's where I was sent when I was in serious trouble. Like the time I punched my brother and had to wait two hours for Mum and Dad to collect me. I was suspended for a week after that.

I take a deep breath then peer through the small, square window, the edges of my glasses bumping the wooden frame. Sure enough, a group of bored-looking adults perch on tiny chairs, their knees squashed under the equally small tables in front of them. My brother Josh, older than me by only eleven months, spots me and gives me a cheery wave. He doesn't bother to hide his smirk.

It's typical that he beat me here. Kiss-arse. He's always trying to make a good impression on the kids' teachers, as if it could undo the trauma we put the staff through. His attempts at being a better man come with the bonus of making me feel inadequate for doing the best I can. He often forgets there's only me; I don't have a partner to share the damn load.

A skeletal face pops into the window and I leap away from the door.

Holy shit.

It says a lot about the power of Agnes Palmer that she can still put the willies in me. She's aged a lot since the last time she kept me in for a lunchtime detention, and the extra lines marking her skin only make her more ghoul-like. She's slimmer than she used to be, her face more pinched, giving me a sharp reminder that she's *always* unimpressed. Especially with me.

She yanks open the door with amazing strength for such an old bat. "Alexander Webster. If you are done making googly eyes at your brother, perhaps you would like to join us?"

Her thin, over-plucked eyebrows raise at the shudder of my shoulders. Josh laughs, and I avoid eye contact with him *and* her, shuffling into the classroom with my gaze fixed on my battered trainers, trying my best to calm my racing pulse.

"Sorry, Agnes, uhm, I mean, Headmistress. Work ran late, and I hit every red light on my way over here. Traffic was awful. You know what it's like. Commuters use the village as a rat run and—"

"Yet everyone else managed to make it here on time. Find a spot so I can carry on explaining why I have brought you all here this afternoon."

With nowhere else to perch, I resort to leaning on the wall next to the door, ignoring the pinprick judginess from the rest of the Perfect Parent Club. They can piss off. I'll never be a member and that's fine with me. I don't want to belong to their stupid cult anyway.

"As I was saying before I was rudely interrupted, the end of term summer fête is in four weeks. In your pairs, I would like you to come up with an original idea for a stall. The goal is to raise as much money as possible so we can upgrade our old playground over the holiday. To make things more interesting for you, there is a prize for the parent-teacher duo who raises the most."

All of the parents in the room are holding on tightly to small slips of paper. One mum leans across to another to show her what's written there, smug and proud as if she's boasting about her firstborn. *Oh, fuck.* If Palmer has already paired everyone up, I might be left to put together a stall by myself. Or worse. I'll have to work with *her.*

I have to get out of here. I could push myself off the wall and sneak out when everyone is buddying up. There's no way I can work with Palmer. I'd be better off paired with Ol' Mop Head, who once threatened to hang me from my ankles after he caught me stealing rolls of toilet paper from his precious supply cupboard. I only wanted to wrap Josh up like a mummy, but Mop Head made it seem like I was cracking on with World War Three. I'd have been better off stealing some of his bleach than trying to lead a rebellion with the stupidly thin tracing paper they like to pass off as bog roll in this place.

Nobody will notice me walking out. At the end of the day, being a member of the Parent Teacher Association is a volunteer position. We're not getting paid for this. Winning a spa day at the big fancy manor in the next village over isn't worth the pain. I mean, sure, if I'm lucky, there'll be afternoon tea, but am I going to subject myself to working with the old witch for a couple of cucumber sandwiches and a scone?

I slide from my spot, ready to make an escape, when my gaze catches on a picture pinned to the wall. The title *Alex and Rory* is printed neatly by someone other than my child, but underneath it stand two stick figures around the same height. All right, pal. I'm short, but not *that* short. They're holding hands, and both figures have smiles that take up all of their pea-shaped heads. A big stomach is the only thing that identifies me as the adult.

Bollocks. My head is now full of Rory's disappointed face, his lower lip wobbling and tears filling his brilliant green eyes when I tell him I'm not taking part in the fête. I promised him I would do it. Stepping out now would make me the worst person in the world.

For whatever reason, my involvement in the PTA is important to him. So much so that he told my mum about it, which means she volunteered to do it instead of me. She doesn't trust me to do a good job, either. So, not only do I have my obligation to him, but there's a point to prove now. It's crucial I try to get on with Agnes Palmer if it'll mean nailing this summer fête shit.

If I was a lucky guy – and I'm not – there would be a backup teacher or a parent who didn't show up. Did I tell the school I was coming? I do the mental maths while Agnes continues her spiel, counting the parents and the staff, but a Sweaty Betty-clad mum paces the other side of the room, messing up my calculations. For fuck's sake, lady, stand still. I'll never be able to work out how much poop I'm in if you keep trying to get your step count up to whatever arbitrary number social media recommends this week.

After a few more attempts to add up the waiting parents and teachers, I give up. Maths was never my strong point.

Headmistress Palmer clears her throat. *Shit.*

"If you have any further questions, please come and find me. Otherwise, feel free to move the furniture around or locate a quiet corner of the school to work from. We have an hour until the caretaker has to lock up, so make good use of the time."

Chaos ensues. Parents and teachers weave around each other, trying to find their matches. There are a lot of hands shaking and awkward hellos, combined with the scraping of table legs as the groups carve out their own spaces. I hover near the wall, a lump in my throat, working up the courage to speak to the headmistress.

Come on, you can do this. I'm not nine anymore. Yes, I was late, but I'm also a grown-up. It's not like she can keep me inside so I miss my playtime. She's not Miss Trunchbull. It's like I tell Rory: it's better to rip the plaster off and get it over and done with.

I'm rubbish at following my own advice, though.

I skirt around the already working teams to her desk, where she has settled behind a mountain of textbooks. Just like when I was a kid, I keep a safe distance from her, stopping out of arm's reach. She was never violent, but TV shows back in the day told us it *could* happen. I wipe my sweaty palms on my jeans. "Uhm, Ms Palmer?"

"What is it, Webster?" She lifts her head from her work to fix me with a hard stare.

"I...I don't have a partner."

"Well, you were late, and you missed the allocation." She harrumphs and sets her pen on her desk, making a big show of looking around the room. "Ah, yes, Mr Jameson. He was supposed to be helping me but it won't hurt if you're partnered with him instead."

My insides freeze when my gaze follows her pointer finger. *Shit.* The only time I've properly spoken to Mr Jameson was at a parent-teacher conference which started badly and ended abysmally. I was late, something Mr Jameson tolerates as much as Agnes Palmer does. In my usual way, I got passionate talking about Rory and flung my hand out, spilling Mr Jameson's glass of water all over his notes *and* into his lap. Halfway through the meeting, he tried to give me feedback on what Rory could improve on. I argued. As if I believed he was the most perfect kid and couldn't do anything wrong.

Oh, but that's not all. Nope. All of that would be embarrassing enough, but once our meeting was over and Mr Jameson got up to shake my hand, I was so rattled that I took it and pulled him into a bear hug. Like a massive, arms right around him, head buried into his chest type of cuddle.

He mumbled his thanks, and we both parted with red cheeks. The shame often pops into my head when I least expect it, haunting my dreams every time I think about it. Which is often.

It didn't help that he's what I could only describe as a sexy librarian. As we spoke, he pulled his hand through his dark blond hair, never messing it up. The locks fell back into place. He was the perfect height for me to fit snugly under his chin. The brown cords and plaid shirt he wore were the epitome of clothes that could put kids at ease – inoffensive, almost boring, yet comforting – and although he wasn't massive, they fit tightly on his broad body. There wasn't an inch of belly fat straining over his belt. He was even wearing those glasses, the kind Clark Kent uses, and I have a kink for men who could be superheroes in disguise.

Did I mention he was nice? Friendly, while I was making a tit of myself. Ugh. It's no wonder I left the place with a crush.

Nope. This can't be my only option to win this thing. I take back everything I said about working with Palmer. Anything but gorgeous Mr Jameson.

Before I can decline, she's waving him over, and the pleasant look on his face – all soft eyes and big smiles – tells me he's better at forgetting things than I am. Or an expert at hiding his discomfort. I shift my weight, trying to avoid eye contact *and* survey the rest of his face for any indication that he remembers me.

He approaches like I'm a stranger. Jeez, I didn't think I was *that* forgettable. I arrange my face into an expression that doesn't look like I'm about to puke.

"Yes, Agnes, did you want me?"

"Thank you for joining us. There has been a change of plans, and you will be partnered with Alexander Webster. I presume you've met before?"

"At the parent-teacher conference last month." His grin grows wider. Gah. He does remember me, which means he can recall every stupid thing I did and is probably waiting for the best time to torture me about it. I have to find a hole to dig myself into. Quickly.

"Perfect. Good luck."

The headmistress returns to her pile of paperwork, leaving me to stare at Mr Jameson, the shame from our previous meeting crawling back into my cheeks. Even if he does recall all of it, even if he does feel ill every time he remembers how I threw my arms around his delightful back, my chubby dad bod pressing against the hard plains of his body, he may not do anything to torment me. He may be more professional than me.

I need to take a breath. Maybe working with him won't be that bad. He radiates a certain calm that tells me that if I were to fall and scrape my knee, he'd be right there to fix me up. It doesn't stop me from cringing, though. My head plays, rewinds, then plays again the moment I thought it was okay to manhandle him. We got on well enough, when I wasn't arguing with him. We even talked about the latest football scores. If I can pretend at least to be a normal person, then we may get along. I'd love to get to know him a little better, perhaps get a friend who isn't a brother. *It might even be nice to get him alone again.*

"Uhm." He clears his throat. "Yeah, I guess we could head to my classroom if you're looking for somewhere quiet."

Did I say that last bit out loud? He fiddles with his notepad. A grimace twists over his face and the pink on his cheeks has deepened to a crimson red.

Well, here we go again. Foot in Mouth Two: Back in the Habit.

Two

MR JAMESON TELLS ME he does his best thinking in his library and leads me straight there, presenting the cubby to me with his arms outstretched. "Tada!"

"Well, this is...nice."

It's not a library, that's for sure. Even calling it a reading nook is a stretch. Squished next to a cupboard full of carefully stacked arts and crafts supplies sit two rickety bookcases. I run my finger over the closest and snap my arm back as it wobbles precariously. How the fuck did the cases pass the health and safety checks? One puff of air, and both will come tumbling down. In comparison to the rest of the tidy room, the shelves are stuffed full of books, with piles overflowing in haphazard stacks on the floor next to them. Handwritten labels tell me Mr Jameson's favourite books, and which the kids should pick if they're in a certain mood. Happy, grumpy, jealous, sad – he has them all on cards in matching colours. Which book should I read for when I have a ridiculous crush on my kid's hot teacher?

It's cosy, at least. I help myself to a beanbag from the pile, letting it drop to the floor with a small *puft*. My knees pop and my spine protests as I ease myself into it. My body shouldn't be giving up – not at thirty-six. I should be lithe and keen to run around, but the creak of my bones reminds me of how inactive I've been recently.

I pick at the Play-Doh mushed into the grey carpet while Mr Jameson sits opposite me with practised ease. The lingering scent of dry-erase pens and disinfectant takes me back to a time when I could throw myself onto the floor and not have to consider how I was going to get up again. Not that I would have been caught dead hanging around anywhere like this.

"It was the best I could do with the limited resources the school gave me." He watches me closely, as if waiting for my approval.

"Maybe we should be fundraising for a proper library for the school, then?"

"A set of books that aren't dog-eared and falling apart would be nice. I usually end up scouring car boot sales for freebies and their condition isn't always great. Sometimes I miss working at the British Library. All those beautiful, fresh books..." He puffs out a small sigh, and his eyes turn glassy.

"The big smoke, 'eh? That's a change to East Beechmill."

"Yep."

I'm not sure why anyone would choose to come here over a big, vibrant city, but I don't push it. As much as I'm fascinated by him, I'm not going to dig for more information. I'm here for the fête, to show Rory and my mum I can commit to something and see it through.

"I guess we should talk about the stall then, Mr Jameson?"

"You can call me Nathaniel."

"And I'm Alex. But you already know that."

"Not Alexander, then?" He holds my gaze long enough to have my stomach squirming like fresh mud wriggling with worms. Help.

"No way. Unless I'm in trouble." Is that…am I flirting? I swallow hard and scramble to get my brain back on track. "Since you're a back-up, I guess you don't have any stall ideas?"

"Plenty, actually. I jotted some thoughts down in case they were needed." He grins as he flicks through his notepad. "How about bric-a-brac?"

"Oh, come on. Nobody wants to buy someone else's unwanted shit."

It's the wrong thing to say. He draws his lips into a tight line, making him look like Agnes.

"One man's trash is another's treasure," he bites, as if a bric-a-brac is the best idea in the world.

I hold my hands up in surrender. "All right. But what other ideas do you have?"

"A garden sale?"

No way. I freaking love gardening, but a sale of any type will only earn us pennies and won't win me the competition or prove that I could join the Perfect Parent Club – even though I don't want to join their cult. He *has* to have something better than that in his neat little book.

"People don't want to spend money on stuff they don't need. So no bottle sales, garden sales, stuffed toy sales."

"But kids—"

"Yeah, kids love it, but as a parent, I'm telling you nobody needs any more stuffies in their house. Or broken toys. Trust me on this. Cross any type of sale off your list."

"Fine." He does as he's told, his pen dragging lines over his ideas like a knife. "Since none of my ideas are good enough for you, why don't you tell me what you have?"

His gaze fixes on me, a little less friendly than it was. The stern look reminds me again of Agnes and its effect is like a cold shower. He must be her new protégé, learning how to make children *and* adults cower.

It's working. I can't admit that I have nothing, that I turned up to the PTA meeting late and unprepared. The threat of getting detention is back – although it'll be a lot easier with Nathaniel supervising me – the hour is ticking by, and I can't leave this place without some idea of what we're going to do.

I run my hand over my face. "I don't have anything. Honestly, I thought I was coming here to be told how I can help set up on the day, not that we'd be fucking running it."

"Really? Because in last week's newsletter—"

I scoff and immediately regret it. His eyebrows fly into his stupidly well-styled fringe. His pen taps on the edge of his notepad. Although he probably knows what I'm going to say next, he waits for the words to blurt out of my mouth.

And blurt they do.

"I don't have the time to read any newsletters. Between working fifty million shifts a week and single-handedly bringing up the world's most hyperactive six-year-old *and* trying to prove to my mother I am the best person for the job, I barely have time to read my emails, let alone every piece of paper he brings home." I don't add that I usually rely on Josh and his wife for anything important, especially related to the school. I'm extra pissed off that neither of them told me about the stalls so I could prepare. Probably kept it from me so Josh could win. Well, I'll show him.

"The newsletter is probably disintegrating at the bottom of Rory's bag with all its cousins and the twelve conkers he collected last autumn, since the only thing he empties from it is his lunchbox and sometimes his homework."

Nathaniel continues to stare at me, a muscle twitching in his jaw. He's probably heard all the excuses from all the parents and is getting tired of them. I don't blame him. Inadequacy – a familiar feeling – replaces my squirminess from earlier. He's the mirror image of my mother, and my need to please her, and him, spurs another round of word vomit.

"Look. All I know is Rory came barreling into the house last week, shouting about the summer fête and how I *had* to get involved. As soon as he mentioned his Uncle Josh would be there, my competitive side kicked in." I soften my face into the pleading look Rory often uses in an attempt to play to Nathaniel's softer, kid-loving side. "This is important to Rory, so I promised I would work hard at it. For fuck knows what reason, he wants this to go well."

It takes a moment, but the rigidity finally dissolves from Nathaniel's shoulders. "It is hard to resist him. He has those puppy dog eyes that make saying no impossible."

"Right? He's the bane of my life."

My quip drags a laugh out of him, and the icy air from my disregard of the newsletter melts. Okay, good. We're kind of on track again. I prise Nathaniel's notepad out of his hands, flip it to a new page then help myself to his pen. Across the middle, I scrawl STALL IDEAS then flick a load of random arrows out from it. Drawing so many is optimistic, but it's nice to have a goal.

"Back to business. What other ideas can we think of?"

He pushes his head closer to mine, and together we empty our brains onto the paper. None of the ideas are award-winning, but at least they're out there so we can sort through the weeds. Time moves quickly, and I pride myself on the fact I've concentrated purely on this and not the waft of his cologne filling my nostrils every time I take a breath.

Half-way through, he suggests face-painting.

"Yes!"

In my excitement at getting a half-decent idea, I throw my arms up in the air and my legs kick out. The pile of books next to my right foot totters and I hold my breath. They tumble to the floor, spreading out in front of us, and I can't help the curse that follows.

"It's okay. They've been threatening to fall over all term. I'm surprised they've lasted this long, to be honest." Our hands almost meet over a copy of *The Little Prince*, but at the last moment, I chicken out and focus on fishing out *James and The Giant Peach* from under the bookshelf. "Could have been worse. You could have kicked over my water."

My head shoots up, clunking against the shelves and threatening to knock more books onto the floor. "Yeah, sorry about that."

He shrugs. "The shirt needed a wash, anyway."

Once all the books are back in a pile safely away from me, we get back to work. I jot *face painting* under one of the arrows, then settle in for more idea hunting, losing track of time again.

"We should revisit the sponsored spelling bee," he tells me for the five-hundredth time.

The school bell rings before I can scoff at his suggestions. "Nah. We have better ideas on the list."

"Yeah, though we haven't got as far as I would have liked to. If only we had another hour."

That would be great, but we're out of damn time. Today, anyway. A spark is lighting somewhere in my tiny brain. We still have four weeks, and not having a concrete idea right now means I can have more time to talk with Nathaniel.

"Since the school is closing and I have to collect Rory from my parents', how about we take a couple of days and get together to chat?"

"Sure." His cheeks flush and his gaze moves to the floor. Well, isn't he cute? "I don't really go out. Marking and prep takes up all of my spare time nowadays."

His voice is more weary now, tired even, and a pang of sympathy tugs at my stomach. I could never be a teacher, not for all the money in the world. Who wants to take work home with them? Not me. It takes some effort, but I resist the urge to give him my thoughts. Mostly to protect how well we've worked together, and how we've moved past the awkwardness of our previous meeting.

"Here," I demand, holding my hand out, "pass me back your pad."

He does as he's told, though his head tilts to one side. For a teacher, he's not very bright. I scribble my number and thrust the notebook at him. My almost illegible scrawl takes up most of the page. He frowns at it for a moment before carefully tearing the page out of the book and folding it neatly. He stows it in his shirt pocket, patting the material as if reminding himself my number is there.

"My phone is in the staff room, so I'll text you later or something?"

"Sure. Don't feel like you have to get to it straight away." I hoist myself to my feet. Sitting on the floor was a bad idea. The beanbags are desperate to keep me with them, make me one of their own. I will not give in to them. I have a child to put to bed.

When Nathaniel pops onto his feet with less effort than me, I scowl. "Aren't you the same age as me? How do you get to be so agile?"

"It's the kids. I *have* to keep up with them, so I hit the gym every morning before work."

"*Every* morning?" I've never set foot in a gym, and the last time I ran for anything other than a bus or the ice cream van was in high school when I *had* to. "Then you do all your marking and shit in the evenings? Do you ever get time for yourself?"

He smiles. "I don't. I'm always tired." Chuckling, he adds, "Nah. Routine is key. If I didn't do it, I'd lose my mind."

"Mum keeps on saying the same thing to me. *Routine is important, Alexander*," I mimic, my voice a cruel imitation of her nagging.

"She sounds like a gem."

A grimace is all I can offer. Things between us are complicated, but I know she only has mine and Rory's best interests at heart. Most of the time. "Text me tonight, if you want. If you find time amongst all your school work and exercising. All I'll be doing is bingeing some inane boxset and falling asleep on the sofa before the final episode."

"All right."

He leads the way out of his classroom, and I can't resist taking a nose at the artwork on the walls. Each display has been put together with the same effort the curators of the National Gallery must use. The kids' scribbles, mostly of nothing, are proudly on show, next to typed-out explanations of the topics they've been working on, all presented in a rainbow of colours. The amount of dedication he's put into them is impressive. You can tell he's a new teacher.

We reach Agnes' classroom as the other parents and teachers spill out. Nathaniel turns to me. "The sooner we decide what we want to do, the sooner we can get to work and make it the best stall ever. For Rory, of course."

"Only for Rory. And not because we want to beat the other parents and teachers."

"Oh no. Especially not Josh Webster."

"*Especially* not my big brother."

I can't resist winking at Nathaniel. *What the fuck are you doing?* To balance out the flirty gesture, I stick my hand out for him to shake.

He takes a step away from me, frowning. *Fuck.*

"You're not going to hug me again, are you?"

Shit. Shit. Shit. All my hard work this evening *didn't* make him forget my weird behaviour at the conference. My palms grow clammy, and I'm about to pull my hand away when he takes hold of it, his eyes lighting up as he shakes hands with me. *Oh.* He can tease, too.

What a git.

"You know, it's mean to use me being an idiot against me."

"True. But I couldn't resist. The shock on your face was worth it."

Well, he's not only a git but an absolute wanker. And I'm grinning like a fool.

"Goodnight, Alex."

I watch him as he retreats from the classroom. Although I try to keep my eyes trained on his wonderful blond hair, my eyes drift to his backside more than once.

Bugger.

THREE

NATHANIEL'S PEACHY BACKSIDE NOW lives rent-free in my mind, distracting me as I cross the village to Mum and Dad's. It's only a short journey, but I'm lucky I don't get myself killed. I almost run a red light imagining how good it would feel to dig my fingers into Nathaniel's firm arse. *Concentrate, Alex.*

The sun is slowly sinking behind the woods nearby, painting the sky with lilacs and oranges, illuminating the leafy trees in gold. Dad used to invent stories about the faeries living in the copse, and with the beams shining past the darkened trunks, it's easy to believe in the magic. I should tell Rory some of those tales. I bet he'd love them.

His face is pressed against the front window when I pull onto the drive, the glass turning his nose up and flattening his forehead, but it doesn't hide his massive grin. A smear on the pane shows where his face has already been. Mum will go mad if she sees the mess he's making. As soon as my engine is off, I hurtle out of the car, trying to shoo him away. He presses harder, only moving when I reach the step.

The front door opens before I can try the handle, and a miniature Avenger throws himself at my legs.

"Hey, Thor." I flick the wings on the plastic helmet that perches on his head. "Where's Rory?"

"I *am* Rory, silly."

"Ah, my bad. You look so much like a Norse God, it's an easy mistake. Are you ready to go home?"

"Yeah."

I head inside to collect his belongings from where he's strewn them around the living room. There's a controlled untidiness in the house, with the eclectic furniture Mum and Dad have collected over the years, piles of shoes at the door and washing *always* waiting to go upstairs. It smells of dinner, like usual, and freshly cut grass, and I bite back a swear. Dad's way too old to drive the ride-on mower now. I told him to ask me and I'll do it. Parents never listen.

"Can't stop," I bellow. If I give Mum the chance, she'll be talking my ear off all evening. "It's almost bedtime. Thanks for having him."

She emerges from the kitchen in a cloud of steam, tossing a tea towel over her shoulder. Her brown curls are puffed out and frizzy, and her face is red. Although I inherited her build, it doesn't diminish the effect she has on a room. She's small but powerful.

"Oh. I assumed you'd be staying since it's a Friday and Rory doesn't have school tomorrow. Surely an extra hour won't hurt him?"

"We would, but Rory has—"

"Nonsense. Come on. I haven't had a good natter with you for a while, and Rory can do his homework on the kitchen table while you help me serve up. How did the PTA meeting go? Is casserole okay?"

It's a done deal, then. Me and Rory will be hanging around until she is ready to see us go home. A tiny voice in my head tells me to stand my ground, like the mid-thirties man I am, but she disappears before I can open my mouth to argue. The kitchen door swings shut behind her, so I follow, my shoulders slumping. This is *just* what I need.

"Did you do the TPA meeting?" Rory calls from the backseat of the car.

"You mean the PTA meeting? Yeah, I went. I told you I would."

"Are you going to do a good stall? Are you going to beat Uncle Josh?"

"I hope so. You'll never guess who I'm working with."

I spot his forehead crinkle in the rear view mirror. "Is it Mr Reynolds? No, wait...oh no! Did you get paired with Ms Palmer? She scares me."

"She scares me too, buddy. But it's not Mr Reynolds or Ms Palmer. One more guess."

"Mr Jameson?"

"The one and only."

He claps his hands. "He's my teacher."

"I know."

"I like him. Today, we got a story about Loki. He's Thor's brother. He's *loads* better than Mrs Boller."

"Mr Jameson or Loki?" Rory doesn't get the joke but I laugh anyway. "We have to come up with an idea for a stall at the fête."

"What's a feet?"

Maybe the kid isn't as into this competition as he first made out, especially if he's easily distracted about it. "Fuh-eight. It's a sort of fair. We'll hold it on the school yard, and there'll be music, food, and places where we can buy things. We're going to need a massive idea to win."

"I can help."

A look of concentration falls over his face, and I turn my attention to the road, letting the routine of the short journey to the house wash over me.

Once Rory is bathed and in bed, I stretch one glass of red wine over five episodes of a regency drama. Nathaniel doesn't send me his number, and I *don't* spend at least four episodes stewing over the reasons why.

Maybe it was the way I rubbished all his ideas or the fact I didn't read the stupid newsletter. Maybe he's mad because I *didn't* try to hug him, or maybe he got run over on the way home. Or he's busy having delightful sex all evening with his gorgeous partner, and he doesn't have the time to speak to me.

Whatever the reason is, the lack of a message tugs on my insecurities. Even in bed, my brain is busy reciting all the ways Mr Jameson must detest me.

It's not surprising that when I do fall asleep, my dreams are fucked.

The morning comes far too quickly, and I wake with a gasp. My whole body is overheated, and I check the bed to make sure I'm alone.

The other side of my mattress is empty, which is both a blessing and a curse, given how hard my cock is. It throbs with the ghost of what Dream Alex was doing before my stupid brain tore me away from it.

My head flops to my pillow and I squeeze my eyes shut in an attempt to cling onto the remaining tendrils. It started off normally enough. Something about Nathaniel. There was a big bag of money on Agnes' desk for us to steal, but Ol' Mop Head wouldn't let us pass the spot he was cleaning. All the while, Headmistress Palmer moaned about nobody coming to the fête. Which was my fault, apparently.

Maybe the before-bed cheese snack was a bad idea?

The dream felt real. Maybe that's what's creating the unease in my bones. The smell of furniture polish mingled with the reek of Mop Head's breath, like he'd tried to wash away the stale coffee and cigarette smoke with a bottle of Pledge. I swear I could hear the tap of my feet on the school's wooden flooring.

Don't get me started on how nice it was having Nathaniel touch me, even if it was only in a dream. The memory of his fingers runs over my arm and I shiver. I'm pretty sure Dream Nathaniel and Alex reached the money and celebrated in style. They must have had a great time, and my cock aches at something vague I can't claw back.

Dammit.

Without opening my eyes, I spit on my hand and ease my boxers down just enough to sort things out. Sure, it'll make looking at Nathaniel that much harder the next time I see him, but there's no way I can go about my daily business with a stiffy the size of a telegraph pole hindering my movements. It's indecent, dealing with my morning wood with fantasies fuelled by Rory's teacher, but I have to do something. My normal wank material – usually Chris Hemsworth – isn't going to cut it.

I stroke slowly, my imagination taking over from the remnants of my dream. Cream silk bed sheets, two pairs of glasses sitting on a side table next to half-drunk flutes of champagne. Nathaniel's brown corduroy trousers crumpled on the floor, the carpet unrecognisable but extravagantly thick when it squishes through my toes. Kisses, wet and hot, travelling down my neck, to my collarbone. Teeth on my nipple, pulling enough to make it tingle. I pinch it with my fingers, pulling on it in the way I hope he would. A groan sounds from somewhere, and I turn my head more into the pillow in case the noise escaped from me. The last thing I need is Rory disturbing this fantasy.

My balls tighten, the pressure almost unbearable and I stroke harder. My spare hand leaves my chest, tracing over my hip and I roll onto my side so my fingers can dig into the flesh of my backside. I pick up the pace, imagining it's Nathaniel's hand wrapped around my cock, pumping me into oblivion. I'm there. I'm so close, and I moan against the pillow, my hips thrusting to find purchase, find somewhere to drive into. I bet Nathaniel is warm and tight, a perfect fit for me.

The slam of a bedroom door and the thunder of footsteps pulls me from the edge of my orgasm. My body goes cold, despite the heat in my face. I yank my boxers up, roll further onto my side and pretend to snore, all the while willing my hard-on to deflate. Fast. My door flings open, and Rory throws himself onto my bed.

"Go away," I mumble. Although I won't be able to finish my wank now that he's awake, it would be nice to enjoy a few extra minutes in my dream world before I face reality. Rory won't allow it, though. He burrows closer. Nobody has told him about personal space yet. I guess that's something else I need to add to the list. Why don't they come fully trained?

"Don't you know what 'go away' means? What are they teaching you in school?"

He laughs. "I'm hungry."

"You know where the toaster is."

"Yeah, but I can't reach it."

I hear his pout before I feel his lips on my bare back, his drooling the last ingredient for quelling my passion. "Grow taller, then."

"I'm gonna sleep here," he tells me. "Your bed is sooo comfy."

Forcing my eyes open, I roll over to face him, almost squashing him in the process. He grins, his dark brown hair sticking out in all directions. He looks like me, the poor bugger, although he has a smattering of freckles across the bridge of his nose where I have none. The kid is short, but he's only six. There's loads of time for him to grow. The overwhelming urge to smush him blooms inside me, and I pull him into a cuddle, determined to enjoy how sleep-warm he is.

"You're not sleeping in here," I say, kissing his forehead. "You keep falling out of bed."

"No. I don't." His face is so serious, his little eyebrows curl together and his pout is back. In the moment, I'd give him every-thing I have in the world, even my bed, to wash away that look.

Still, I tease. "Yeah? Prove it."

"How?"

I shrug, trying not to smile. "I don't know, but until you do, you can't sleep in here. Sorry, I don't make the rules. What time is it?"

"The big hand is on the six and the little hand is on the seven." He peers over my shoulder at the old-style alarm clock sitting on my bedside table. No digital in this house, he has to learn properly.

"And that makes it?"

He thinks, but only for a moment. "Half-past seven."

"Great work. What time do we have to get to football?" I only get a blank stare in response so I ruffle his hair. "That's okay. You've already done a lot of thinking for so early in the morning. Football starts at nine."

"When the big hand points at twelve and the little one points at nine."

"Yes. You've got it. I think you might need some breakfast after all those thoughts."

"Can I have eggs *and* bacon?" His eyes light up. He's food motivated like me.

"Since you've been brilliant all week, I'll toss on a sausage, too. Can you get yourself dressed while I grab a shower?"

He pulls himself out of my grip. "I've been dressing myself for ages now."

"All right, off you go. It's your blue kit today. Make sure your boxers are the right way around."

"Yessir."

Despite Rory's initial eagerness to get out of bed, he drags his heels pulling on his trainers and climbing into the car, making us late for warm-ups. Aimee, Josh's wife, coaches the under-sevens team, and she stops helping one of the kids to watch our approach, her hands on her hips and a scowl on her sepia face.

"You're late," she shouts, loud enough for the Perfect Parent Club to hear.

"And you're grumpy." After helping Rory with his jumper, I give him a small push towards the rest of the team. "Don't piss your aunt off too much, will you? She always takes it out on me and Uncle Josh. Good luck, kid."

There's no enthusiasm. He trudges over the pitch and I sigh. He never enjoys playing, and has confessed a few times that he'd much prefer to sit on the sidelines with me to watch. I spoke to Mum about it, but she assured me it's good for him to play a team sport. He's so downtrodden now, though, his head ducked low, a stark contrast from this morning's happiness, and it sows more seeds of doubt.

His mood does brighten a little when he reaches his friends, and after giving him a thumbs-up, I wander along the sidelines to find Josh and the rest of his brood. We're a huge fucking family. Josh and my other two brothers are all married off with kids of their own. Don't tell the rest of them, but Josh is my favourite. We were in the same year in school and share a lot of the same friends. Plus, being the youngest means we're spoiled rotten. He was always cooler than me – still is – and I followed him around like a puppy dog.

His daughter and son sit with him on the halfway line, ready to cheer on Lottie, the youngest of the three. A sizable distance lingers between their camp chairs and their dad's. Ella has her head stuck in a book, a crown of springy curls bobbing over the edges of the pages, while James is glued to his handheld games console. Standard. Josh fishes a travel mug out of the carrier bag by his feet. I flick out my seat, plonk it next to him and take the offered cup.

The scent of freshly made coffee hits me straight away, pushing away the last of the sleepiness. He bought one of those fancy machines last year, and having free proper coffee has made being stuck in the park on Saturday mornings a lot easier. That, and the fact the weather has been unseasonably nice for a few weeks now. Caffeine doesn't help when you're stuck in the rain.

"Morning, family." I'm extra cheerful to annoy the kids. Ella lifts her head from her book to give me a small wave, but James doesn't grunt a single hi to me. "It's nice to see you, too."

"How did the rest of the PTA meeting go?" Of course, Josh wastes no time getting into it. No, how-are-yous, or nice-to-see-yous. Nope. There's no time for niceties if you're my brother. "You and Mr Jameson buggered off as soon as Palmer dismissed you, and we didn't see you for the rest of the evening."

The way he wriggles his eyebrow annoys me. It's clear what he's insinuating. I've been single for eighteen months, and if I so much as breathe next to another bloke, my brothers have us matched up and are planning the wedding.

"*Mr Jameson* is Rory and Lottie's teacher, mate, so please wipe that look off your face. All I want is to make the most money for the kids to have a better playground."

"I thought you said you were there to beat me to the prize? Wasn't that the only reason you signed up?"

"I signed up because Rory wanted me to. Beating you is a Brucey bonus. What are you and Heatherton doing?"

"I don't know." Josh fiddles with his cup. "The old guy is losing it. I mean, he was ancient when he was teaching us and that was thirty years ago. The meeting was fucking pointless. He muttered something about making school-themed cocktails and wandered off to ask Palmer if we have a liquor licence. He never returned."

"Ah man. I wish I could have seen her face."

"No drinking in the school grounds," he says in an awful imitation of Palmer's nasal drone.

"No beer before maths."

We burst into laughter and the kids divert their attention to glare at us.

"I'm going to let him get on with it, and collect stuff for a bottle raffle. Less effort for me when I'm inevitably stuck on my own. I'm busy enough without having to argue with the old codger over a summer fête."

"*You're* busy?"

"Oh, don't pull the *woe-is-Alex* card. You know that shit doesn't work with me. There are three kids and only two adults in my house. So I think we have it worse." He takes a sip of his coffee before continuing, "Is everything all right with you two, though?"

"Me and Rory? Yeah, we're fab."

We watch the teams scatter across the pitch. For today's game, East Beechmill Under-Sevens, or the Baby Beechers, are playing Aller Grove. The Grovers are the best team in Devon, so I don't have much hope we'll win. The Beechers look good, though, as they spread over the sunburned grass, kicking up dust clouds. Until Rory trips over an untied shoelace.

I clap along with the other parents. "Come on, Rory. Come on, Beechers," I yell across the pitch. Perhaps if he hears me cheering him on, his accident won't put him off. He can tie his own laces now, but I usually check before we leave the house. I'd hate it if my distractedness this morning put him off.

He takes a knee, his tongue poking out of his mouth. I keep on telling him if the wind changes, his face will get stuck like that, but he never falls for it. Once he's sure both boots are secure, he hurries to catch up with the rest of the team.

The referee blows his whistle, and the Beechers start off strong. I watch for a while, but as soon as I'm sure Rory is happy enough on the pitch, I sink into my seat and close my eyes, determined to enjoy a little of the morning sun which is already warming my skin. I can follow the game from the sounds of the kids shrieking, and the Perfect Parent Club bellowing at their minions to "*Get the ball.*"

My brother's gaze burns into the side of my head, but I ignore his waiting questions. It doesn't take him long to explode. "So will you be seeing Mr Jameson again?"

"Oh, fuck off, will you? I swear you're like a dog with a bone."

"Come on. I've seen that dopey look on your face a hundred times. You fancy him."

A smart retaliation doesn't come as quickly as I'd like. So, I scoff. "I barely know him. The only other time I saw him was at the parent-teacher conference a few months ago. I mean, he hasn't been at the school for a full year yet."

Josh scratches his head. "Oh yeah. He replaced Boller, didn't he? Poor dear never could handle naughty kids. I'm surprised she lasted as long as she did. Are you saying you've had a crush on Mr Jameson since the parent-teacher conference thing, then? Why didn't you tell me? I'm a great wingman."

"I don't need a wingman because I do not, and have never, fancied Mr Jameson."

"It's a shame you missed the open house a few weeks ago. He made an amazing curry, with rice and—"

"What open house?"

"You know. The other fundraising thing. All the dates were in the newsletter."

Right. From now on, I have to make sure I check Rory's bag for this blasted newsletter. Important shit is supposed to go on the fridge. Bloody hell. The list of things you need to keep track of when you're responsible for a tiny human is fucking endless. Why can't the school send a text? I'm good at those.

"Nat— Mr Jameson gave me a lecture about that stupid thing, so don't you start, too. Why don't you try helping instead?"

I sound like Rory when I try to feed him broccoli, but I can't help my whining. It's like there are a hundred barriers in place, preventing me from doing the best I can. The family doesn't always see that. They only notice the times I'm late, or the events I miss, and they never recognise that most of the time, Rory is a healthy and happy kid.

"Fine. I'll try and remember to text you the next time something's coming up. Okay?"

"Yeah. Cheers, mate." I shoot my brother an appreciative look and he nods.

"Tell you what, let me and Aimee take Rory tonight."

"Are you sure?"

I resist the random offers to babysit if I don't have anything planned because one, I don't want to take the piss; and two, if I'm desperate, I don't want anyone getting fed up with always having Rory.

"Of course. It's been a while, and we can return him tomorrow at Sunday lu— Aimee!" He jumps to his feet. "It's not half-time yet. How is one of the kids crying already?"

After making sure it's not Rory in tears, I take advantage of the break in play to check my phone. A message from an unknown number waits, and although I try to stay away from texting or scrolling if I'm with Rory, I can't resist the temptation.

> **Unknown:** Heya, it's Nathaniel. Rory's teacher. Sorry I didn't text yesterday. I was wiped out after a long day. I promised to send you my number, and here it is. Hope your evening was good and you have a nice weekend.

I save his number under Mr Jameson – I'm nothing but professional – and hammer out a response.

> **Me:** no worries at all :) not like i was staring at my phone all night

> **Mr Jameson:** Do you have any ideas yet?

Oh, he's impatient. It's not even ten o'clock, and he's already bugging me for answers. I picture him sitting at home in a modern-looking flat, tapping his foot the same way he rapped his pen on his notepad yesterday. Does he live in East Beechmill, or in one of the other villages? I'm not sure I'd be keen on living within a hundred miles of the kids I teach. Probably one of the many reasons I'm not a teacher.

I debate not texting again, leaving it a little longer until the game has finished, but the urge to reply is too strong.

> **Me:** nope

It's a good job I reread my message before I send it because, without context, it comes off as blunt. I always forget the tone is missed in messages. I think hard about what to add to make it seem friendlier, and okay, to impress Nathaniel a little. After all, we do have to work together for the next month. A smiley face doesn't feel enough.

And then it hits me.

> **Me:** dont worry if ur busy but Rory is staying at my brothers tonight fancy a takeaway at mine? my treat? we can work on our plan

A cheer rises around the pitch, bringing my attention back to the game. Lottie has scored the first goal of the match. I leap to my feet, only a little guilty about missing her goal. She scores all the time.

Rory is nowhere near the celebrating team and for a brief moment, I panic. I scour the field, finally spotting him having a natter with the goalkeeper at the other end of the pitch, completely oblivious to everything else. A side of me, the one I inherited from Mum, longs to shout at him to pay attention, but what's the point? If he's having fun, I'm not going to stop him. It's not like it's the World Cup.

The game carries on, but I don't hear from Nathaniel so I sour. By the end of the match, he hasn't replied, and now I'm the grumpiest Alex.

What the fuck was I thinking? It's such a bad idea to invite Rory's teacher over for a takeaway on the weekend. Or any day. He's probably got a loving partner, two or three perfect children, or a million friends he'd rather hang out with during his rare time off. In fact, he's probably sitting in a fancy cafe right now, eating brunch in a lemon-coloured polo shirt with a smarmy-looking wife in a posh dress. My message is displayed on his phone, and they're laughing at it while they sip stupid lattes and eat avocado on toast. There's no way I'm in his league – there's a permanent mud stain on my jeans, I'm chunky, and I *always* end up with food down my top.

The final whistle blows, and I'm surprised to see the Baby Beechers have won. When did that happen? *Fuck.* I hope Rory doesn't ask me any questions about the game or how well he did, or didn't, play. Not that he would. He's usually more interested in filling his stomach after a game. Like he is any other time, too.

I gather my stuff, and I'm about to head over to celebrate with everyone else when my phone buzzes in my pocket. My intestines tie themselves into a great big knot, but I pull the device out, preparing myself for the letdown.

> **Mr Jameson:** Takeaway sounds great. I've been craving Chinese for ages. Send me your details and I'll be there.

Yes! I almost drop my phone, but by the time Rory throws himself at my legs, I've replied with my address and a time for

Nathaniel to come over. At least I can blame my massive smile on the Beecher's win.

FOUR

THE DOORBELL RINGS AT bang on six. *Fuck.* I'm nowhere near ready for Nathaniel. Fresh out of the shower, and with a clean pair of shorts on, I've been pondering my wardrobe for the last ten minutes, trying to determine if a button-up shirt or a T-shirt is more appropriate for a *working dinner*.

I close my eyes and shove my hand into the wardrobe, rifling around until my fingers land on something. The hanger clatters on the rail, drowning out the second ring of the bell. I pull the top out, satisfied. Good job, blind me. An ancient Nirvana tee will show that I'm *chillaxed* but also a little trendy. Not that it matters. I'll look like a weed next to him.

I yank the top over my head and leave the room, racing down the stairs to the tune of the doorbell ringing again.

"All right, all right. I'm coming. Give me a chance." I tug open the door, pasting on the widest smile I can possibly muster. It grows more genuine when I lay eyes on him, although that could be the last of the summer sun he brings with him.

He's gone for a T-shirt, too – plain and dark grey – and he's swapped his school-friendly chinos for a pair of black jean shorts that are too tight to be real. How do his balls cope with the confinement? The denim is practically painted on. I swallow my murmur of appreciation. Oh, sweet Jesus, tonight is going to be hard. My shower wank earlier wasn't enough to help me survive the next few hours.

I know I should greet him with something nice, or at least with a simple hello, but all of my words are stuck in my dandelion-fluff mouth. So I stare at Nathaniel for a moment longer.

He's the first to break the silence. "Hey."

"Hey. Sorry it took me a while to answer the door. Only just got out of the shower."

"I can tell."

His eyes rake over my body, lingering on my still-wet hair before moving over my face, his gaze tickling my skin. If I'm not mistaken, his cheeks are pink, but maybe he legged it up the street to the front door. There are never any parking spaces on the road, and the taxis here hate dropping you off right outside for some unknown reason.

Or perhaps he walked across the village from wherever he lives. *Oops.* I didn't offer him a lift. That's not very chivalrous of me.

We stand like this for what feels like ages, both of us drinking our fill of each other. The silence isn't awkward. It's nice, like we have all the time in the world.

Eventually, he steps forward and reaches for my face. My heart stutters, but I angle my head to make it easier for him to cup my cheek. Minty-fresh breath hits my skin, and I pull in a mouthful of it. It's a natural reaction, one I have no hope in stopping. My eyes are wide, so I force them into something more sultry and sexy, although I probably end up looking like I have a tick. It doesn't put him off. Okay, Mr Jameson, this is a bit forward, but I'm not going to complain. I'm that touch-starved that we can fuck now and talk later if you want. I lick my lips.

"Oh," he says, breaking my stupor. I open my eyes more to see what the hold up is and spot his face growing redder. "You've got a bit—"

His fingers graze my cheek, but it's only a fleeting touch. The pad is soft over my skin, and I imagine it drifting down my neck, over my chest, and—

He wipes away a smudge of leftover shaving cream, his fingers rasping in the tidy stubble I left behind.

"Th–that will teach me to leave my room without checking my face." A bead of sweat trickles down my back. Because it's old, the house never gets properly warm, but suddenly it's as hot as the Sahara. "Although you being so punctual doesn't help."

He wipes his finger on his shorts, the white mark lewd until it melts away. "I know. It's one of my many flaws. My friends in London always encouraged me to be late, but it never worked. Once, they told me a party started half an hour later than it did, but with some diligent social media stalking, I managed to uncover their lies. At least it's not a bad flaw," he adds. "There are a lot worse things a person can be. Like a murderer, or a con artist."

"And are you either of those?"

"Not that I know of. Although there was one time in uni when I got a little too drunk and woke up with blood on my hands. To say I panicked would be an understatement. When I tried to get out of bed so I could give myself up to the authorities, I discovered deep cuts on both my legs. I needed stitches in the left one. Apparently I fell over a curb and my housemates didn't think to get help. They love retelling that story."

"Note to self, put the wine away."

I open the door wider for him, delighting in the way his arm brushes against mine as he enters the house. A delicious scent trails after him, more earthy and fresh than the pens and

Play-Doh from yesterday. He sits on the bottom of the stairs to untie his trainers – a pair of Converse, not the sensible shoes I expected from him – and places them neatly beside the jumble of mine and Rory's. That's the one thing I forgot to tidy up. I knew it was too good to be true when I finished cleaning the house with enough time for a wank.

My little terraced cottage isn't big, but I pride myself on it being homely. When me and my ex bought it, it was a mouldy shell of a building. It was so cheap, and Mum thought we would never be able to make it decent enough to live in. But we painted every inch of it, bought a ton of second-hand furniture, and even installed a new bathroom by ourselves. Okay, so we had a little help from my dad for the big stuff, but that was to make sure we didn't blow ourselves up. Now that Rory lives here too, I've tried hard to keep it a place he can always call home.

"Did you have a nice day?" Nathaniel perches on the edge of the sofa once I've led him the three steps to the living room.

"Yeah, not too bad. The Beechers won their game, so you'll hear all about that Monday. Then I took Rory to McDonalds. After I dropped him off for his sleepover, I got a few errands done and that's it."

"Where is he staying tonight?"

"At Josh's. Rory is close with Lottie, so he's super chuffed he's there and not with me."

"Oh, of course. Charlotte Webster belongs to your family, too. Are you like the mafia of East Beechmill?"

"You have no idea. Josh has another kid, Ella, in the year above Lottie and Rory, and one that moved to high school last year. I have a million other nieces and nephews, and all of them have been to Beechmill Primary." I rest on the opposite arm, neither of us willing to go for complete comfort. "How was your day?"

He runs his hand over his face. "Nowhere near as fun as yours. I had a pile of marking to get through."

So he *didn't* spend the day with his hot partner, laughing at my keenness between having lots of great sex. Of course, his admission doesn't give me enough to rule out a wife or a husband, but maybe if I ask more of the right questions, I can get to the bottom of it.

And then lure him into bed.

Shut up, horny brain. That's *not* why we're hanging out tonight.

I do my best to shove my indecent thoughts out of my head. "So this evening is the highlight of your day?"

"The whole weekend. I had so much work to do, I didn't get to enjoy the sun at all."

"Ah, man. It was gorgeous out."

"Yeah. My flat has the tiniest balcony and when I first moved here, I made the mistake of trying to mark out on it one afternoon. A gust of wind blew half of the kids' work away. Fortunately, at six they don't care much about their grades and most of their homework is to draw a picture or finish some spellings. It's not exactly going to make or break their career. I was distraught enough to never try again. It's a shame. I love being outside in the summer."

Nathaniel has put an opportunity for me to impress him right into my hands. Getting back to my feet, I gesture out of the living room. "Well, Mr Jameson. I'm about to make your day."

My living and dining rooms merge into one where the carpet changes from dark grey to the horrible paisley brown I can't afford to replace yet. At the end of the long room, though, past the scratched old table, is a set of French doors leading out to my pride and joy – my garden.

The sun is enjoying an encore before it turns in, painting the sky a deep pink. My flower beds – full of carefully chosen daylilies, peonies and coneflowers – wave in the light breeze. At this time of year, it'll be warm out there for a while longer.

"Why don't we sit outside to work for a couple of hours? At least you can say you managed to get a bit of sun. You never know when it's going to piss down."

"Mr Webster" – I shudder at the use of my surname – "how can I say no to that?"

He's already on his feet, hurrying to the hallway to pull his shoes back on. I don't bother with mine. If I could, I'd spend all my time barefoot, especially around the house. The paving slabs carving a path through the beds will protect my soles from the gravel, and I'm not too bothered about a bit of dirt.

"All right. I'm ready."

Nathaniel appears by my side. I lead him through the house, grabbing a bottle of wine, glasses and the menu for the only Chinese in the village. When we get outside, he gasps.

"It's stunning, Alex. Are you a trained gardener or something?"

"I fucking wish. When Rory came along, I had to pick a regular income. So it's just a hobby."

He sets off along the path and I take a seat at the rattan table to watch him. Every so often, he stops at a flower bed, leaning in to sniff at the buds or run his fingers over the green leaves of the bush next to it. The garden – the sole reason I *had* to have this house – winds around itself then down a small slope towards a brook that babbles lightly. It's easy to get lost in it, but his exclamations tell me exactly where he is.

"This lavender smells amazing. And it's full of bees."

The floral scent wafts towards me, twisting around the smoke from a barbecue a few houses down. His next stop will be the Japanese grass. I picked it because next door's cat likes to come over for breakfast and Rory loves watching her chow down on it.

"Isn't it great? Mum comes over once a week to help look after it. I did all the planting and sowing and shit. I really want to put a pergola or something out here, give us some shade so Rory can spend more time outside. He loves it. He's always digging in the beds for bugs. I make him put them back once he's worked out what they are. Otherwise, there'd be a small insect graveyard in his bedroom."

"He brings all manner of beasts in from the yard, too. You should see his face when I tell him to return them to where they belong. It's adorable. The kid is great."

Everyone loves Rory. He's a good wingman, even when he's not here. I must remember to stick another quid in his piggy bank for a job well done.

Nathaniel reappears next to the small hawthorn that used to live at my grandparents'. The sun illuminates him as he walks towards me, stopping to explore the deep pink – Mum's favourite colour – hydrangeas. The light sharpens his features, and from this angle, he looks like an old Hollywood heartthrob. If I wasn't already sitting, I would swoon.

Focus on the damn job at hand.

"Nathaniel. Wine." I hold out his glass, now filled half-way with my favourite red, to coax him to the table quicker.

It works.

After sinking into the chair opposite me, he takes a long sip and smacks his lips together. "Oh, this is good. I can't remember the last time I sat outside and enjoyed a drink with another adult."

"Do you drink often with the kids, then?"

He's like a cat. He reclines in his seat, throwing his head back and stretching out his limbs to bask in the last of the warmth. Being close to the man is going to drive me mental. I wiggle my toes in a sunbeam. It does feel good.

"Only the small ones. They're less likely to tell on me."

The saucy look he throws me triggers more of those squirming worms in my stomach. I swallow hard, fighting to regain my wits and fire a retort before he thinks I'm an idiot.

"Ah. I see." I stumble. "You're a comedian, are you?"

Yeah, that's not my best work.

"No. Not at all. Sometimes I can make the kids laugh, but their humour levels are basic. Their current favourite is, 'What's brown and sticky?'"

"Rory told me this one twenty times last week. It's a stick, right?"

"Got it in one."

I grimace. "That's an awful joke."

"Clearly I need to put more effort into it. I didn't need jokes in my old job."

"What brought you to East Beechmill, anyway?" I lean into the conversation. We have plenty of time to plot later. I want to learn more about this man I'm sharing a bottle of wine with. "Couldn't have been the opportunity to terrorise our kids with your shit jokes."

"I have a PGCE, and was all set to teach back where my parents are in Hertfordshire, but then a position came up at the British Library and I couldn't resist. Books are my jam, you know? Living in London was fun, and I was there for twelve years, but there were cutbacks and they let me go. So I started looking elsewhere. When this job popped up, it felt like a sign. Not that I believe in fate. But a small village school seemed right up my street after such a long time living amongst the hustle."

"Don't you miss your friends or your family? Or did the wife and five kids come with you?"

He laughs again, raising his eyebrows. Maybe he's onto me? Abort. Abort.

"It's only me here. And I do miss everyone, but they come to visit. It doesn't take long for me to catch the train to London if I want a taste of it. I love East Beechmill already, even though I've only been here for a couple of months. It's so quaint."

"Quaint is one word for it. Everybody knows everyone else's business and the traffic is shit, especially at this time of year because the whole of the UK would prefer to be at the seaside and we're right smack in the middle between the M5 and the coast." I roll my eyes. "It *is* steeped in history, so I guess it has that going for it. Did you know the village is listed in the Doomsday book?"

"No. Perhaps I should teach the class about it?"

"Definitely. Rory is obsessed with history, especially if he can link it to something about him. He's been begging me to start a family tree, but—"

I pause and pull my drink closer to me. Although I've enjoyed learning more about Nathaniel, I'm not sure I'm ready to explore my family's past.

He saves me from divulging. "I know I've already said it, but he is something special."

"Yeah?" I know I'm biased because Rory is mine, but I think he's the best out of all his cousins.

"We didn't get much time to talk about it at the conference the other month—"

My groan interrupts him. "That was the worst evening of my life."

"It was the *best*. Honestly, every time I tell my mates about it, they laugh so hard."

"Well, I'm glad *they* laugh about it, because I cry when I wake up in a cold sweat at three in the morning and shame scares away any hope of getting back to sleep." I take a sip of my wine, hoping the dark cherry will out-bitter the after taste of my fuck ups. He told his friends about me. What does that mean? I'd love to ask, but I'm not that brave. In fact, I'm a cowardly coward.

"Don't feel ashamed. It was awkward, but it was cute."

His cheeks turn pink again, matching the heat radiating from mine. Our eyes meet across the table and his grin eases me into my own. For a moment, the world slips away and it's only me and him. To an outsider, we must look like idiots, but I don't care. This is nice.

Then he continues, breaking the magic. "Yeah, so I didn't get to tell you at the conference, but Rory is heads above the rest of his class. But that's not what impresses me. He's creative, and comes up with the best ideas for stories. The other week, he told me a tale about a giraffe who got roller skates stuck on its feet. It was brilliant. The poor animal rolled around supermarkets, disrupted traffic, and travelled down street after street in her search for the cure. So imaginative. Give it a few more years and you could get him an agent and make a million from him."

My cheeks ache from the amount I'm smiling. "That's good to know. I'd love to give up work and live a life of luxury. It's always a battle to stand out in our family, so it's nice Rory has something that could carve out his own little niche, get him noticed."

"And what about you?" Nathaniel moves forward in his seat, toying with the stem of his glass and watching me with a burning intensity I've never seen from anyone. Nobody has ever paid me this much attention. Not even my ex. "What makes you special compared to your brothers?"

The question makes me squirm. I had a lot of goals and dreams for my life, but when Rory came barrelling into it, I had to put them aside and focus on him. My gaze shifts from Nathaniel's, searching for a way to redirect the conversation. When I clear my throat, I spot the menu I brought outside with me and slide it towards him.

"I'm starving, that's what I am. What do you fancy?"

He regards me for a moment, scratching at the bridge of his nose. His grey-green eyes feel like they might pierce right through to my soul. Eventually, he sighs and takes the offered menu. There's no missing his disappointment, though. Yeah, yeah, I know it's cowardly of me to avoid answering him, but if Nathaniel Jameson learns how boring I am, he'll be scared off before I can make him my friend.

"You're telling me that you had all afternoon to come up with an idea, even if it's more rubbish than what we put down yesterday, and you have *nothing* on your piece of paper?"

Nathaniel reclines in his seat, cradling his second glass of wine. After ordering dinner, he kicked off his shoes and curled up, managing to fold his tall body into the rattan chair without breaking it.

He hasn't revisited his earlier question, but, as the sun dips lower and our bottle of wine empties, our conversation has grown louder and more animated. There's only been two breaks – when our food turned up, and when he had to answer a quick call. After apologising profusely, because it was someone he *apparently* couldn't decline, our conversation picked straight back up, increasing in volume. It's fine. The neighbours on either side of me are old and deaf. Rory screams blue murder sometimes, and there are never any complaints.

"Look," I retaliate, "I'm not a teacher that only works nine 'till three every day."

He scoffs. "I don't leave when the kids do. And did I not just tell you I spent all of my *Saturday* marking?"

This is clearly an argument he has regularly and I have no hope in winning, but I continue poking at him anyway. Others may call it flirting, but I have zero skills there. Being single for eighteen months is proof of that.

"Well, I'm sorry my brain is empty, but my day was busy, too. I was lucky Josh offered to have Rory early enough for me to do a food shop while he wasn't with me. Every time I take him, he piles the trolley full of shit and I end up spending a fortune. It's freaking hard to say no to him. Then once I packed the food away, I made my house presentable. The last thing I need is you reporting me to Social Services for living in a toxic wasteland. Do you know how hard it is to keep a house tidy with a kid like Rory running around?"

Nathaniel's laugh fills the garden with noise and my belly with warmth. "I've seen the mess Rory makes around the classroom. He's a whirlwind. Especially on arts and crafts days. There's glitter everywhere."

"Oh, so that's your fault, is it? I keep finding the stuff in every nook and cranny."

"Mmm." He drains his glass. "Glitter is the gift that keeps on giving. I'll pull a book off the shelf and a pile of it pours from the pages. And don't get me started on what happened to poor Sammy the hamster. His poop was shiny for days."

I lift my head from the Chinese container I've been picking at. It's more to give me something to do with my hands. There's no way I can fit any more food in; we went overboard with how much we ordered. I'll be eating leftovers all next week.

"I have a bone to pick with you." I jab my chopsticks at him. "That bloody hamster. Rory adored having him stay with us when it was our turn, and now he's desperate for a pet. Although fuck knows how he got from hamster to dog, but as you said, he has a *great* imagination."

"You don't want a dog?"

"I'd love one. A big Labrador or something that can keep up with Rory. But with work, I can't. It wouldn't be fair to leave the poor thing alone all the time."

Nathaniel tops up our glasses, concentrating a little too hard on opening the second bottle. Once it's done, he pushes my drink towards me.

"What do you do? If you don't mind me asking?"

"I work in my brother's pub. Have done since I was sixteen, apart from a short break a couple of years ago when I—"

A flash of a dark body lying in a pool of blood invades my mind, as unexpected and disarming as the moment I came across it. The draw of my wine is longer this time, and I focus on the velvety way it caresses my tongue to return me to the garden, and back to talking to Nathaniel.

I swallow. "I was saving to start my own business as a gardener, but when Rory came along, I abandoned those plans. My brother, Simon, owns The Watering Hole on the outskirts of the village, and I've worked my way up from busboy. Now I'm in charge of marketing the place, including managing all the social media accounts. And I'm great with coming up with new concoctions with my stomach of steel. My job title should be Chief Tester."

A million questions burn behind Nathaniel's eyes, but he holds back from asking them. He must be happy to follow the conversation in the direction I'm taking it.

"I ate there on my first night in the village. Hands down, the best food in Devon, although I've not been anywhere else yet. The menu does have some strange combinations, though. There was a cheese and peanut butter toastie, chicken-loaded fries, *and* a strawberry and pineapple tart for dessert. I wouldn't put any of it together for a meal, but somehow, it worked."

"That toastie was one of my best ideas." I grin. Although I didn't expect to be there all my life, I'm as proud of the work I've done with the pub as I am with raising Rory by myself. "Me and Simon sometimes spend days working out new flavour combinations, and..."

This time when I trail off, the smile stays on my face. An idea runs smack into my brain, and I kick myself for how long it's taken me to come up with it. I grip the table. In response, Nathaniel frowns.

"What?"

"I've got it. The idea for the stall."

"What? What idea?" He unfolds himself quickly from the chair, and I find myself getting to my feet too.

"Do they ever serve food at these things?" I *should* know, on account of all the nieces and nephews that have passed through the school doors before Rory, but I haven't been to any of their fêtes.

"The local butcher brings a barbecue, but some of the parents were moaning that the food is never any good. And an ice cream van. Why?"

I reach across the table for the notepad we were scribbling over yesterday, flip it to a new page and add my idea. At any moment, it could leave my head and we'll be stuck at square one.

As I write, I talk. "I practically own the restaurant with Simon. What if I use my charm and persuade him to cater for the day?"

"I'd say you're a genius, but this is your actual job, Alex. This should have been your first idea. I can't believe it took you this long. If everyone hates the barbecue, they'll be desperate for something else."

"Exactly. And with our weird combinations, we have curb appeal. Most of the families in the village visit regularly, so they'll know and love what we can offer."

While he peered over my shoulder to read my notes, Nathaniel's hand found its home between my shoulder blades. His touch, even over my T-shirt, feels good and he makes no effort to move it when we're both upright.

"Will Simon be up for it?" he asks.

Maybe? My brother is the only thing standing between us and success, and he's a shrewd businessman. He keeps a close eye on all our expenditures. Just the other day, I wasn't allowed to order our usual pens because the price per box has gone up twenty pence.

I blow out a shaky breath. "I fucking hope so, because otherwise, we're screwed. And this will be brilliant if we can pull it off."

We both sit again. The massive satisfaction that it was me who came up with the winning idea pushes my great mood into overdrive. I slide the paper to his side of the table then, without considering any of the risks that might come with such a ballsy move, shove my chair over so I can sit close to Nathaniel. The excited jiggling of my leg must catch his attention because he looks at me and gives me a knowing smile, telling me that moving was exactly the right thing to do.

That bag of excited worms erupts in my stomach, but I try my best to ignore their squirming, and duck my head closer to his to plot.

FIVE

"**R**ORY," **I SHOUT UP** the stairs, "if you don't get your butt here in five minutes, I'm going to eat your breakfast."

Fridays are always a struggle for him. As usual, he's dragging his heels while getting ready for school. It's not that he doesn't want to go. He loves it there. He just loves his bed more. Something he must have got from me.

I return to the kitchen, my eyes flicking to my phone sitting silently between two bowls of Frosties. Nathaniel's first message of the day is late.

Of course, I could text him first, but we've fallen into a routine over the last few days, a pattern of messages zipping between us. If I'm the first to break it, I might seem needy. So, I'll wait. I'll stare at my phone. And I'll try not to let all the negative thoughts break through the carefully built boundaries in my brain.

His first text usually comes through before my alarm clock goes off, and I send the last message since I prefer staying up and watching shit TV over going to bed at a decent time. We've been talking about everything, not only the stall, and I even think he's flirting back. He could just be being nice for the sake of the stall. I'm a rubbish judge of anything over text. You need to add 'by the way, I'm trying it on with you' if you're being a flirt, because I mistake obvious signs of attraction for friendship, and cordial offers for the guy being in love with me.

Not that it matters. We're only in it for the fête.

As I'm about to go and nag Rory about how late we're going to be, my mobile pings. The speed at which I race over to the counter is embarrassing. I'm not *that* desperate to hear from Nathaniel. Not at all.

Okay. Maybe just a little.

> **Mr Jameson:** Good morning. The gym took forever today. A bunch of bros were hogging the one machine I wanted to use. Had to give up in the end. Can't be late for school.

He was delayed at the gym. Not debating how to stop texting me without risking the success of our stall. Stupid brain and stupid thoughts. A witty reply is already at the tip of my fingers, and they tapdance over my screen.

> **Me:** how will ur muscles recover? :'(

I know, I'm so damn funny.

> **Mr Jameson:** I will be significantly smaller the next time you see me. Try not to be too grossed out by it.

> **Me:** will have to see if I puke at drop off i'll try to hide it tho so u dont get upset

> **Mr Jameson:** No drop-off for me today. Ms Palmer has called me into a meeting first thing.

> **Me:** what have u done?

Mr Jameson: Killed a few kids yesterday. They had it coming.

Mr Jameson: She's probably looking for an update. She's been nagging EVERYONE about their stalls this week.

Me: will my joke of the day help?

Mr Jameson: Maybe. The kids weren't fans of yesterday's.

Me: kids have a shit sense of humour

Me: y dont circus lions eat the clowns?

Mr Jameson: I don't know. Why don't circus lions eat the clowns?

Rory chooses this moment to make his appearance, arriving in the kitchen doorway with his red school jumper on back-to-front. I tut, abandoning my phone to sort him out.

"Thought you said you could dress yourself?"

"I can. I got stuck and my arms stopped working. I was so, so tired." He follows his words with the biggest fake yawn he can muster. "Do I *have* to go to school today?"

"Yup. If I have to work, you have to learn. It's how life works, buddy."

"But you get paid to work."

"Pfft. Not a lot. Classes are way more fun than working with Uncle Simon." I tug the jumper back over his head the right way. "I would rather be at school with you than melting at the pub. But you gotta do what you gotta do. We have to eat, and you can only sell a kidney once."

"But I don't want to sell my kidney." He frowns up at me.

"That's okay. It's too small right now. We won't get much for it. On the stool." He follows me like a duckling to the breakfast bar and I give him a boost onto the tall chair. "At least it's a Friday. Mr Jameson says you do fun things at the end of the week."

We eat our breakfast together, and Rory tells me about all the different Friday activities Nathaniel has put on for them since he joined the school. Rory is animated and some of his creativity shows itself, only making me more jealous that I don't get to enjoy the day with him. Sometimes, I wish I was six again. Although it would make the continued sexy dreams of Mr Jameson even more inappropriate.

Even though I know Nathaniel isn't on duty this morning, I still look for him when I drop Rory off. There's a noticeable gap where he usually stands, his hands jammed in his cord pockets with a friendly look on his face to greet the kids. I've gotten used to seeing him there, and his absence makes me all discombobulated.

The lack of him does remind me we were in the middle of a text conversation, so I slide into the car and check my phone.

> **Mr Jameson:** Can't believe you left me hanging.

> **Me:** because they taste funny

> **Me:** how was the meeting?

His reply comes in when I'm watering the window boxes and checking my carefully chosen violas and oriental poppies for weeds at the restaurant. Everything that blooms here matches our colour theme.

> **Mr Jameson:** As expected, it was about the fête. She confirmed the only food stalls will be ice cream and soft drinks. There won't be a BBQ this year because Mr Famer, who usually does it, fell off his ladder and broke both his ankles. So perfect for us.

> **Me:** poor mr farmer

> **Me:** just Simon to win over now

> **Me:** ready for later?

I don't expect a reply from him, since the bell for school rang ages ago, and he's not allowed on his phone in the classroom. Not that I'm deluded enough to expect his attention on me when he has a room of hyperactive kids to look after. I'm not *that* selfish.

I take a deep breath of the floral perfume, closing my eyes for a moment to enjoy the morning sun. It's gross being inside on such a lovely day. Someone else comes to mow the lawn around the picnic benches, so I can't even use that as an excuse to get out of the office. *Dammit.*

"I've been here an hour already," Simon tells me when I finally drag myself inside. He doesn't look up from whatever he's typing. His shoulders are hunched over his keyboard, his nose practically touching the screen and his face is fixed in the frown he always likes to wear. If he smiled more, he'd look like Josh and me. Although he has more freckles than the two of us combined and a skinny strip of a moustache I often refer to as his little nose caterpillar.

"Yeah? Did your kids need dropping off at school?"

"You know well enough they can wa—" He cuts himself off, but there's no shame at the recognition of what I'm digging at. Simon doesn't have the time for that.

"Anyway," I continue, "we don't have a meeting until four this afternoon. What's the rush?"

"You're on set up and we have to finish the summer holiday menu so I can send it to print."

"Yeah, yeah. I'm gonna log in, sort out front of house, and then I'm all yours."

Nathaniel's next message doesn't come in until I'm eating my lunch.

> **Mr Jameson:** Yep. I'm prepared. Just want the school day over and done with now so I can get to the pub.

> **Me:** to see me?

I only register what I've sent when I press send. It goes straight to read, so I've no hope of getting it back. *Fuck, fuck, fuck.* Where did that come from? My stomach tries to join the local gymnastics team with how many flip flops it does. The pulsing three dots that tell me he's typing back appear, then disappear, before starting again, and the swirling in my belly doesn't stop until my phone pings.

> **Mr Jameson:** Yes, I want to see you. But also, I want to get Simon's approval so we know we're not back at square one.

Of course.

> **Me:** it'll come soon enough

> **Me:** how are the kids?

> **Mr Jameson:** One of them vomited and now the rest of them are queasy. I think we'll spend the afternoon outside. My classroom stinks.

> **Me:** gross

> **Me:** was it Rory?

> **Mr Jameson:** Nope. I had to stop him examining the puddle though. He wanted to count how many carrots Felicity threw up.

> **Me:** that's my boy

There's a lot of work to get through, but it's hard to keep my attention on Simon, and the day drags. As we contemplate whether we should make the *Sunshine on a Rainy Day* cocktail, or the *Green, Green Grass* shot a feature, my attention drifts to the clock above Simon's desk.

"What is your problem today?" He reclines in his chair, huffing.

I snap out of my daydream. "Nothing. We should use the cocktail. The reds and blues stand out against the rest of the colours in the background. The shot can go on the back."

"Good idea. Do you have a reason for watching the clock? Usually, you hate attending meetings with me."

"I don't want to miss this one. It's important."

His permanent frown grows. "I've never known you to get so involved with a PTA event. What grabbed your interest this time?"

I won't roll my eyes at him. One day, I'll do it too hard and will lose my eyeballs for good. He knows what's grabbing my interest. The fact I spent last Saturday night with Nathaniel has been a running joke in the family group chat all week. The idea that a handsome man is the motivation I need to work hard has got everyone in stitches. Ha, bloody, ha. It's all a load of bullshit, but I ride the wave of abuse without complaining. Eventually, Henry – who still plays rugby even though he's closer to 45 than 35 nowadays – will break another wrist or get another concussion and I'll stop being the focus.

Simon's questioning has me rankled. I'm about to bark that I'm doing it all for Rory, that a successful stall is my only goal, when a gangly waiter bursts into our office.

"Not learned to knock yet, Freddie?" I tease before Simon can open his mouth. He doesn't like the staff barging around the place.

"S-s-sorry, Mr Webster, but someone is here to see Mr Webster."

"Which one?"

It's a pointless question from Simon. I'm on my feet straight away. A glance at the clock confirms it's five to four, and Nathaniel *can't* be late. Simon chuffs some sort of laugh, but I brush the biscuit crumbs off my jeans, take a deep breath and walk out of the office, trying to maintain what I hope is a normal pace. My stomach squirms again, but I put it down to the anticipation of the meeting and not about seeing Nathaniel after almost a week. The glimpses I steal at drop-off just don't cut it.

He's waiting at the bar, looking out of place amongst the bright green and purple uniforms whizzing around him. His dark chinos blend into the rusty-red wood. A large tote bag full of books waits by his feet, and a bottle-green jumper is folded over the top of it. I bet he'd look amazing in the sweatshirt, but I'd be more focused on removing it.

Stop it. He's here for the stall. Not me.

"Hey, Nathaniel."

I close the gap in five quick paces, but as soon as I reach him, I'm not sure whether I should shake his hand or give him a quick hug. What stage of our friendship are we even at? He stares at me, expecting *something* so I panic and do nothing.

"Alex, hi." He thrusts his hand towards me, his toned arms flexing under the tight material of his dark green polo top. "How have you been?"

"Since your text twenty minutes ago saying you were leaving? Fine. The day has crept along, but I'm sure it'll get better." It *already has.*

His flush races past his cheeks, across his sexy, sharp jawline and disappears under his collar. "Ah. Sorry. I forgot I'd already asked."

"No worries. How was your afternoon in the sun?"

"It took me forever to plaster the kids in suncream, but then we read *A Kid in My Class* and acted out all the different characters. Not what I originally planned to do with them, but worth it for their performances. I'll be putting the videos on The Hub some time this weekend."

The enthusiasm he uses when discussing his students captivates me. I wish I was this passionate about my work. I can't help but stare at the way his eyes light up, the genuine smile filling his cheeks with colour. Nathaniel is a new teacher, and his enthusiasm is never ending.

"You win," I tell him when he raises his eyebrows at the delay. "I'd ask for a job swap, but I reckon I'd last an hour tops. Still sounds a hundred times better than my day."

The smile he gives me in response is weak, and it drops when his eyes flit over my shoulder to the door behind me. I offered to speak to Simon alone, but Nathaniel wanted to come along. Even when I warned him about how much of a shrewd business person my brother is, and how he'll want to grill us, Nathaniel was adamant he wanted to be a part of this.

"It's frustrating having to wait all week to speak to Simon." His gaze remains trained on the STAFF ONLY sign on the door. "It means we'll only have a few weeks to put everything in place if he says yes, and if he doesn't agree, we don't have any other ideas."

The lost look on his face – the downward turn of his mouth and a distant stare – tugs at my heart. When I reply, I make sure I'm using the most confident voice I can muster.

"Sure we do. Bric-a-brac." His second attempt at a smile isn't as enthusiastic as when he was talking about his students. I sigh and squeeze his arm. "We're going to be fine. We have a solid plan, just like you told me last night. Plus, despite my best efforts to annoy him today, he's less grumpy than usual. He loves Fridays. Let's get this over with, yeah?"

I hold the door open, gesturing for Nathaniel to head in first. I know, I'm such a gentleman. How can any guy resist me?

Simon is already standing behind his desk and he crosses the small office quickly, holding his hand out for Nathaniel to shake.

Their grips are firm, more formal than my greeting, and the skin on the backs of their hands turn pale.

"You must be Mr Jameson," Simon says.

There's no invite for Nathaniel to make himself comfortable. Instead, Simon guides him towards the meeting table, which sits in between the only window and a pile of boxes from our overflowing stock room. He barely gives the teacher time to hang his jumper on a hook. Nathaniel abandons his bag of textbooks next to my tatty rucksack, and slips out a plastic document wallet before following my brother.

I take my seat next to Nathaniel and pour everyone a drink of water. When I pick up my glass, it almost slips from my sweaty grip. Simon's overly formal introduction has thrown me for six. He's like this with our suppliers and contractors, but I thought he'd offer a friend of mine something warmer.

Fuck. Does this mean we're not going to get him on our side? I know he's careful with his money, but I figured since it's for Rory, we wouldn't have too much of a battle on our hands to persuade him.

"So." Simon splays his hands across the table. We're in a reverse interview set up. He's directly opposite us on the rectangle table. "Tell me about this idea of yours."

Nathaniel rights his shoulders and matches Simon's rigid, upright posture. His hands remain next to the wallet as he takes the lead. We rehearsed this twenty times over, then decided it would be better if he does most of the speaking. I would have messed up straight away, especially with the way Simon drags over a pencil and a notepad, ready to listen. He means business.

"In three weeks, East Beechmill Primary School will be holding a summer fête to raise money to refurbish the playground."

"Is that old thing still standing? I used to get splinters every time I used the climbing frame."

"Well, exactly. This year's fête is going to be the pinnacle of three years of fundraising. Headmistress Palmer wants to replace the whole thing this summer, so she's turned the event into a competition, challenging us to raise the most money with our stalls. She paired every teacher with a parent on the PTA, and there will be a prize at the end for the winning team."

"Sounds interesting. But what has that got to do with me?"

"We want to give the attendees something different to eat this year."

"What about Mr Farmer? Won't he be bringing his barbecue?"

Here comes the grilling. For every point, Simon has a counter argument. The corners of his mouth twitch, although he doesn't break into a smile, it's clear he's enjoying this.

It doesn't seem to be putting Nathaniel off his stride. In contrast to Simon's weakly held frown, Nathaniel's smile is bright and unwavering, and he maintains eye contact with my brother as he slides our plan out of the plastic wallet and across the table. Simon picks it up, quiet for a moment as he reads through it.

"Mr Farmer is injured, and there is nobody else willing to cater the event on such short notice. We, that is, Alex and I, are proposing that we take The Watering Hole to the fête. Our idea is a 'make your own' style grill. See what concoctions the kids come up with. They choose the flavours, we cook the food, and their parents pay. Alex assures me the pub has all of the equipment, so we just need your permission."

"You need my wholesale account, and my licence, since Alex isn't covered to cook. You need *me*. Also, you're missing an important part of your plan." He folds his hands over the pristine pages.

"What's that?" I decide to intervene. We went through everything with a fine-tooth comb, so what the fuck did we leave out?

"How will hosting a stall under *my* business's name make *you* money?"

"We're asking for you to donate half of the profit."

At least Nathaniel is clear on the answers, since they have all leapt from my brain, screaming *nope, nope, nope* as they tumble to the floor. He must have spent all night preparing, while I was killing my online buddies.

Simon whistles and flicks through the papers again, his lips moving in soundless words. I've seen this before – the calculating, plotting, thinking three steps ahead of everyone else. There's a reason he's the family chess champion. It'll take him all of half a minute to work out how much our venture is going to cost him and whether it is worth it.

The silence must kill Nathaniel, because he doesn't wait and instead spills out, "Of course, there are more benefits than only raising money for the playground. Publicity, for one. We can put banners and flyers all over the stall to promote the business. Not that you need it. Alex tells me the pub is always busy, that it's hard to get a table. The only reason I've been able to eat here is because I turned up close to closing. Also, Alex and I will do all of the work. If you have to come, you can relax. Plus, making the playground safe is important. It's been condemned for the past three years, and the kids miss it. You should hear the complaints I get when they ask every Monday if it's fixed yet, and I have to tell them it's not. Especially Rory."

Although his voice is unwavering, he's talking faster than normal and is playing with his pen. I may find his fluster cute, but Simon's frown deepens. Fiddling is a waste of time, and every word should be measured and efficient. As Nathaniel continues rabbiting on about ensuring we follow proper health and safety and food hygiene practices, and how his library work will help him monitor everything, I reach along the table and squeeze his arm.

The word vomit stops and I'm rewarded with a small smile. Simon doesn't miss this. His frown melts into a more neutral look as he taps the pages of the plan into order.

"It's a good idea." His gaze remains on the hand resting on Nathaniel's arm but I don't yank it away. Fuck Simon and fuck my brothers for always laughing at me. Some things are worth the punishment, and the feel of Nathaniel's skin – even if it's a little clammy – under my palm will carry me through a million jokes. "Messy but fun. I will donate everything you need for free and I won't take a penny of the profit."

"Seriously?" Me and Nathaniel speak at the same time.

"Yes. The school is fantastic, and although my children have already left, my nieces and nephew still attend. I will work the stall with you, too. I'm sure they can cope here for the day without the two of us."

"That is— Thank you, Simon. It means a lot to us."

"I'll leave Alex to make all the arrangements. He knows where everything is. I'll have a contract written by close on Monday." Simon is already on his feet, wandering over to his desk and I resist the urge to laugh. A contract for a charity event? He turns his PC off and pulls his jacket on. His shift is over, the meeting the last item on his agenda. "Have a nice evening, Nathaniel. Alex, I'll see you Sunday."

The minute we're alone in the office, my hand leaves Nathaniel's arm and we scramble to our feet. We move in sync, closing the tiny gap between our chairs, and fling our arms around each other. *Bloody hell.* I sink into the embrace, letting out a deep breath against his chest. He's warm and his hands slide to my back, rubbing softly. It's like we've been doing this every day of our lives, and it makes me mad that this perfect hug is not our first time.

We pull away, and I notice with great satisfaction that his cheeks are as bright as mine feel. I grin at him. "Well done, Nate. It was a tough one, but you smashed it."

"So did you." He nudges me with his shoulder. "You were the one who told me last night that Rory is Simon's soft spot. Speaking of which, Rory is going to be excited when we tell him."

When *we* tell him. The thought makes my head spin, and gives me wonderful mental images of me and Nate, working together as a team on more than the stall. Securing Simon's agreement means we have a lot of work to do, but that means more time with Nathaniel. Even though it's going to be hard fitting it in with everything else, I can't wait.

"I wish we could tell him tonight. He's staying with Henry, my other brother, because I'm picking up a shift and—"

Nathaniel's smile fades from his face, and he takes great interest in the tiled floor. "I didn't realise you had plans."

Oh. In all the messages we've sent this week, we never discussed doing anything together this evening. Maybe it was a given and I was too stupid to realise it? The look on his face causes the buds of excitement to wilt. There's nothing more I want to do than spend the evening with him, but I have to work. I can't arrange cover this late in the day.

I sigh and take a step away from him to tidy my desk, unable to stand his disappointment.

"Yeah. One of our waiters called in sick yesterday, and I offered to cover the shift. I need the extra cash if I have any hope of taking Rory anywhere this summer, and luckily, Henry was willing to have him."

Nathaniel doesn't lift his head to look at me, and I fight the temptation to march over to him, slide my fingers under his stupidly hot jawline and force his eyes upwards. I'd end up kissing him, and I'm not sure if he's interested in me *that way*. Although it's clear he wants to spend time with me, for all I know, he's looking for another mate date. Or maybe he wants to get straight to work on the stall.

"That's okay," he says in a way that tells me it's absolutely not. "It's not like we made plans or anything. I have a ton of work to do. I didn't have time to squish it into my *nine-to-three* workday."

The joke feels more like a dig, enforced by the grimace that accompanies it. Is he having a strop? How adorable. His reaction makes me hate working in the pub even more.

I drag myself over to the coat hooks so I can get ready for my shift and catch my foot on the massive bag he dragged in with him.

"Is this your marking?" I lift my head from it long enough for his nod. "Well, you're welcome to stay here and work if you want? I can't promise it'll be much fun for you, but I might be able to stop and chat now and then, especially if it gets quiet. I might even feed you if you behave."

His face relaxes. Maybe I was wrong? The speed in which he cheered up *must* be an indication he wants to spend time with me in a more-than-friends kind of way. Could Nathaniel be as interested in me as I am in him?

"As long as you don't mind? I'm happy to pay for my meal."

"Absolutely not. What's the point in being forced to work with the brother of the guy who runs this place if you can't get a free meal out of it?"

"You paid for the Chinese last weekend."

"Then you can buy our next meal."

"Fine."

"Fine."

My cheeks warm at the prospect of getting *another* meal with him. The way he's holding my gaze confirms my suspicions. He wants it, too. Fucking amazing.

While the Alex in my head dances, I tear my eyes away from Nathaniel's to rummage in my rucksack, eventually finding the snot-green shirt I shoved in this morning. It's creased, but I'm kind of the boss, so it doesn't matter.

"Go find a spot at the bar. I'd offer you a booth, but they're all booked. Now shoo, or I'll be late. I know you're desperate to see me naked, but we've only just met."

His eyes linger on me for a moment longer, and he chews on his lower lip in the most delightful way, as if he already has that image in his head. Horny Alex will have time to think about that later when I'm finally home alone. Nathaniel takes a step towards me, pauses then shakes his head and scoops up his bag. As he walks away from me, my eyes linger on his backside but this time, I feel a little less guilty about it.

The pub is busy from the minute I tie the electric-purple apron around my waist and head into the dining area. I usually hate shifts like this, because I can spot a million things that need doing, but can't get to them due to the mass of customers. Tonight, though, the snippets of conversation I grab with Nathaniel help. As well as the looks we share over the sea of diners. It's nice knowing he's there, perched on a stool at the end of the bar, waiting to talk to me. This could become a nice part of our routine. He could bring Rory here for dinner when I'm working. With Nathaniel around, I could see more of my kid.

Woah, hold on there. The guy agreed to sit here while I worked because he was getting a free meal. There is *some* attraction between us, I'm 99.5% sure of it now, but I can't consider making him a permanent feature. I don't know what he wants for a start. And even if Nathaniel is looking for something, we have to move slowly, if not to protect my heart, then to shield Rory. It'll be confusing if I introduce his teacher as his new parent.

By ten, the crowds have thinned out. I'm collecting the last of the plates from the table in my zone when Matt, the shift manager, stops me.

"You can wrap up early if you want, Alex," the youth says. His confidence comes from being given a tiny amount of respon-sibility at such a young age, and he has forgotten I practically half-own the pub. I guess it's nice he feels he can get on with his job and treat me like the rest of his team.

"Can I?" I raise my eyebrows.

"Y-yeah. The other Mr Webster says we only need five people to clean up after ten. I'm on lock-up, and since you've got your friend here, I thought you'd want to knock off. W-we still pay you for a full shift."

"Well, that's nice of us. Thank you, Matt."

I dump the dishes in the kitchen for the pot-washer to deal with and hang my apron next to the others. I sign out and make my way over to Nathaniel. My dirty tea towel hits the bar with a louder-than-expected *thwack*, disturbing him from his phone. Without asking, I scoop up a spoonful of his leftover apple and cheese crumble and eat it. I was fed earlier, but it's never enough.

He doesn't complain. Instead, he presses his thumb one more time against his screen then slides his phone on the bar next to my towel. "That's how a Friday night in The Watering Hole goes, huh?"

"Yep. My feet ache and my body is howling and I only did a five-hour shift. It's a sign I'm getting too old for this shit. What did you think?"

"It was nice. Friendly. The food was great."

I press myself back against the bar so I can look at him properly, hyper-aware that I'm a hot sweaty mess, especially after a toddler emptied a whole bowl of orange-flavoured custard over me. Because of the state I'm in, I can't believe the next thing that comes out of my mouth.

"I feel guilty about making you wait around for me. How can I make it up to you?"

"It wasn't a chore. I've had a brilliant evening."

"You and me need to have a conversation about what's brilliant and what isn't. Watching me work all night is on the *not good* end of the scale. So, please, I know it's late, but I'm Rory-free and rarely go to bed before twelve. What do you want to do?"

"I don't know."

Although he's packing his stuff, his eyes keep on flitting to me. The action, and our flirting earlier – or what I think was flirting

– makes me bolder than I usually am. I've *never* taken the first step, but there's no way I'm saying goodbye to him yet. *Something is building between us, and we need some decent time together for me to work it out.*

"You don't know if you want to spend time with me, or you don't know what you want to do?"

He puffs out a hard breath and straightens on his stool. "I don't mind what I do, as long as it's with you."

Yes. I was fucking right and I'll not back away from him. I'm pulling on my big-boy pants, and facing whatever *this is* head on.

"Well." I swallow hard, hoping it'll quench the heat coming from his burning gaze. "There are no other bars around here, and I've spent all day stuck in this place. I need to get out. Why don't you come to mine for a film? I have another bottle of the red you enjoyed." When he cocks an eyebrow at me, I rush to add, "No dodgy intentions. But we talked all Wednesday about the *Cornetto Trilogy*, and I found the box set in my attic. I was going to let you borrow it, but how about watching *Shaun of the Dead* with me instead?"

"What about Rory?"

"He's a little too young to get the jokes." I smirk when he rolls his eyes at me. "Nah. It's not fair to make him stay up and wait for my shift to finish so he'll sleep at Henry's. My house is empty. You don't want to send me home alone, do you?"

I give him the same puppy dog eyes and pout Rory uses on me, and to my delight, it works. Nathaniel chuckles. "Fine. Can I get a lift to yours?"

"Don't you drive?"

"I've never learned."

"I guess you don't need a car in London. Okay, Mr Jameson. Not only can I give you a lift to mine, but I'll only have one glass so I can get you home safely."

"You are such a gentleman."

"Aren't you the lucky one?" Although he's taller than me and able to get himself off the stool, I hold my arm out for him, tingles spreading from where he hooks his hand into the crook of my elbow and slides off the seat. He doesn't remove his grip as I lead him towards the backroom. "I need to grab my stuff then we'll be out of here."

Six

NATHANIEL DOESN'T WAIT TO be invited in. Once I've opened the front door, he breezes past me and plonks himself on the third step to untie his shoes.

I remove mine in the hallway, not wanting to get too close to him, the grime of my shift having fully sunk into my skin. Sure, he sat next to me in the car for the ten-minute journey, but my broken air conditioning forced our windows open, keeping the vehicle fresh. If he gets a whiff of me now, he'll run away.

"Is it all right if I grab a quick shower?"

"Go right ahead. I can sort the wine."

The way he makes himself at home is cute, and he moves with ease despite only visiting once before. He toes his shoes off and discards them next to mine before trotting on socked feet towards the kitchen. I allow myself only a second to watch him, my eyes dipping quickly to his backside, then race upstairs to wash.

My shower is quick, motivated by the need to get back to him. I want to see if he curls up on the sofa in the spot usually reserved for me. We have a strict hierarchy of who sits where in my house, but I find myself not minding if he's stolen my seat. In fact, I like the idea.

Five minutes later, I'm downstairs, now wearing a clean T-shirt and a pair of green joggers. If he complains he's too smart – since he's still in his work clothes – I'll offer him something else. He'd look good wandering around in the grey sweats I have. My cock twitches at the image and I pause at the door to the living room to quench my spicy thoughts. *Football was invented in China. Devon has more roads than anywhere else in the UK. I must remember to buy slug pellets before the bastards eat my hydrangeas.*

That'll do it.

When I enter the room, I'm surprised to see the sofa is empty. A glass of wine, full to the brim, waits for me on the coffee table, and I'm greeted with the same peachy backside I was fantasising about. He's browsing the photos hung on the wall.

I help myself to the glass and sink into the sofa. "What are you looking at?"

He jumps a mile. Straight away, he checks the carpet. No wine has been spilled. Phew. It's brand new and red is a bugger to get out.

"You've talked about how big your family is, but I didn't believe you until I saw it for myself."

He taps his finger over the massive family portrait sitting pride of place on the middle of the wall, like he's counting the members in there. I study it too, my eyes travelling from person to person. Mum and Dad have their arms around each other. No matter what shit we've gone through, it's clear they're as much in love as the day they got married. On one side of them is Josh, Aimee and their kids as well as Simon with Jaya and the five

children they've spawned. Next to Dad stands me with Michael, the ex I bought this house with; Henry, his wife and family, and—
Luke.

On his hip sits a much younger kid, but it's clear it's Rory. Same hair as the rest of us, same pattern of freckles as Luke, and the toothy grin that reminds me every day of my brother.

Nathaniel's eyes stay on the picture. "Can I ask you something?"

"You just did." Despite my teasing, my insides freeze. It's not that I've deliberately kept stuff from him, but the picture paints a hundred stories, and some of them are a gut wrench when I have to tell them.

He looks at me, and I can see the full extent of his confusion. He's thinking, his eyebrows furrowed, and he pulls his lower lip between his teeth over and over in a move I'm learning is a tell. But his question doesn't come, though it looks like it's burning at the tip of his tongue.

After a moment of pondering me, he shakes off his befuddlement, although the smile he gives me is weaker than normal and doesn't shine in his eyes. "It doesn't matter."

He crosses the rug in the middle of the room and settles on the opposite end of the sofa. Like last week, he sits rigidly and now it's my turn to feel disappointed. I want him to ask. I want the chance to talk to him about my family – even if it might hurt – but I can't find the words to steer the conversation in the right direction. At least not naturally. Perhaps my joking wasn't the right time.

"*Shaun of the Dead*, then?" The dejection in my voice disgusts me.

He's already loaded the DVD into the player, so I press play and take a long sip of my wine. Jaunty music plays as the zombie-like characters go about their daily business. It's one of my favourite films; I've watched it so many times, I can quote it line for line. Now, I'm struggling to concentrate.

You could tell him. But what if it's too soon to empty all of the skeletons out of my closet? We're on the precipice of something more and I'd be gutted if we don't get a chance to see that blossom.

Given that Rory lives with me, Nathaniel has probably connected the dots and come to his own correct conclusion. He's smart. I'm sure I've mentioned that there used to be more of us, but I don't think I've ever insinuated that Rory isn't mine. It wasn't intentional, though. Beechmill is a small village – everyone knows each other's business. I'm used to not having to tell people because they were there. They mourned at the same funeral I did. Everyone loved my brother.

I puff out a hard breath, my eyes drawing back to the photo. The way I see it, I have two choices. I could ignore the massive elephant in the room – another of my special skills – and watch the movie. We'll have a lovely evening, I'll drive Nathaniel home and that will be that.

Or I could take a risk.

Michael left because of Rory, because of the strain everything put on *us*. My focus has been on making sure Rory is okay, on trying to fill the gap my brother left behind, so I've not let anyone else in. Nathaniel is the first person I've entertained getting to know more in a *long* time.

I press pause on the movie before Shaun gets a chance to suggest they go to The Winchester, have a nice cold pint, and wait for it all to blow over. After returning my now half-full glass to the coffee table, I pivot my whole body to face Nathaniel.

"Ask your question."

It takes a lot of effort to keep my face neutral, to not anticipate the pain I know will twist through my gut when I tell him what happened. With every silent moment that ticks by, I find my courage failing, but he doesn't open his mouth. Instead, he stays quiet, chewing his lip again. I wish he'd stop it.

"Nate. Please?" Emotion leaks into my voice and it must work because his shoulders drop. Curiosity has got the better of him. Teachers are all the same.

His words are slow and deliberate. "In the picture, you're standing with a redhead and no Rory. He is on the hip of another man, who is identical to Simon but isn't him, because *he's* standing with his wife on the other side of your parents. There are five of you, all with curly hair in various shades of brown."

I stare at the photo for a moment longer, trying to get the words in order. Eventually, I sigh. "I'm surprised the school didn't tell you, but Rory isn't mine. At least, not by birth. I'm his legal guardian. I didn't steal him."

"And the other man in the picture? The one that looks like Simon. Is that Rory's dad?"

"Yeah. Luke. Simon's twin. He's not with us anymore."

I'm not sure if it's wishful thinking because I desperately want to be touched, to be comforted, but Nathaniel twitches more towards me. At least, I'm positive his knees are facing me more, when they were pointing at the TV earlier.

"What happened?"

"Luke...he didn't do anything wrong. He definitely didn't deserve it. It–it was my fault, actually."

A gentle touch traces over the back of my hand, and when I glance up, I'm surprised to see Nathaniel is leaning towards me. Usually, I would pull away out of fear I won't be able to tell the story. But this once, I let him tangle our fingers together, a flare of relief coming from his squeeze. I can do this.

"It should have been me. I was supposed to be on lock up that day, but it was the start of Christmas and Mike lured me out and...I guess I wasn't very reliable back then. My brothers should have fired me. Probably Mum stopped them. Luke covered my shift, and by the time I remembered I was supposed to be there. I— Well, I was too late. Luke was alone, and some thug must have thought he was cashing out or something. The guy broke into the place, stabbed my brother for fifty quid."

"That's...awful."

"When I got to the pub, the alarm was blaring. It was dark and I was the first person to find Luke. I...I...practically tripped over his body. He was left there, in the cold and the wet and— I've been trained in first aid, but it wasn't enough. The ambulance was too slow to come. I couldn't stop the bleeding. I couldn't—"

My hands tremble and when I look at them, all I can see is my brother's blood staining them, how it dripped off the tips of my fingers as I tried to stop the life draining out of him. Not even Nathaniel's tightening grip can erase how it felt to place my hands over Luke's deep wound, how I pushed hard to stem the bleeding, the warmth as it weeped through the hole in his stomach.

"Fifty fucking quid. They didn't even catch the prick who did it. Who the fuck kills someone at Christmas?"

"Alex..."

A tight pain throbs behind my temple and my nostrils burn. Dad taught us to be stoic, unwavering in the face of our problems, but I deserve a pass when it's my brother lying dead on the floor.

"What about Rory's mum? Where is she?" Nathaniel's thumb rubs circles over the back of my hand. He's so close to me now that our knees bump together.

"Katie?" I run my hand through my hair, taking a shuddering breath. "Fuck. Rory didn't have a great start in life. There were complications when she had him, and she bled out. Didn't even get to meet him. Luke was on his own. Rory lost both his parents in the most horrific ways."

"Christ. That is... What a... I'm sorry, Alex. That's really sad. How did you end up being Rory's guardian?"

My palms are slick with sweat, reminding me of the way Luke's blood stuck to them. It took me hours to wash it away. *You're clean now.* Nate wouldn't be touching me if I was covered in blood. Yet I tighten my grip on him anyway, so he can't recoil from me.

"At the time, I was with Mike. We'd been together for years. Since college. We were in love." I can't stop the scoff slipping from my mouth. Fat load of good *love* did for us. "Although I couldn't face going back to work after...after what I saw, I was still getting paid. We didn't open the pub for a whole month, but it took me longer than that before I could face it again. Simon looked after me, though. Rory stayed with Mum and Dad for a while, but everyone had their plates full, a riot of kids to support, and my parents are getting old. Luke's death hit them hardest. Of course it did. They weren't coping."

Neither was I. But I don't voice that. Neither do I tell him about how Mum was adamant I wasn't the right choice for Rory, or about her concerns that I wouldn't be able to provide a stable home. She never said it, but on my worst nights I wonder if it's because I am gay and was living with another man. There was never any question about whether any of my straight siblings would struggle with an extra family member.

Admitting it would mean I would also have to tell Nathaniel about how her concerns had me questioning my sexuality and the deep shame it brings me, even two years later. I had never been ashamed of who I was before then, and was bullheaded in accepting Rory, keen to make up for what I'd done. I wanted to prove my mum wrong.

No, I won't say any of that to Nathaniel.

I take another sip of my wine, trying to quiet my jangled emotions. "We agreed to take Rory on, and eventually, Mum got tired of protesting. I was already the kid's godfather, and we had a great bond so it made sense. At least my brothers supported it. They made parenting look easy" — my laugh is thin and short-lived — "so it was a no-brainer, and we got the adoption papers signed straight away. But a four-year-old who's lost both of his parents comes with problems. Bed wetting, night terrors, sleepwalking.

It put too much of a strain on my relationship, and Mike walked out. Was so desperate to get away from us he left the village he'd lived in all of his life. We don't speak to him anymore, and he's never tried to get in touch."

The remaining air leaves my lungs, and I find I have no more words to say. Nathaniel doesn't let go of me as he shifts so we're sitting next to each other, shoulders, hips and knees pressed together. My hand remains in his, and without thinking about it, my head drops to his shoulder.

"You don't have to go on if you don't want to," he tells me, his breath ruffling through my hair.

"No, it's fine." I clear my throat, lifting my head from its comfortable spot. There's not much else to say. "It's been me and Rory for eighteen months now, and we get by well enough. It's hard. I guess I don't make a big deal out of our situation because I don't want anyone to treat him differently. But I can't hide it. The news was all over the village papers the next morning. There was no getting away from it."

It's Nathaniel's turn to release a long breath, and we linger in the silence that follows. I like that he doesn't hurry to fill the space with half-assed platitudes, or to assure me that it's not my fault. When he finally speaks, his words are gentle, measured, and full of the same compassion that flashes in his eyes, lightning striking amongst the green.

"It's a tragic story, Alex. You gave up your life for Rory, but I truly believe it's paying off. He doesn't stop talking about you in class. And I guess a lot of things are clicking into place."

"Like what?"

"Like the fact he never refers to you as Dad, only Alex."

"Yeah. I'll never be his dad, and I wouldn't want to be, either. Only to—" I shake the thought out of my head. I'm *not* going there tonight. "I'll always be Uncle Alex to him, but I don't mind if he drops the Uncle. It's not important and there are other things I have to focus on. Like making sure he remembers Luke and

Katie. The whole family is invested in it. We always speak about them, no matter how hard it can get sometimes. I try my best to make sure Rory gets plenty of time with Katie's side of the family, too." I wipe my eyes with my spare hand. "Here, let me show you something."

I keep a firm grip on Nathaniel as I stand and pull him to his feet. The smile I give him is watery, but it grows when he returns it. It gives me enough confidence to lead him upstairs to Rory's room, the weight of his touch comforting.

A bright blast of colour hits us when I open the bedroom door. Everything in the room is orange – Rory's favourite – including the bedspread and the curtains. I was against painting it this way when he first asked, but now I find it warm and sunny, even if it does make my hangovers a hundred times worse.

Not that you can see much of the paint. The walls are plastered from ceiling to floor with posters and drawings, some sun-bleached. Thor, Loki, Matthew Smart — North Devon's hit striker — stare at us amongst the scribbles and cutouts. Next to Rory's bed is the space we've dedicated to Katie and Luke. Rory has pestered family members for every photo of his parents they have, and every time we find a new one, we stick it on the wall, alongside the drawings he does of everyone. Some of his photos are duplicates, but we can't help it. He gets so enthusiastic when he gets one that we sometimes print multiples of the same shot, just to keep him happy.

Nathaniel pulls his hand from mine to venture further into the room, and I feel the loss of him straight away. It's like pulling weeds without my gardening gloves. I allow him to explore on his own. The pictures are ingrained in my mind already. Sometimes, when the grief gets too much, when I miss my brother the most, I find myself here. It helps me to remember, too.

"I wouldn't be surprised if he's got a couple of drawings of you up there somewhere. You're his favourite teacher *ever* apparently. Although, I never remind him you're only his second."

"Well, Rory is one of my favourite kids, too. Definitely one of my favourite Websters." He stops his exploration of Rory's room and wanders over to me, resting a hand on my arm. "Thank you, Alex, for telling me about Luke. And for showing me Rory's room. I can tell it was hard for you."

The lack of pity in his face helps me relax. Every time I've told someone about my family, they're over the top with their sympathy. I hate people feeling sorry for me.

"Well," I pause, my breath hitching as I take in how close he's standing to me. "You're easy to talk to. You're a brilliant listener."

"It wasn't a chore. I like talking with you. I promise it's all safe with me. I won't let on to Rory that I know."

"I mean, that's good, but he knows he's not mine."

My face flushes as he laughs, throwing his head back.

"Stop making jokes when I'm trying to be serious. We were having a moment then, Alex," he chastises me but doesn't remove his hand from my arm. His thumb is back to drawing comforting strokes along my skin, leaving a trail of goosebumps in its wake.

"I'm sorry." I'm not. I straighten out my face. Or I try. We've gone from a serious conversation to me feeling giddy and warm, like my head is wobbling on my neck or like a bee drunk on nectar. "Tell me who your favourite Webster is," I goad.

He's trying hard not to laugh again. "No."

"Nate" — when he raises his eyebrows at the pet name, I grin. I'm keeping that one, then — "it's not fair for you to keep something that big from me after everything I've told you."

"I will never tell you. And it's mean to use that against me."

"Is it?"

He takes a step closer to me, and suddenly, I find it hard to breathe. He is intoxicating, the smell of dry-wipe pens, something woody and musky, and the custard from his crumble earlier draw me in, erasing any last ounce of control I might have.

Fuck it. I'm going to take another risk, since the last one paid off. This could go even better. I crane my head up and use his arm to yank him more towards me, desperate for more contact.

He gets his moment to decline, to step away from me and brush this all off as a silly mistake. If he does, I'll be gutted but I'll understand. We're only hanging out because of the stall, after all. It's easy for emotion to steal us away, whisk us into a fantasy world where we might stand a chance. If he says no, we can go downstairs, finish the film and then I'll take him home.

The protest doesn't come, though. Instead, he lowers his head towards mine and tightens his grip on me. Our slow dance continues until our mouths are almost touching, his spare hand resting on my hip as my hand slides to his elbow, holding him in place. Our breath warms the air between us and fogs up our glasses. I wet my lips, and push up on my tiptoes to finally get on with the kiss.

As I take my final breath, he speaks.

"It's you. You're my favourite Webster."

Seven

TWO SENTENCES. SIX WORDS.

It's you. You're my favourite Webster. I didn't know I had a praise kink until he said that. Well, he could do anything and it would turn me on. I am *his*, and he's my favourite, too.

Without pulling in another breath, I close the final few millimetres between us and gently press my mouth to his. God, his lips are so soft, and they glide against mine as if they know their way, like I'm the only man he's ever kissed and we've already been doing it forever. We're slow and hesitant together, yet warmth blooms from where we touch. His grip on me tightens as he returns the kiss, and I stash how he feels in my brain for the days when I am deprived of him. I slip my hand from his elbow, trailing the cords of his bicep then up his neck until I can trace his jawline. My fingers rasp over day-old stubble. When he grazes his lower lip against mine, I capture it, relishing in his taste. Dark cherry wine. Cinnamon.

Fuck, I could devour him.

We finally pull away with shuddering breaths. He looks all the more handsome like this: lips parted, his eyes dewy and soft, and a flush highlighting those stupidly perfect cheekbones.

"That was better than I imagined," I blurt out.

The heat filling my face has nothing to do with the kiss, and all to do with how fucking stupid I am. My cheeks are lava-levels of hot. I'm an idiot. Only I can say something *that* ridiculous. Now all I'll get is one kiss. I'll never get to experience fucking him, or snuggling with him in bed. All because I can't control my bloody mouth.

I stare at Nate, waiting for him to turn and run. But it doesn't come. He doesn't leave. A wide smile graces his face instead, and he rubs his thumb over my lip.

He's still here.

"You've pictured us kissing, too?"

People are always talking about moments like this and how their hearts leap into their throat, or pound in double time. Mine has fucked off. I'm dead. RIP Alexander Webster. Killed by the idea of a gorgeous man wanting him.

We're both idiots. If I'd known he'd been thinking about kissing me, if he would have told me, we could have spent all week doing it.

Now I'm irritated that I've been deprived of *him* for longer than necessary.

"Yeah."

His thumb continues rubbing soothing lines over my cheek. "Is it wrong that I've spent *a lot* of time thinking about it? About you?"

"No. Not at all. I—" I puff out a sharp breath, trying to arrange my thoughts a bit better. "You're so tantalising, Nate."

"Tantalising? I warned you that you were watching too much of that show. It's turned you into a Regency Earl. Are you going to ask to court me? Get my father's permission to take me on a promenade?"

"Only if he'll say yes."

He buries his head against my neck, and I'm not annoyed at his lack of response. His kiss fully confirmed the answer would be in my favour, and I can't fucking wait. I'm off to Hertfordshire straight away to ask his dad the damn question.

"Can you imagine if I just rocked up at your parents' house? 'Excuse me, Mr Jameson. Please may I take your son's hand and walk him up the Thames. And maybe fuck him senseless behind a tree.' I'd probably give the old man a heart attack."

A snort escapes Nate and I laugh too. "It would be the death of my father, for sure."

He nips my collarbone, the hand on my hip sliding further around to my backside, the hand that was caressing my cheek moving down my body. He kisses, licks and sucks his way up my neck. I thread my fingers into his hair so I can guide his mouth, keen to show him all the places I love to be touched, what turns me on. Teachers are fast learners. Before long, he's taking the lead, letting me sink back into the doorframe to *really* enjoy it. He finds the sensitive spot below my pulse point and clamps his lips over it, sucking as if it's giving him life. I'll devote everything to him, every drop of blood in my body, as long as I can enjoy this forever.

"Nate." My hips lift to seek him out. My skin burns when he sucks harder. He's going to leave a bruise at this rate. *Good.* Let the world know he's branded me.

I don't want this to stop, but when I peel open my eyes, eager to see how he looks while he's torturing me, a flash of orange reminds me exactly where we are.

Nope. We can't go any further here.

"Nate."

"Mmm?"

"Although I'm really enjoying this, it feels wrong doing it in Rory's room."

The suction noise he makes when he pulls away from me is obscene. He looks at me, his cheeks colouring, and I almost say fuck it, tear his clothes off and take him right here on the tangerine carpet.

"What about your bedroom?"

My eyes must bug out of my head, because he chuckles softly at me.

"A-are you sure?" *Great playing it cool.*

"More than anything."

I untangle my fingers from his hair and lace them with his. With another check, just to be sure, I tug him out of Rory's room and across the hallway. My spare hand fumbles for the doorknob as Nate seeks out my lips again, and I abandon my attempt to let us into my room.

This kiss is hungrier, unleashing a week's load of sexual tension. All my lame attempts of flirting over text, the banter, and the teasing are paying off.

Another moan reminds me of my mission, and as I swipe my tongue over his, I finally locate the handle and push the door open with such force that it bangs against the wall, taking a chunk of plaster with it.

The noise forces me from him. "I'm never fixing that hole."

"We can frame it," he replies.

There's that word again: *we.*

Focus on the task at hand, Alex. Fuck the guy first. Propose later.

Once we're inside the room, his hands are on me, running over my top, his lips chasing mine. I lose myself in him; his scent, his touch, his taste overpowering everything else in the room. I don't think twice as I move us towards the bed, tumbling to the mattress with him. I respond to his heat eagerly, climbing onto his lap to straddle him.

Oh fuck, he's as hard as me. His *tight* tight jeans leave nothing to my imagination. I grind against him to get the full lay of the land, my vision darkening around the edge as I take in how thick and hot he is under the starched denim. Every inch of me screams to unfasten his fly and get my hands on him.

Or my mouth.

"We've only just met."

What the fuck, brain? My cock deflates faster than a birthday balloon. Go for it, Alex. Stick a wall up right between you and the sexy man who is hard for you, who clearly wants to fuck you. Why not give yourself another eighteen-month dry spell?

Nate pulls away from me, and I whine. It's a pitiful noise that's only going to gross him out even more. His elbows drop to the bed to prop him up, his chest heaves, and his gorgeous hair which never falls out of place is *finally* wild and unruly. And I've gone and messed things up. Still, my hands, which are paying no attention to what I'm saying or what's going on around them, move over his belt and untuck his shirt.

When he cocks an eyebrow at me, I add, "I'm not a one-night stand kind of guy."

"Alex," he whispers. He sits up properly, his fingers sliding to the base of my skull. One of his thumbs rubs my cheek and I lean into the touch, revelling in how we went from spicy and horny to gentle and loving in one breath. Although there's a light sheen of sweat on my skin, something that used to turn my ex off, Nate doesn't flinch. He's here, no matter what spit spews out of my mouth, no matter how gross and clammy I must be right now. Chubby boys don't do well when things get heated. But he doesn't care. That must mean something, right?

"Neither am I," he continues. I force my smile away. He doesn't want me grinning at him like I'm the Joker. Even though finding out he's on every same page as me is better than all my sunflowers blooming at once. "I don't know about you, but I'm hoping this will be more than a one-time thing. But if you want to wait, I can. It's been a hard evening for you and after a long old day, too. We can take it slow – lie here and cuddle or something. Or I can go home, or…"

The heated look he gives me sets me ablaze, igniting at my crown and flushing right through to my dick, which is now back in the game. Although Mike looked at me like this, I never believed it. The way Nate's pupils are blown, lined with green so dark it's almost black, the way he pulls his lower lip through his teeth. Nate *sees* me.

I shudder, but I don't close my eyes to block the intensity out. Instead, I hold his stare as he leans forward until our noses touch, forcing me to go cross-eyed so I can keep on watching him. I never want to take my eyes off him.

Eventually, he covers my mouth with his, and my eyelids flutter shut. Our lips part as I wind my arms around his neck, drawing him closer. He's all hard muscles, and I push him into the mattress so I can enjoy him properly.

His fingers run along the hem of my T-shirt, asking permission to move this forward. I lift my hands in the air and he pulls it off. Then I take over. His top, his jeans, his briefs. God, this man wears the most form-fitting boxers that show off his girth perfectly. His cock is even more glorious without them. Uncut, thick, a bead of precum shining at his tip. It takes all my self-restraint not to cover him with my mouth and suck him until he's screaming my name.

Not yet.

With all his clothes on the floor, I concentrate on returning all the bites and licks he gave me earlier, showering his body in praise and adoration. My teeth nip on hard, corded thighs then my tongue slides down his calves. When he growls my name, I move up his body so quickly, my head collides with his jaw, and sharp pain bursts over my forehead.

"Shit."

"Are you okay?" Concern bleeds through his words as he runs his fingers over my scalp, searching for lumps and bumps.

"Fine. I'm fine." I'm also a fucking idiot. Trying to make it up to him, I kiss along his jaw, taking it a little more slowly to get to his lips again, just in case. We can't have sex if we have a concussion.

A sigh tickles my cheek then we fall into another deep kiss, our limbs tangling together. We work with each other to remove the last of my clothes, planting kisses wherever we can get them. Our fingers fumble, and there's at least one more clash of teeth and noses, but each slip of my hand or bitten lip only fills the room with laughter. It's perfect in its imperfection. I can't get enough of him. We only stop to be careful with our glasses, placing them next to each other on the side table.

When we're both naked, I climb over him, settling on my knees between his legs. He's breathtaking, unabashedly exposed to me, yet he doesn't move to cover up as I devour his body. It's been a long time since I've wanted someone this badly.

I run my hands up his legs as I imagine all the ways I could take him. Should I use my mouth first, or my hands? Oh, but it would feel so good to push my dick against his and dry-hump him like an inexperienced teenager. That first frot is always the sweetest. The ideas rush at me, tugging me in a hundred different directions, all of them with one goal in mind: to draw all the pleasure from him.

I must frown, because Nate's hands skim over my thighs. "What now?"

This time I don't swallow my smile. He's exasperated and it's the hottest thing ever. I lift my head, making sure I have his full attention, and I say in my lowest, sexiest voice, "I can't decide how I want you first."

He laughs, sitting up enough to slide a hand to the back of my neck, anchoring himself to me. There's a kiss on my collarbone, my pulse point, my jaw, my lips, my cheek then a soft bite at the bottom of my ear. He whispers, "I need you to take me. Hard."

I cannot get to my bedside table quick enough, and he flops onto the mattress. I root in the drawer, digging deep. I'm always careful to hide things like lube and condoms from Rory, and when I can't find them, I panic. I don't want to have to leave my room, leave this man, who is stroking himself slowly as he watches me, being the most distracting person ever to exist. It doesn't help that he's lazily tracing a hand over my body, tickling my hip, squeezing my butt cheek.

Fucking hurry up, Alex. I refocus my efforts, delving deeper until *finally*, my hands fall on what we need. I don't waste any more time, and I'm already uncapping the bottle as I return to him on the bed.

"Have you bottomed before?"

"Yes," he replies around a soft moan as I slide my lubed-up fingers through the cleft of his cheeks. "But it's been a while. Take it slow."

"Always. Let me know what's feeling good."

I circle him gently, my eyes trained on his face to gauge his reactions. Regardless of if he's experienced or not, I press a kiss to his hip bone, determined to make this the best for both of us. The hand not caressing his backside dances along his chest, following a light trail of hair from his pecs and down. His abs jump and react to my touch, his cock bobbing when I slide my first finger into him.

His whimper is loud, and I look up, my own dick twitching. My ex was unresponsive and quiet, but Nate couldn't be further from it. His hands clench the pillow – *my* pillow – and his eyes are open. Keeping my gaze on him, I lower my head and *suck*.

"Oh fuck. Alex." His eyes scrunch up tight.

Adding an extra finger is easy, helped by how deep his dick is in my mouth. I focus on thrusting my fingers inside Nate, losing myself in his tightness. He moves with me, forcing his cock deeper into my mouth. I try my best not to gag, even when he hits the back of my throat and tears burn in my eyes. I want to give him everything he needs and he shows me how well I'm doing by how he reacts. His hips thrust, rumpling the duvet. At some point the pillow falls off the bed.

"You have to—" The rest of his words are swallowed up in another gasp and he pushes me away, panting. "Fuck, I need you inside me. Now."

He helps me with the condom, his fingers shaking. Their tickling on my already sensitive dick drives me insane. I long to surge forward, press myself into him.

Be patient.

Using my already lube-slicked hand, I stroke my cock. He peels my fingers away and takes over. *Fuck.* Having my fingers inside him was hot enough, but this. His touch is more than I could ever imagine. He caresses me with just enough pressure, testing his grip, his thumb swivelling over my tip on every upward twist.

"Yes. That's it," I moan. Nate's hands leave too quickly. I'm about to protest when he pulls me closer and spreads his legs for me and I pause for a moment, drinking him in. This is going to be...out of this world and I want to savour every moment of it. "You ready?"

I lean over him, kissing him slowly as I place my hand under his legs, pressing them towards his shoulders. My knees plant under his hips, and I let go of him only to line myself up, the head of my dick throbbing as it grazes over his entrance.

"Please. *Please,* Alex."

I edge into him inch by inch. He's so fucking tight, and it takes all my self control not to slam into him. His words of encouragement spur me on until I'm buried deep inside him.

My fantasies were *nothing* compared to this. I dig my fingernails into his thighs and take a couple of breaths, trying to cling onto my last ounce of composure. Something more than pleasure races through my body. Our eyes are trained on each other, and those silver streaks flicker through the green, telling me he's feeling the exact same way. That he *knows.*

"Move, Alex."

He's pretty bossy for a guy with my dick inside him, but I'm a people-pleaser. I release his legs and brace my hands on either side of his chest, grinding into him. "Like this?"

Sweat glistens on his forehead and I lean in, licking the trail of salt from the corner of his mouth to his temple.

"Yes. *Fuck*, yes. So good. You're so fucking good."

I pull out almost all the way, fitting our mouths together at the same time I thrust back inside him. With his arse clenching around me, it's hard to keep it slow. I want to pound into him, take every ounce of pleasure from him. But I want him to come too. *Fuck.* It's been too long since I've had this, and I shake with the effort of keeping it together.

Nate's breath is forced out of him in sharp bursts with every drive of my hips. "My legs," he tells me after a while, "I need to—"

Before I can consider how I want him next, he wraps his thighs around me, pushing me deeper and further into him. His hard cock lies between us, hot and leaking onto his stomach but I daren't touch it yet. I want him to ask for it, to beg and plead for my caress. Pleasure knots in my stomach, threatening to explode and I can't imagine how it must feel for him. When I nudge against his prostate, he swears loud enough for the whole village to hear.

Fuck. I want that *next.* Let that homophobic old witch on Jamie's street hear how perfect Nate and I are together.

"Nate," I whimper. He continues to move his hips in time with mine, our moans filling the room. "I—I want..."

"Do it." His voice is as needy as mine, and I lift one hand from the mattress to wrap around his cock, groaning as it throbs in time with our thrusts. I try to warn him with my touch that I'm nearly there, *nearly* fucking there, so close to exploding into a million pieces.

He whispers my name, his hands on my shoulders, clawing down my spine, and my pleasure builds and builds. Beads of water drip from my body, and I trace their journey through the valley of his stomach muscles, pooling in his belly button, allowing it to distract me from my impending orgasm.

Not yet. Just a few more—

"Now. Alex."

His command sets me off. I come so hard my body shakes with it. Pleasure shoots up my cock, my hips snapping to his as I pin him down and fuck my orgasm into him, my declarations to whoever is listening bursting out in loud grunts.

Nate's peak comes a nanosecond after mine. He pulls me to him, opening my lips with his own. His tongue slips inside at the same time his body shudders and hot come spills on his belly.

I must be dead. I sag on top of him, collapsing and letting every ounce of my weight rest on his strong, wide body. His arms wrap around me, and we ride out the aftershocks until they blow away, like leaves on the wind. I'm heavy, my limbs overused, and my insides jelly. I'm also the happiest man in the world. I sigh, a content noise, and nuzzle closer.

In all the ways I've imagined having sex with him, I forgot about the afterglow. With Nate, it's even more perfect, like soaking in a hot bath after having a deep-tissue massage.

"I could fall asleep right here."

"Right on top of me?" He chuffs a laugh. "But we're all sticky and gross."

He strokes his fingers through my hair. My eyelids droop and my breathing grows steadier, calmer. I won't be able to move if he keeps on doing that. I'll never leave this spot.

"I guess we should go shower. But you're cosy and I don't want to leave."

He moves anyway, sliding out from underneath me and standing naked next to the bed. My eyes are drawn to his body, and I wonder if I can go again already. I'm given the promise of more with a small twitch of his cock. Yeah, he's right. I'll need at least twenty minutes before another go.

"If you don't want to wash my come off your stomach then at least you can feed me. I'm always hungry after sex."

"Seriously?" He holds his hand out to me and I take it, grumbling my complaint. I contemplate closing my eyes again anyway, but then his belly growls and I laugh.

"Alex. Please." He drags me out of bed without waiting for any more protests, and starts to lead me out of *my* bedroom as if this house belongs to him too. "What if I promise you we'll snuggle as soon as we're out of the shower? Do you snore? You better not. I prefer sleeping in silence."

He's staying the night, then.

Fucking brilliant.

EIGHT

I AM THE LUCKIEST fucking guy in the world.

For the first time in forever, I'm woken by the sun streaming through my window and birds chirping outside. I must have forgotten to close the curtains before drifting into the best sleep of my life. Although, can you blame me for not remembering when the man tempting me into bed is as stunning as Nathaniel fucking Jameson?

The bright light paints stripes on his face, highlighting his sharp cheekbones and the creases on his forehead where he's frowning in his sleep. He snuffles, igniting a flutter in my heart, and I wriggle over the mattress so I can watch him better. He moved away from me during the night, pulling most of the duvet into his arms and cuddling up to it. It should be *me* he's snuggling, but I can't be mad given everything we did.

Oh, yes. It was phenomenal. My confession, accepted without pity, and with understanding and compassion; telling Nate I fancied him, and the elation that he felt the same. And the sex. The fucking sex.

Yawning, I stretch out, my limbs winding under the duvet and prising it from him. He stirs straight away, moaning his complaint. I wrap my arms around him in a tight cuddle and nuzzle my greeting against his neck, following it with a line of butterfly kisses, working up towards his lips.

"Good morning to you, too, handsome." I don't have to look at him to know he's smiling. His voice is peaceful and happy, if full of sleep, and he presses his lips to my forehead. "How did we end up here?"

I push a wavy blond lock out of his face. He admitted his hair is blow-dried and straightened, every damn day. He was worried about going to bed with it damp. Ugh. It's even more perfect this way, unruly, sleep-tangled, and it reminds me of everything we got up to.

"Well, Mr Jameson. When two people drink a bit of wine and admit they fancy the pants off each other, certain things happen—"

"Shut up. No way?"

"Yep. But wasn't it fun?"

"So much fun. We did a lot of great things together."

His cheeks turn pink. After I fed him – and he needed a three-course meal before he was full – he took me in the shower, pounding into me while my hands were splayed across the wet tiles. My limbs, already tired from fucking him, were useless afterwards. He dried me off, wrapped me in my towel, then hitched me over his shoulder like I weighed nothing more than a bag of rice and carried me to bed. We changed the sheets, fucked once more anyway, then fell asleep, limbs entangled. There was no telling where I stopped and he began.

"Do you regret any of it?" I continue to stroke his hair.

"Never. If anything, I want more."

"Me too." I've never been more certain about anything before. "You know, when I first met you, I wasn't sure you were gay."

"I— I'm bisexual." He takes a sudden interest in my duvet, which is as plain and boring as they come.

"I wasn't your first man, was I?"

I prop myself on my elbow, trying to get his attention back on me so he knows he can be as open and honest with me as I was with him.

"You asked me that last night, too. No. I—" He sighs and lifts his gaze. When he finds me staring at him, he smiles and kisses me softly. "Did you think you were my first?"

"Absolutely not." The things he did to me come with experience. He knew all the right angles to hit, the exact right way to pull my cock into his mouth. How to draw the loudest groans from my lips. My body flushes at the memory of it all.

Flopping onto his chest, I run my hand over his tight pecs. All his time in the gym is paying off. Not that I can imagine him without a solid body. I'm happy to sacrifice time for texting if it means I get to enjoy all his muscles. My fingers bump over a scar that sits above his ribs. "How did you get this?"

His fingers join mine, rubbing over the same spot. "My gay awakening didn't come until I was twenty-nine. It...it was difficult, to say the least, and coming out didn't go that smoothly. One of my friends didn't take it too well. He thought I'd been misleading him. Even went as far as to suggest I was taking advantage of him when we were working out or changing together."

A sigh breaks through his words, and I glance at him to make sure he's okay. His smile is gone, and his eyes have a distant stare, but his fingers still work along the scar with mine. I add pressure to let him know I'm still here.

"Things got a bit out of hand. I'm not a fighter, but some of the things he said...the words he used. He was my best friend, but I didn't have a clue he was a raging homophobe. We both threw a few punches, and when he shoved me away, I caught my side on a rusty pole. Serves me right for brawling like a kid."

"What happened with him?"

"We stopped talking. For the most part, people were understanding, but he managed to drag a few mutual pals with him. It made things difficult with—" The words catch in his throat and he puffs a wave of hair out of his eye. "Whatever. I'm better off without them."

"I agree." I rest my head on his pec. His heart thumps under his skin. "I'm sorry you had a bad experience. Not everyone is like that, though."

His hands link together and settle on the small of my back. I'm practically lying on top of him now, but if I'm squashing him, he doesn't complain. "I know. But it's hard for me to make friends, so when people walk out, it sucks even harder. My parents treated me like a mini-adult when I was younger, which is why I'm so boring and rigid n—"

"There was only one thing rigid about you last night."

The tickle attack comes hard and fast. He uses his strength to roll us over, pinning me to the bed. His hands run all over me, and no amount of kicking my legs can stop it. "You're a pain in the backside, Alexander Webster," he says between laughs. "Here I am, telling you something important, and all you can do is joke."

Is it wrong that his using my full name turns me on?

"I'm a comedian." I giggle-snort, trying to fight him off. "It's what I do best."

It takes him forever to run out of steam, despite the workout I put him through last night, but he finally plonks himself on top of me, his head resting on my chest and his legs straddling my thighs. His full weight is on me, his hands now stroking my sides, and it feels like one of those massive blankets. Warm and solid. Comforting. I embrace the silence for a moment, using it to catch my breath.

"I don't think you're boring," I continue. "Or rigid. You're caring. A brilliant teacher. Fun."

"I'm glad *someone* thinks so."

I frown as he closes his eyes and lets out a deep sigh. The man he's talking about is the complete opposite to the one I've been getting to know recently. Sure, we have a long way to go in discovering our ins and outs, our icks and yums, but so far, there's nothing I've seen that'll scare me off.

Not that I'm a great judge of character. I once thought me and Mike were forever.

Don't get me wrong. I'm not naive. Every person in the world has one thing that is annoying as fuck. But I can't see Nate's being *that* bad.

"Well, I'm right and everyone else is wrong," I tell him.

He scoffs. "I've had a few partners since coming out, Alex. And they've all called me hard work. The need to be on time, the dedication to my job. Did you know this is the first Saturday since I moved here where I haven't woken up early for the gym. I don't think I could have left you in bed alone, but there's still a part of my brain niggling me to get to my workout." Although he snuggles closer to me, he groans, turning his head so his long nose is digging into the soft skin between my moobs. "I shouldn't be telling you any of this. You'd be running for the hills if we weren't lying in your bed."

"I'm *not* going to run away, Nate." I tug on his hair gently, forcing him to look at me. His face is bright red, and it takes him a breath before he'll meet my gaze. "What I said is true. I don't do one-night stands or flings. For me, sex means something, and I save it for the people who I want to know better. So, believe me when I say I'm not going anywhere."

"Thank you." He gives me a quick peck.

"Since we're in a sharing mood. Before yesterday, there was...well, a dry spell. There hasn't been anyone since my ex."

"Really? The only reason I didn't tell you earlier that I fancied you was because I was sure men were throwing themselves at you. I thought you wouldn't be interested in me because you had much better offers."

It's hard but I bite back my scoff. The dating pool in East Beechmill is extremely small, and for a gay guy, is full of older conservative men married to wives suspicious of their husband's sexuality but who would prefer to keep it hidden so they don't get kicked out of the WI. It's not worth having a gay dating app on my phone, unless I'm desperate for a dick pic from the butcher *and* the postman. Sometimes, if I'm really lucky, I get pictures of both of them together, living their best hidden-queer naked lives. Add in my pudgy body, my glasses, my awful dress sense and Rory, and I'm limited in choice. Men only throw themselves at me in my dreams.

"Nobody is interested in sleeping with a single dad-hobbit, Nate."

"Stop it. You're perfect, Alex." He kisses me before his head returns to my chest. "I feel the same, by the way. About sex, and, well, about you, too."

His soft peck wasn't enough. I use my hand in his hair to draw his face to mine. This kiss is slow and unassuming, but I have a desperate need to persuade him that I mean what I say. I'm staying right here. With him. And there are no other men in my life.

We pull apart and his smile is back, wide and dopey-looking. If he wasn't lying on top of me, I'd be kicking my legs and screaming with how adorable he is.

"Can you do me a favour?"

"What's that?"

"Will you give me a chance to learn about you and make my own decisions about whether I think you're hard work?"

It takes him a moment to answer me, his forehead wrinkling. Finally, he relaxes and his smile returns. "Okay."

I'm about to pull him into a hungrier kiss when the alarm clock on my bedside table rings. I push him off me and reach over to shut it up. Stupid analogue clock. Stupid me for wanting to teach the kid properly. It hits the floor but goes quiet, and I turn back to Nate, sighing. "I need to go get Rory."

He pouts. "But it's not even nine yet."

"I know. I told Henry I'd be there at half past."

"Do you *have* to?"

The gleam in his eyes is something I haven't seen on him before – mischievous and alluring. It's telling me we should stay here in bed for a lot longer than I had planned.

"Do I *have* to pick my six-year-old up?" I smirk. "Well, yeah. He's far too small to be wandering the streets alone, and he can't read a map. Plus, if my mum found out I abandoned him to stay in bed with you, she'll finally have her way and take him off me."

"Do you really think that's going to happen?"

In a massive betrayal to her, I stop and think about it for a second. Sure, there are a lot of things pointing that way, but I always attribute them to my insecurities as Rory's guardian. Mum would never do that to me.

I shake my head. "No."

"So," Nate continues, trailing a finger along my arm. There he goes, being tantalising again. "Why not ring your brother and ask for a little bit longer? Say you've got a headache or something. I'm sure he won't mind since he already has him. A few more hours won't hurt."

It's a fantastic idea. I'd love at least one more round with Nate. But a niggle of doubt tugs at me too, filling my head with how awful it would be if my family found out I lied, that I put extra pressure on my sibling because I wanted more sex.

Luke would never.

No, but he would have been the first to tell me that finding someone is important, that getting a new boyfriend would make me happy. Especially someone who is everything Mike wasn't.

Though, if Luke were here, I wouldn't be in this predicament. Bastard.

Nate continues to tempt me, his hand now sliding over my hip. My dick stirs, agreeing with his idea.

"Come on, Alex. You're a brilliant parent to Rory, and you sacrifice a lot for him. I promise it's okay to do something for you once in a while. Nothing bad will happen. We can spend a little longer in bed, shower again, get some food then you can drop me home on the way to pick him up. It'll be fine. Let someone look after *you* for a change."

I'm the weakest man in the world. Either that, or he's weaving some sort of magic spell on me. His lips clamp onto my neck, sucking a gasp out of me, and my hands slide over his back, my fingernails digging into his delightfully firm arse cheeks.

"Okay, but not for too long." Although, if he asked me to stay in bed all day with him, I would. His bites are already moving down my body and he shoves the duvet to the floor. "Hold your horses. I need to ring Henry."

But he doesn't stop. Hands trembling, I reach for my phone and dial my brother's mobile number, not wanting to risk one of the kids answering the house phone.

The call connects at the same time Nate takes me into his hot, wet mouth and I suppress my moan.

"Alex? Is that you? What's wrong?"

I swallow hard, trying my best to stop my voice from wavering. But Nate's nose presses against my pubic bone, his eyes closing as he takes all of me straight away. Then, he hollows his cheeks.

Fuck. I can't keep my hips on the bed. My spare hand slides into his hair, holding him there while I fight the urge to fuck his mouth. I bet he could take it hard. Last night, I was gentle with him, but there is a rough side of him I'm eager to explore.

I cough to clear my throat. "Henry. I've got a migraine. Can you keep Rory for a little bit longer?"

NINE

MY STOMACH GRUMBLES OVER my panted breaths. It's been a few hours since I spoke to Henry, and me and Nate have been making the most of our time alone.

He lifts his head from the foot of the mattress, his eyes lingering on the mess on my stomach before moving up my body to my face. His smile is blinding, and I fall for him a little bit more. This is why I don't do one-night stands. I'm not in control of my emotions.

"I'm starving, too." He's stroking the bottom of my leg as he talks, his words dragging over a yawn.

I roll over to check the time. "I'm such a bad host. It's gone eleven."

"Do you have the ingredients for pancakes?"

"Yeah, I think so."

"Brilliant. I'm a pancake connoisseur."

He shifts with a groan and drags himself up the bed, giving me a long, lingering kiss. His tongue swirls through my mouth. Along with the coffee I crawled out of bed for a while ago, he tastes of me. I'm not put off by it, though. Instead, I yank him closer, my hand creeping down his back. Although I'm too exhausted to go again – well, my dick is at least – part of my brain pleads for one more orgasm. Nate is *brilliant* at extracting them from me.

When he withdraws, he's still beaming at me. He drags his hand behind him, as if he can't stop touching me as he slides off the bed and uses one of last night's discarded towels to clean himself.

"I'm tired, and everything hurts," I complain. "But seeing you standing there naked makes me want more."

Not even his chuckle stirs any more horniness. I am satiated. But if he were to ask...

"*Please* let me eat, Alex. And get some water. I'm going to have a sex hangover if you keep me this dehydrated."

"I didn't hear you grumbling about it five minutes ago."

"That's because you were working me too hard."

"I had to make up for you missing your precious gym time."

"Bold of you to assume I won't be going once you've dropped me home." His wink sends goosebumps erupting over my skin.

Bloody hell. How does this guy have so much energy? I am ready for the longest nap right now. "Didn't I give you a good enough workout?"

"Of course you did. But I need to balance out the rest of my muscles or I'll be wonky. Now, do you want food or not?"

"Yeah, I'm hungry. You gonna put some clothes on?"

He glances down at his bare body and grins. "No. It was fun cooking naked last night. Are you going to get dressed?"

"Nah. But I do need to use the loo. See you downstairs?"

"You bet."

We share one last kiss and then he's heading out, my eyes fixed on his backside. It's too peachy and firm, and now that it's emblazoned with red handprints – *my* handprints – it's harder to resist.

"I know you're looking at me," he calls out, the pound of his feet on the stairs punctuating his words.

Well, I was, but now he's disappeared, I haul myself out of bed. My legs tremble and ache as much as the rest of my body. I need to work out more. Yuck. As much as I want to see Nate sweat in other ways, I cannot bring myself to enter a gym.

Not that I mind the soreness. It serves as a hopefully temporary reminder of how good sex with him is. I wander, zombie-like, across the hallway, pee, then clean myself off with a cloth. My reflection catches my eye and I barely recognise the person staring back at me. I'm a fucking mess. My hair looks like a bird has made a home in it, and a necklace of love bites sits above my collarbone. My cheeks are red and there's nothing I can do to wipe the satisfied smirk off my face. *Brilliant.*

I debate taking a swig of mouthwash or running a comb through my hair, but instead, I quickly wash my hands. I take the stairs two at a time. Maybe I can find enough energy to bend Nate over the counter and—

"Are you sure you're hungry? Because I can think of something better we can do with that pancake mi—"

Oof.

The man I collide with is not the man I've spent all morning having sex with. No, this man is far too tall and spindly to be Nate. Also, my visitor is wearing clothes.

Oh fuck, oh fuck, oh fuck.

"Alex." Henry takes a step away from the door. Behind him, Nate cowers behind the kitchen island, his face as white as the countertop. "I didn't know there was going to be a pancake lunch."

The life drains out of me and whatever is left inside freezes.

No. Not now. And not fucking Henry.

Rory stands next to my brother, dancing from foot to foot in the excited way I usually find cute. Right now? I'd rather see anything else. I don't blame him, though. If I wasn't so fond of having my balls attached to my body, or if it was happening to anyone but me, this whole scene would be hilarious. I probably wouldn't have minded if we were caught with clothes on. But naked? Fuck. My. Life.

Henry continues, since nobody else is brave enough to speak. "Does nobody wear clothes in this house?"

Acting on instinct, I cup my dick – although everyone in this room has seen it all more than once, just in less ridiculous circumstances – and skirt around the counter, determined to reach Nate. My brain is in turmoil. I'm not sure what to say or who to apologise to first.

So I resort to my usual. Defensive blabbing.

"I thought I was coming to grab Rory in a couple of hours?" I stand in front of Nate, as if my small stature will be enough to protect his modesty. My family might have seen my naked arse before, but I don't want them getting a look at him. That view is for my eyes only. Perhaps if I turn to the side, my beer belly will help, but it would mean breaking eye contact with Henry, and he wouldn't appreciate it.

"Yep." He pops the p to make his point. "That's what we agreed. Because you had a migraine after work and needed more time to recover. This little guy" – he runs his hand over Rory's head – "has been poorly. I figured since you were both feeling rubbish, I'd use my key to chuck him into the house. He wanted to cuddle in bed with you, but it seems you have a waiting list."

Kill me now.

My brother has been a grump all his life. He was born with a scowl on his face and I don't think I've ever seen him crack a smile. I'm usually used to it, but today his tone is greeted with a wave of guilt that crashes over me. Nate promised me it would be okay to be selfish for once, but Rory is ill, and I've neglected him. For what, a few hours of sex? I'm such a bad parent.

Henry's touch must remind the kid he has a voice. He scuttles over to me and uses my hand to pull him to his level.

"That's my teacher," he whispers in my ear, before growing in confidence. He pulls himself up as tall as he can and looks Nate dead in the eye. "Mr Jameson. Why are you here? Where are your clothes?"

I'm sure the neighbours are keen to know too, kid.

My brother's eyebrows might as well be in the sky with how high they are. And is that...did the corner of his mouth just twitch? He's probably wondering the same thing. At least Rory had the guts to say it out loud.

Before Nate can open his mouth, I jump in. "We were, uhm, doing some work on the stall, and decided to have breakfast. Only we got the batter all over the place so I put his clothes in the washing machine. Mine too."

"Oh," Rory replies. "Is it broken? Because it's not making the whir-whir noise."

I want to disappear. Why the fuck can't the linoleum split in two and swallow me up? The cost of repairing it will be much better than *this*.

"I did text you," Henry adds, further stoking the poker-hot shame creeping over my body. There's a glint in his eyes that tells me he's determined to make this worse for me. I'm pretty sure my phone fell down the side of the bed at some point during mine and Nate's activities. I didn't give it a single thought once I'd hung up on my brother. Nate had my cock in his mouth, and all I was focused on was returning the favour. *Fuck*. My whole body is on fire. Perhaps if I'm lucky, I'll spontaneously combust. "I also asked if you needed anything, but it's clear you're being *well* looked after."

Where's the damn apocalypse when you need it? To try and save face, I run a hand over Rory's forehead. Perhaps I'll look like a better parent if he gets all of my attention. "You don't have a temperature, buddy."

"It was probably all the running around and junk food they ate. Perhaps leaving them with Sal while me and Soph went out wasn't the best idea. It was chaos when we got back. Sorry." Henry softens as he shoulders some of the blame, grimacing. But his focus soon drifts from me and back to Nate, as if he's waiting for an introduction.

No way. It's not going to happen. Not today. If my family is going to meet him, it's going to be when we're all fully dressed. No. I need to get Henry out of here to save Nate any more embarrassment.

"Well," I say, "thanks for having Rory. I'll see you tomorrow, yeah?"

At least my eldest brother is good at taking a hint. "Yeah. Of course."

He turns to leave, his phone already out of his pocket. *Shit.* Grabbing a pair of drying boxers off the radiator, I stumble into them as I follow him. "Henry, wait. You're not going to—"

"Put this in the family chat? Why not?"

I groan. "Because *Mum* is in there."

"If I had to suffer through seeing your naked backside, then everyone else should experience it, too."

"*Please*, Henry. He's Rory's teacher."

His eyes flit to the kitchen, where Nate has taken a cue from me and located another pair of pants. He's trying to squeeze into them without exposing himself to Rory, but isn't doing a great job. Rory, either oblivious to his teacher's nakedness or just not caring, assaults Nate with a barrage of questions about Captain America. His enthusiasm would be adorable, if this wasn't such a shit moment.

Henry's lips grow tighter, like he's about to experience his first ever laugh and isn't sure what to do about it. After a moment and a couple of deep breaths, he turns back to me.

"Fine. But only because I'm happy you're *finally* getting some. I'm annoyed you lied to me about it, though. If you'd told me the real reason, I would have offered to have Rory for longer. And I wouldn't have brought him home early."

Maybe I've underestimated my brother.

"If I catch you again," he adds, "especially if you've been telling porkies, *all* of this goes in the chat."

Maybe I haven't.

Part of me thinks I deserve the extra ribbing. I took a chance, an opportunity to have some time to do something for me, and it blew up in my face. That's what you get for being selfish. For now, my brother is affording me the chance to do this in private, to tell the family when I'm ready. It's not like I want to keep Nate a secret – I really don't. I'm fucking ecstatic we got to sleep together. But I want to wait until I know what we are first.

"At least Rory doesn't seem too traumatised by it all," I offer.

"Wait until the nightmares. I know I'll be having them tonight."

Git.

I don't bother to see him out. Instead, I return to the kitchen, stopping next to Rory. The kid is still grinning widely at his teacher, although I haven't heard any more questions yet. At least Nate has some pants on now.

I crouch to Rory's level. "Hey, buddy, I need to have a chat with Mr Jameson. Why don't you go and dump your stuff in your room and get settled on the sofa. We can watch *The Avengers* if you want?"

"Can he stay? We could watch all the *Thor* movies?"

"No. Not today."

"*Iron Man*?"

He doesn't give up. Maybe I've been spoiling him too much recently. "Not *Iron Man* either. Mr Jameson has to go home."

I would love for Nate to spend the rest of the day with us, but if things are going to carry on – and I hope they do – there have to be some strict boundaries. At least there are only a few more weeks of him being Rory's teacher. Maybe we can start hanging out together during the summer holidays. I want to take it slowly. I have to protect Rory.

"But, Alex," he whines. I grit my teeth at the noise. He rarely annoys me, but the high-pitched nasal tone gets right to my last nerve.

"I said no."

He turns on his heel with the loudest huff he can muster and storms out of the kitchen. Yeah, there's no way he's sick. I've heard of miraculous recoveries, but never this quick. Every step he takes towards his bedroom is a hard, angry stomp, using too much energy for a kid who's been chucking up this morning.

Sighing, I switch my attention to Nate, who lingers in the middle of the kitchen, grimacing. At least seeing my baggy boxers on his stunning body is a turn off. Yesterday, I dreamed of seeing him in my clothes, but instead of being excited, I'm fucking miserable. Not only have I potentially scarred my kid for life and let my brother down, but I've put the man I'm keen to see more of in a shit position.

Maybe I'm the problem?

"Nate. I'm *so* so sorry. It's not like Henry to let himself in. The key is only for emergencies." I guess it could have been worse. Mum could have been looking after Rory. I don't voice it though. It won't make things better. "That's not the point. I shouldn't have put you in this position. I need to be more responsible. I should have made you put some clothes on. Or gone to pick Rory up when I first agreed to. I was selfish, and it backfired on us."

"It's not your fault, and you weren't being selfish."

I ignore him, fully committed to my spiralling. "I should have been keeping a closer eye on my phone. I have a kid. It's not like I'm twenty with zero responsibilities. I can't stay in bed with a man all day, no matter how much I want to."

Tears of frustration, of shame and embarrassment, burn in my eyes, but I don't step closer to him for comfort. I'm beating myself up a little too hard over it, but he's the first guy I've been interested in since Mike who's available. Who's interested in *me*. Now I've fucked it all up.

"I should go," is Nate's only reply. *Oh.* He won't meet my gaze, which fuels my disappointment. We've failed at the first fucking hurdle.

"Yeah, I guess. Why don't you find my phone and I'll order you a taxi?"

"You sure?"

"It's the least I can do."

As he passes me, he squeezes my arm and I risk a proper glance at him. His lips are turned down, and it's clear he's feeling the same way about how things have ended. He reaches the door and stops. For a moment, I think he may lean in for one last kiss, but Rory thunders downstairs and into the living room, the door slamming behind him.

Nate lets go of me and slips upstairs. This time, I can't watch him.

The clothes horse is in the kitchen, waiting for our freshly washed clothes to be put away. Yet another task I neglected for having sex. I dress in whatever I can grab first then settle on the sofa with Rory, scratching at my beard as I contemplate this morning.

It doesn't take long for him to interrupt my thoughts.

"Why were you working on the stall without me?"

I lift my arm and let him cuddle into my side. "Uncle Simon liked our idea, and we wanted to get some of the boring stuff out of the way."

"Did Mr Jameson really get pancakes on his clothes?"

I pause for a moment, debating how much to tell Rory. Lying to him feels wrong. I always try to tell him as much age-appropriate stuff as I can, encouraging his curiosity. But he's only six. He doesn't need to know I was boning his teacher less than an hour ago, and I *cannot* tell him that Nate is my boyfriend without his permission. I don't even know if he *is* my boyfriend yet.

Plus, that's something we should do together. *When* we agree things are more serious between us.

"No. He came over after work because we wanted to celebrate the good news. We watched a film, drank a bit of wine and then it was too late for Mr Jameson to go home. Only he didn't have his pyjamas with him."

Rory nods, looking too wise for his age. "He could have borrowed mine."

Some of the tension leaves my body. It takes a lot of effort to reply to him with a straight face. I love his view of the world. "I'm not sure they'd fit."

"Did *you* get pancakes on your jammies?"

"Yeah, you got me. You know how much of a mess I make."

"You always get your dinner down you." Bloody hell, he's getting too much like Mum. "Did Mr Jameson sleep in my bed?"

I shake my head. "I don't think he'd fit there, either. He stayed on the sofa. I've already tidied away the spare duvet."

He runs his little hand over the cushion next to him, as if he's searching for indents or any other clue to confirm my story. Once he's satisfied, he turns his body more towards the TV, pushing all his weight into me.

I cast my eyes upward, following the creaking of the floorboards above us. Nate hasn't been gone long, but I already miss him like crazy. It's mental that someone can walk into my life and upend things in the most wonderful way, especially after only a week. I have to tread carefully, though.

Lighter footsteps on the stairs indicate that he's returning. I refuse to let him leave under a dark cloud like this, and I want to salvage some remnants of an otherwise perfect night and morning with him.

"I'm going to go and say goodbye to Mr Jameson, okay? You stay here." I kiss the top of Rory's head then wander out to the hallway, catching Nate as he sits in his usual spot to tie his laces. "Hey, you."

He doesn't look at me. He's too busy gathering his things. "I ordered a taxi off the app on your phone. It'll be here in a minute."

I don't have to question how he worked out my PIN. It's Rory's birth date. Guess he knows me pretty well already.

"All right. I'll wait with you."

My hands twitch, eager to take hold of him, but I resist. I'm pretty sure if I turn my head, there'll be a tiny spy watching us. I linger at the bottom of the stairs, one arm tucked around the newel post. "Listen, I'm sorry again about earlier."

"You don't have to keep apologising, Alex. This sort of thing is going to happen, right? I don't mean being caught in your kitchen naked. That will never happen again. But being interrupted. You have a kid. He's going to be around. It's not like you can get a babysitter every time we see each other. I get it. And it's kind of my fault for persuading you to call Henry and pretend you were sick." His voice is calm, barely above a whisper, but I tune into the thrum of anguish it creates in my body.

"Yeah. I guess it's going to be tough. And about last night—"

"Oh. Do you regret it now? I mean, I understand. Rory's appearance has reminded you about how awkward this could get. I'm his teacher, at least for a few more weeks, and I—"

"No, wait. That's not what I wanted to say." I take a few more steps towards him. We're so close we could touch, but neither of us is brave enough to bridge the gap. I keep my voice low, in case little ears are listening. "Our time together was amazing. I wondered if...I thought maybe we could— Do you want to go on a date with me? If I can find a babysitter now that my brother knows I'm a liar, that is. I'd like to make a proper go of...this..." I gesture hopelessly between us.

"What is this, Alex?"

"Dating. Some romance. A lot more sex. Eventually. I want to do this properly. Maybe I could call you my boyfriend, you know, if we decide we want to."

His eyes burn into me, but I refuse to back away from his gaze, even if it feels like he's trying to X-ray me. I'm putting it all out on the table, there is *nothing* for me to hide.

"Yeah," he breathes out. "I'd like that. I'm free all week after school. Let me know what's best for you. Either way, we have to get together to work on the stall."

Oh shit. The stall. I've barely given it a thought since the meeting yesterday.

"We need to involve Rory, or he'll feel left out and that won't help our case when – *if* – we decide to be boyfriends. When I say a date, I want it to be me and you, in a restaurant that isn't The Watering Hole. Is that okay?"

"It sounds perfect. Thank you."

"You're very welcome." My heart pounds in my chest, and I want nothing more than to steal a kiss from him, but a snuffle at the door scares me off at the last minute. "Bloody kid."

"Good luck explaining everything to him."

"Oh, he's already been firing awkward questions at me." I roll my eyes.

"Perhaps you could call me later and let me know what you say to him. Then I can corroborate in school on Monday?"

A taxi beeps outside the house. Our time is up.

"Yeah. I'll speak to you later."

"Okay. Bye, Alex."

"Bye."

It's hard to let him go, especially without a kiss. I stay on the doorstep until he's inside the taxi and it's pulling away, watching until it's disappeared down the street.

As predicted, Rory is peering around the doorframe, his eyes wide. The cogs in his brain must be going a million miles an hour. I groan. It's going to be a long afternoon.

"Right, you monster," I say, closing the front door. There must be something I can distract him with. "Do you feel well enough for a sandwich?"

TEN

RORY DOESN'T FIGHT HIS bedtime. We spent the afternoon sprawled over the living-room floor, designing rainbow-coloured signs for the stall while *The Avengers* played in the background. But the closer we got to dinner, the paler he grew. By the time I helped him into his seat, he looked like a Victorian ghost child.

After watching him pick at his food for a solid ten minutes, I sighed. "Come on, mate. I think it's time we get you to bed."

I carry him upstairs to his bedroom, plonk him on his bed then fish out clean pyjamas for him.

"I feel yuck," he tells me, missing his armhole for the second time. I step in, wishing I could protect him from all the sickness bugs. It's awful seeing him this way. He barely has the energy to climb under the duvet when I pull it back for him, and he doesn't ask to be tucked in with Mjölnir.

I don't get time to say goodnight to him. As soon as his head hits the pillow, he's fast asleep. His snores – like a train rumbling through the countryside – fill the room, and I tuck him in tighter. Although he remains pale, the creases smooth out of his face and his lips relax out of his frown. I could watch him sleep all night.

I run my hand over his head one last time before leaving the side of his bed. As an afterthought, I grab the washing-up bowl from the kitchen and leave it on the floor with a towel in case he pukes. There have been a few incidents in the past two years where he hasn't made it to the loo, and it takes forever to get the stink of sick out of the carpet. Leaving the door open, I head downstairs to tidy up.

Once all my chores are done, I settle in front of the TV, at a bit of a loss for what to do. After the high of yesterday and this morning, staying in all evening by myself is a downer. No amount of half-naked regency men is going to cheer me up and not even the hope of a date with Nate is enough to stop me deflating. I'd always hoped that when I finally found someone interested in me, my weekends would be more entertaining.

I shake my head, trying to clear away my grumps. I spent *a lot* of time with Nate over the past twenty-four hours. I'm a parent first, and Rory *has* to be my priority. Luke was always sacrificing his time for him. Anyway, we saw what happens when I'm selfish. It backfires.

After flicking through a couple of shows, I settle on a mindless reality TV programme, but as rich housewives yell at each other about their *awful* lives, my silent phone catches my attention.

Would it be too much to call Nate? I could text, but it doesn't feel enough now I've experienced what his voice is like in my ear, all silky-smooth, almost growling.

Yeah, I can't resist. My phone is in my hand before I give it a second thought, and he answers on the first ring.

"Is everything okay?"

"Well, hello to you too, handsome."

"Sorry. Hi. I saw you were ringing and panicked that Rory might be really unwell and you needed me to come to the hospital or something. Not that I'd be the first person you'd want there. Your mum comes before me, of course. But, still I'd like to be there, if you needed me. Whatever helps."

My parents *would* be the first people I call. Mum is probably down as Rory's second next of kin, anyway. It's nice to know that Nate would be there for me too, if I needed it. He's good at comforting me. I'm not sure how I'd react if something was seriously wrong with Rory. I'm a bit of a panicker, but Nate would calm me down.

"He's okay-ish," I reply. "I put him to bed twenty minutes ago 'cause he looked like he was going to puke over his dinner."

"Bless him. What do you think is wrong? Maybe he's got whatever Felicity had yesterday?"

I shrug, but when the line stays silent – *because he can't see you, doofus* – I say, "Yeah, perhaps. It's probably a twenty-four hour thing. He eats pretty much anything he can get his hands on, and although I've tried to tell him to stop munching on worms, he won't listen to me."

"I get it. You should see the stuff I have to pull out of my pupil's hands. It's so stressful, making sure they're not shoving pennies up their noses, or challenging each other to a woodlouse eating competition. You don't seem too worried about Rory, though, so that's a good sign."

"I wasn't always this laid back about it. The first time he was ill, I watched over him most of the night. Every time I texted the group chat about it, my brothers just replied that Rory will be fine, but each cough, sneeze and grumble wound me up. I couldn't shake the feeling that something was terribly wrong with him, and that he was close to dying. I broke down at about three in the morning and called Mum, barely able to get my words out over my tears. She was horrified that I was still awake, and that I had bothered her in the middle of the night over a cold. I got such a bollocking." I chuckle. "Then she gave me her most valuable advice to date: unless something is broken, or his temperature is above thirty-eight degrees, he'll be fine. Sometimes, just like adults, kids get sick for absolutely no reason. Unless I learn to relax, being a parent will be hell."

"She sounds like a wise woman."

"Well, birthing and keeping alive a hundred of us means she has a lot of different experiences. Unfortunately, her advice is almost always unsolicited."

He laughs. "There are not a hundred of you."

"No. But it's close."

"Did Rory ask any more awkward questions?"

"He only stopped asking when he was feeling poorly again. Is it bad I'm kind of glad he had to go to bed, because it shut him up?"

"Jeez. I'm not sure I can face him on Monday. And if I ever get a chance to see your brother again, I'm not sure I can ever look him in the eye. I can't believe he saw and heard what he did."

Yeah, all because of me and my big fucking mouth. "At least you don't have to go to a family dinner tomorrow. It's going to be the second worst experience of my life. This morning has pushed our disastrous introduction into third place."

"As I keep on telling you – my recollection of that afternoon is a lot different than yours. I thought you were adorable. Seeing you splutter and cringe after you forced a hug on me is what triggered my crush on you."

"Seriously? You're so fucking weird."

"Maybe. You were so embarrassed and pink, practically squirming where you stood, but you looked me in the eye when you said goodbye. That takes balls. I would have run a mile, and never been able to see you again. Someone else would be helping you with the stall."

"It's because I'm used to looking like an idiot. It's second nature to me." I relax more into the cushions and for once, my cheeks don't burn when we talk about it. He doesn't have to be nice to me about it. I *know* how awfully I behaved. How awkward it all was. "I wanted to be on good grounds with you, given how much Rory talks about you."

"It's not that hard to be in my good books, Alex."

Okay, now my cheeks are a little warm. I clear my throat. "Anyway, when he wasn't asking questions about this morning, he was talking about you. He's seriously chuffed you were in his house. Thinks it'll put him in good stead with the rest of his class on Monday."

"You don't think he'll mention that I was naked, will he?"

Oh, shit. He hadn't mentioned Nate's lack of clothes again, but it doesn't mean he won't. I'll have to work out how best to warn him off. I don't want Nate to lose his job over this. But, if I talk about it too much, it'll remind Rory and it'll be in the forefront of his mind.

Dammit. Kids are tricky.

"I'll make sure he doesn't. I promise."

"Thank you."

We fall into easy conversation, and we spend hours catching up. Yes, Nate went to the gym when he got home. No, I will never join him, no matter how many blowjobs he offers me as a reward. Yes, my mother does make the best roast dinner in the village. In the world, even. Yes, *eventually*, I will invite him over to try it and to meet the rest of my family. Henry will be on his best behaviour. Anyway, it's only Mum and Dad he still has to meet. As well as all the wives. Sometimes, though, they're the trickiest. Aimee loves to tease me.

"It's almost eleven, Alex," Nate says around a yawn. "I know you don't mind staying up, but it's not like we got a lot of sleep last night. I'm exhausted."

"I didn't hear you complaining."

"I will never complain about spending my night having sex with you."

"I feel the same about you. I'd go without sleep for a week for more of you. But you're right, I should go to bed. Who knows if

Rory will be awake in the night, and if he sleeps right through, he'll probably be perky as fuck. He has a sixth sense for when I've had a late night. It's hell all day if I'm tired and my little sleep thief is around."

"The cutest sleep thief, though. But remind me never to sleep over at yours if he's there."

"Oh, you won't be staying here if he's here too. He adores you, and I don't want him stealing you from me. I'm jealous and possessive like that."

"I love that, though."

"Yeah? Not in a psycho way, of course. More like a 'I don't want my kid stealing my time with my boyfriend' kind of way."

"Boyfriend, huh? That's the second time you've brought that up today."

"Yeah, sorry. I guess I got—"

"Don't apologise. I like it."

"Yeah?" The grin that spreads over my face makes my cheek ache. "Then I'm going to officially change your name in my phonebook." Who talked about taking it slow? It couldn't have been me.

"Maybe you can show me on our date. We'll do that soon, yeah?"

"I'll ask my family about babysitting tomorrow. Try and get something sorted for this week. But for now, I guess I should say goodnight."

"Goodnight, *boyfriend*. Sweet dreams."

ELEVEN

I **GET A LAZY MORNING** to myself the next day. Rory must
have been ill, because there's no way he'd allow me to lounge
about. If he hears so much as a sniffle from my room, he comes
barrelling in to disturb my peace. Instead, I get enough time to
take a long bath and indulge in some indecent texting with Nate
once he's back from the gym.

I kind of like mornings like this.

When it turns nine and Rory still isn't awake, I head into his
room, stirring him back into the land of living with the promise
of eggs for breakfast. Once he's alert and fed, he's a lot brighter
and back to his usual hyper self. He didn't puke during the night
either. Which is fantastic. Sure, it would have been nice to have a
ready-made excuse for avoiding Henry at my parents' today, but
it's better to have a germ-free kid.

Congregating at the farmhouse on a Sunday has been a tra-
dition for as long as I can remember. No matter how busy we
all were, the call would come up the stairs at one on the dot,

and we'd all tumble to the kitchen, crowding around the gnarled wooden table for Mum's dinner. It didn't matter what season it was, there would always be a roast with all of the trimmings, and an opportunity for us to catch-up and realign as a family.

I was the last to move out, and Mum was adamant the lunches continue. Sometimes, there are only one or two of us. Other times, like today, all my siblings, their partners, and their children descend on the house.

By the time me and Rory turn up, my brothers have nabbed all of the parking spaces outside. On a day as nice as this, I should have walked Rory over but we were running late. Again. This time, it's because he couldn't find the shield to go with his Captain America costume. He didn't want to leave the house in normal clothes, so I had to tumble dry the Hulk for him to wear. He's obsessed, and I *have* to limit his time with those movies. They're not really age appropriate and God knows what he's picking up on.

I dump the car in the passing spot halfway along the lane, wrapping my fingers around a stuffing-filled muscle to stop Rory-Hulk from running off. Although it's usually quiet, the lane is shared by the next farm over, and Farmer Cole is as blind as a bat. I'd need my fingers and toes to tally the number of times he's almost squished one of us under his tractor. He'll just emerge from his field and trundle along without any care or attention. He's a fucking menace. Flattened by a tractor is no way for Rory to go, especially not outside Mum and Dad's house, with everyone watching.

I'd never hear the end of it.

"You know, the costume doesn't give you superpowers, kid." He wriggles against my hold, grunting in a way that I think is his Hulk noise, but who knows.

I only release him once we're safely inside the front garden and the gate is shut behind me. He races through the clutch of chickens loitering around the lawn, laughing maniacally as they flee with a chorus of clucks and shrieks. *You deserve it, you viscous arseholes.* If I had a quid for the number of times they nipped me while I was sneaking in after curfew, I'd be loaded. Dad refuses to get rid of them, no matter how abusive they get, and they hate staying in their run. They're always breaking free.

We're confronted with absolute chaos as soon as I step over the threshold. Children run from one end of the house to the other, tripping over each other in the fight for whatever toy they all *have* to play with. An assortment of shoes, wellies and jackets are abandoned next to the already loaded coat rack.

A waft of Mum's roast chicken pulls me towards the kitchen, and I find her standing at the stove and stirring the vat of gravy bubbling away. I plant a kiss on her cheek.

"Help yourself to a beer, love," she says. "Where's Rory?"

"Oh, shit. I knew I forgot something." The look she gives me is enough to have me buried under the tulips. "Kidding, Mum. He's in the front room with the rest of the brats. Why are they all inside?"

"To ruin my peace and quiet," Dad mutters from behind his paper. "Too many bloody kids in this house."

He doesn't mean it. He fucking loves being a grandad, and is always giving out piggy-back rides, playing football, or joining in with the inane games the littles invent. I pat him on his small shoulders. We could be twins, if I was thirty-odd years older and had grey hair.

"Ah, Dad. Before long they'll be all grown and won't want to bother with you."

"Unlikely. You lot still hang around here, don't you?"

"Yeah because you keep on feeding us."

Mum ignores us. "Go join the others, Ally" – I shudder at the pet name she uses for me – "I'm keeping an eye on the small ones."

As soon as I'm outside, Henry sidles up to me, already halfway through his own beer.

"All right?" His spare hand is in his pocket and he rocks on his feet.

I can't make eye contact with him, so I focus on the next field over, where a herd of cows is enjoying its lunch. "Yeah. Fine. Why?"

"Just wondered if you were tired from Mr Jameson's pancake batter."

"Oh. Gross. Stop it." My skin crawls with a million centipedes. I fight for a witty response to stop his torture before he gets a chance to go full Henry. He may be the grumpiest out of all of us, but he loves winding us up. "No, only Rory being sick."

My brother sighs. "Ah. He *was* ill? I thought perhaps he was faking it, that he was fed up with my lot running him ragged and wanted to come home."

"Wait. You brought him home even though you thought he was putting it on?"

"What was I supposed to do? If he says he's sick, I have to listen. How pissed would you have been if I ignored him? Since you were supposed to be recovering in bed, I thought it would be fine. It's not my fault you were busy doing extra-curricular activities with his teacher."

Ugh. Here we go. "If I'd seen your text, I would have made sure Nate wasn't there. Believe me, it wasn't how I imagined you finding out I was dating someone." I sigh. Nothing ever plays out the way I want it to. At least I can try to get some control over how my brothers see Nate. Hopefully, it won't be too long until he's a part of the family and I *need* it to be an easy transition.

"Can I ask a favour? Can you not talk about him like that? I really like him, Henry."

"All right. Fine. But he *is* Rory's teacher. You should be careful."

"What do you mean by that?" Henry has never judged my parenting skills before now.

"Well, won't it be a bit strange sleeping with your kid's teacher? Won't it be weird for Rory to have Mr Jameson at home *and* in school?"

"Jeez. We've only started seeing each other. I haven't invited him to move in with me." *Yet.* "Give me some credit, will you?"

"Fine. But aren't there rules about it?"

"That's not *my* problem, is it?" I make a mental note to check with Nate anyway. I wouldn't want him to get in trouble.

"I guess not. Look, you're old enough to make your own mistakes, but be careful with him, yeah?"

With Rory or Nate? But I don't need to ask the question because I already know the answer. "You're talking like I never put him first when all I do is prioritise Rory."

"I know, I know." He puffs out a hard breath. "Listen, I have to warn you. Sophie knows."

"Oh, for fuck's sake." She's the most gossipy out of the lot – the worst person he could have told. I shoot him a look that will hopefully maim him. Or at least stop his dick working for a while.

He has the decency at least to flinch. "I couldn't help it. She was in the car and I was laughing so hard, she demanded I tell her. You're lucky I managed to stop her coming in to see it for herself."

"Great. Cheers for that, bro. I'm glad someone got a laugh from it all."

Huffing, I step away from him to seek out Josh, giving Sophie a wide berth just in case.

Lunch is its typical noisy affair. We eat on the patio, on a variety of chairs and tables that Mum and Dad have collected throughout the years. The scent of roast dinner mingles with the smell of cut grass, blown in on the light summer breeze. Rory is better, if the way he zooms around the garden with the others is anything to go by. He pops back every so often, scooping a mouthful of food into his mouth before racing away again.

"I brought you up better than this," I shout after him when he darts from the table with a whole Yorkshire pudding in his mucky grip.

Mum tuts.

"Let him be, love. It'll be hard to get him to sit still while the rest of them are running about. Now, help me tidy up, will you?"

I agree, but immediately regret it when we're in the kitchen and she licks her finger to rub at something on my neck. The spot hurts.

"Ow, Mum. Gerroff!"

I squirm out of her grip, hurrying to the mirror hanging in the hallway and almost knocking over the coat rack. *Shit.* There's a hickey at the top of my neck, under my left ear. I covered the ones I found yesterday with my highest necked top, and have been focused all afternoon on stopping them from poking out. But there's nothing I could have done about this one, even if I had discovered it earlier. It would look weird if I wore a scarf on the hottest day of the year so far. Turtlenecks are out of the question, too. I can't pull them off, not like Steve Jobs.

"Come here." Bloody hell, she's followed me and now she has a dishcloth in her hand. "It's only a bit of spit."

"I'm thirty-six. You know it's not dirt." I keep my eyes cast down, following the Victorian tiles back through the house to the kitchen, painfully aware of Mum on my heels. She won't drop this. To put her questions off longer, I sink my hands into the bowl, whistling while I scrub at the chicken pan a little more aggressively than I need to.

"So, what I heard about you having a little sleepover with Rory's teacher Friday night is true? You'd think he'd have a bit more decency, given his profession."

Because teachers don't have sex? Arguing with her will get me nowhere so I scrub a little harder while staring out of the window, examining Henry for any hint of guilt. He keeps his back to me, but, as if she knows I'm out for murder, Sophie turns from her conversation and locks eyes with me. Her grimace tells me everything.

Bingo. There's our culprit.

I keep my voice level to stop Mum picking up on how much I want to kill Sophie right now. "What does Nate being a teacher have to do with it?"

"Well, he's not just any teacher, love." Mum dries the plates as I wash them. "What did Rory have to say when he saw you?"

"He was excited that his teacher was in his house, but otherwise, he didn't really care. I told him Nate was over to help me with the stall, and it's not a complete lie."

I risk a glance at her. Her eyes are narrowed and cynical. What's got her dishcloth in a knot? I'm a grown adult. I can sleep with whoever the fuck I want. The frown makes the lines around her eyes a lot deeper, showing how much older she's getting. It's a shame her opinions aren't changing with her age.

"I don't think you've thought this through properly, Alexander."

My fingers dig into the sponge, my knuckles bleaching with the effort of keeping it together. "What do you mean?"

"It'll be confusing for Rory. This *Mr Jameson* is with him all day at school. Your house is supposed to be Rory's safe place. How will he feel if his teacher is there too?"

"Rory doesn't need a safe place. He goes to *school*, not war. And it's not like he's in trouble every day. He loves Nate, and I'm pretty sure it's mutual. Anyway, he'll be going up a year in September."

"But he still has three years in East Beechmill. What will happen if you and Mr Jameson split up? Won't that make things awkward for the three of you? What if he moves to a different year group and ends up with Rory's class again. How would that be fair?"

All of the breathing through my nose, of reminding myself how much I fancy Nate, and the smile he puts on my face, can't stop my temper. My patience fractures and I slam the sponge onto the draining board. A plume of bubbles hit both me and Mum.

"It's not like we're getting married, Mum. I've only spent one night with him. You're talking like I haven't thought this through, or that I joined the PTA only to sleep with him. *If* something more serious comes of this, Nate and I will tell Rory together. Honestly, he'll be over the moon about it. But it's something we have to decide *if*, and only if, we become something more. Right now, yesterday morning aside, I plan to keep both parts of my life as separate as I can. For Rory's sake. Actually, I was hoping you could—"

"Don't you think Rory has been through enough?" She's softened her tone but I know it's a trick. She has a million tools in her arsenal – emotional blackmail, tugging on my heartstrings – and she'll use all of them in her mission to control me. "It'll be confusing to bring another man into his life, especially if he admires him. If things get messy, it will break his heart."

"And what about *my* heart, Mum? Don't I deserve happiness?"

"Oh, love," she coos. "Part of being a parent means you have to sacrifice what you want for the sake of your child's wellbeing. Look at me. You were in and out of hospital when you were born and I gave up my job to look after you. I'm so very glad I did. I'll never regret it. Luke understood what that meant. He abandoned all hope of finding someone else after he lost poor Katie. His sole goal was to make sure Rory grew up healthy and happy. A relationship can come after that."

And there it is. The mention of my perfect dead brother she knows will get her what she wants. She's right, too. I've already messed up. I wasn't there for Rory when he was feeling sick because I was too wrapped up in Nate. And although she doesn't say it, the whole family knows that Luke died because I let Mike distract me. I let him tempt me away from work to have fun. *Fuck. Fuck. Fuck.* The next time my hands sink into the steaming hot water, they stay there, no longer scrubbing at anything. I deserve to have my skin melted off. I'm a shit uncle and a shit brother.

What if something worse had happened to Rory? He could have fallen down the stairs, or electrocuted himself. He could have fucking choked on the junk my brother was feeding him.

Mum's right, and I bloody hate it. She's always fucking right.

When I wanted to adopt Rory, she wasn't sure if me and Mike were mature enough. She didn't trust him to stick around. But I was blind to it all, and I ploughed ahead anyway, determined to prove her wrong. I *had* to make up for what I'd done, for causing Luke's death, and I didn't stop to think about how having Rory would change our lives.

And look where that got me.

At least she didn't say "I told you so" when Mike walked out on me, even though she was desperate to.

I'll never reach perfect parent status if I keep on failing this way. The bar set by my brilliant fucking brothers — alive and dead — is way too high. *They* never get told off, or told that they're not doing their jobs properly. Even though some of their kids are a lot worse than Rory.

But they're in hetrosexual relationships.

I study my mum. Is she only concerned because Nate is Rory's teacher, or because he's a man? I'm not naïve. If things were to get serious with him, it could be hell for Rory. When the rest of the class find out he has two dads, they could be awful to him about it. I'm not stupid enough to think everyone is as progressive as me, especially not in a conservative village like this. The fact Nate is Rory's teacher just makes it a hundred times worse. Rory gets on with most of the kids, and as far as I'm aware, doesn't get bullied because he's well-rounded.

And what about when Rory is older and more aware of what's going on around him? How will he feel seeing someone who works in his school walking around the house in his pyjamas – or worse, *nothing*? Am I really that fucking selfish?

Nate's words yesterday fight with what Mum's telling me now.

You're a brilliant parent to Rory...you sacrifice a lot for him...I promise it's okay to do something for you.

Part of being a parent means you have to sacrifice what you want for the sake of your children's wellbeing.

Well, he was wrong. Yesterday ended up being the most embarrassing moment of my life. I don't know yet if I've scarred Rory for life. And look how upset he was when I said Nate couldn't stay for the rest of the day. If I had to tell him we were over, he *would* be heartbroken. When Mike left, Rory was too young to notice the difference, but now...

God. Why is this so hard? I wish there was a clear path, an indication of who I should choose. I know, *I know*, Mum only has Rory's best interests at heart. But who's looking after mine?

Nate would. If you let him.

The conflict rolls around my head, and I continue the washing up in silence. When I finish, and the last of the water gurgles down the drain, Mum stands next to me. She sighs and hangs her tea towel on the hook for it to dry.

"I wish things were different, Alex. We all miss Luke. It's not fair you have to give up your freedom to look after Rory. But you signed the adoption papers. You knew what you were taking on. That means that while he is under your care, you have to listen to your head and not your heart."

I can't remember that being in the paperwork, nor in my affirmations as Rory's godparent but I nod anyway. I guess I have a lot of thinking to do. "Thanks, Mum. Can you have Rory after school tomorrow? I can go and speak to Nate, then. Do it face-to-face."

Her nod is over the top, and with the way her eyes light up, I can tell she's trying hard not to gloat out loud. "Of course, love."

There's nothing more for me to say to her. With everything tidied, I wander away from the kitchen, swiping another beer as I head outside. Josh is sitting with Aimee in a cluster of deck chairs, enjoying the last of the sun before it disappears behind the trees. I plonk myself in the empty seat next to him, and breathe in the rose-tinged scent of late June.

"You and Mum were having a serious-looking conversation."

This time, I let my eyes roll. *Of course,* someone snooped.

"It's nothing."

"Sure? Don't want to talk about anything with me?"

My gaze slides to Aimee, who is taking too great an interest in her phone. "Nope. Thanks."

He opens his mouth once, twice, then sighs and returns to his conversation with his wife. *Good.* I don't want to talk to anyone, anyway. I'm all talked-out and they'll only fill my head with more doubts, more reasons to stay with Nate, and many more reasons why I can't. Josh and Aimee rabbit on, and slowly, the rest of the seats fill up.

I must be throwing off an air of misery, or a strong "do not approach" vibe, because nobody else asks if I'm okay. My beer disappears in only a few gulps while I watch the kids playing, Mum's words on a continuous loop in my head.

It's only when she passes through, on the lookout for empties, that I reach my limit. She must notice my sulking because she stops in front of me and pats my knee. "It'll all be fine, love. Everything happens for a reason."

The other conversations stop, and I shrink into my seat, trying to ignore the prickle of a thousand eyes on me. Nobody dares ask for any further information, but I can tell from their faces they're working it out for themselves. Henry takes a side-glance at Sophie, who in turn raises her eyebrows at Aimee. For fuck's sake. Does everyone know about my love life?

The only noise in the garden is the sound of the kids shrieking and the rustle of leaves. I've had e-fucking-nough.

"I'm going to head home." It takes all my self control to keep my voice even.

"Really, love? Rory is having fun. Why don't you stay for a little longer?"

"No, thank you. He has a spelling test tomorrow, and needs to revise."

"Got to stay in the teacher's good books, 'eh, Al?"

Josh's teasing is innocent enough, but my head spins around faster than a poltergeist to glare at him.

I take a deep breath and let it out over the count of five, all the time fixing my gaze on my trainers. The last thing I need is to make this worse by overreacting or getting into a fight, even if throwing a punch at *someone* feels pretty tempting right now. A dismissive wave of my hand is all I can muster before I storm down to the bottom of the garden, where I last saw the kids.

They're in the treehouse. Another fight is going on, boisterous and loud enough to tell me it's a part of their playing. It's a good job Farmer Cole is a few fields away, or he'd be complaining about the noise.

"Rory," I call. "It's time to go home."

The rowdy thumping stops, and a set of footsteps creak across the ageing wood. Rory's face appears in a misshapen window. "I don't want to."

"Tough. We need to go over your spellings before school tomorrow."

He lolls against the wooden frame, his eyes rolling back in their sockets. He looks like a damsel in distress, the way he's draped over the window sill. This floppiness is the same reaction I get when I tell him he *has* to eat his broccoli before he can have ice cream. It's like if he pretends his limbs aren't working, and that his spine has disappeared, he won't have to do something he doesn't like. He puts his whole fucking weight into it too, so he can't be moved.

"B-b-but, Aleeeexxxx." My eye twitches. The x takes forever to sizzle out. I know what's coming next, and I brace myself for it. "Lottie isn't going home, and she has spellings, too."

I rub the back of my neck. A child in a strop is the last thing I need. "Lottie's home time isn't up to me. I'm in charge of *you*, not her."

Thunder crosses his face, and for a moment, I worry he might Hulk-Smash out of his costume and take the treehouse with him. He pulls in a massive breath, filling his chest with as much air as he can, but his face turns red, not green.

"THAT'S NOT FAIR," he bellows. The quiet murmur of conversation at the top of the garden stops. Heck, the residents of the next village over can probably hear him.

"Yeah, well." I kick at a daisy before looking back up at my nephew. "Nothing is fair, mate. The sooner you learn that, the better. Now, come down, *please*, or I won't let you help me and Mr Jameson with the stall."

If there is a stall to work on after tomorrow.

The threat hits the target. He scrunches his face up, and tears spill over his cheeks. But instead of arguing again, he mumbles, "Fine."

He's a professional at dragging shit out, though. His steps are snail-paced down the ladder and back up the garden, and no amount of coaxing will make him move quicker. When he reaches everyone else, the tiny arsehole makes sure to give all his aunts and uncles the longest hugs known to man. Especially Mum, who he clings onto like a baby spider monkey. Over the top of his head, she gives me a look that's reserved for when I've really fucked up.

Great.

"You know, love, it's not his fault that—" I tune her out. I've had enough of her advice today.

The brat needs pushing in the right direction when he finally lets go of her, and I try my best to regain some of my cool as I gather his things and lead him out to the car. It's hard work. Every forced step, every grumble of complaint stokes the electricity in my storm. It's not going to take much more before I let loose.

"Get in your seat then, mate." I summon the friendliest tone I can.

Instead of doing what he's told, he crosses his arms over his chest, his lower lip wobbling. "No."

My swear comes out as a breath. *Fucking wanker.* I squat in front of him. "Do it, or I'll do it for you."

"Fine."

The force he uses to yank open the door would make a strongman proud. I would be impressed, if he didn't almost clonk me on the head. Once he's fastened into his booster seat, I mirror all of his aggressive movements, marching back around to my side of the car, hauling myself into the driver's seat with a huff, and forgetting to check my mirrors when I pull out of the lane and onto the main road. My actions get me a loud honk from the passing car I almost hit, and I throw two fingers up at the driver.

"Piss off."

TWELVE

AS IF HE KNOWS I'm in turmoil and struggling with a shitty child, Nate rings me five times. There's no way I can speak to him, though, not with Rory acting the way he is.

The tiny wanker continues to be a nightmare when we get home – refusing to do his spellings, taking only a mouthful of his supper, and digging his heels in at bath time. I retaliate by turning the lights off without tucking him in or giving him a kiss. It's childish, but I'm at the end of my patience with him. I lean against his closed door, a sigh leaving my body and taking my soul with it. His crying bleeds through the thin walls, but I ignore it. We both need some space.

I'll have to work double hard to fix things in the morning, but for now, at least, this fight is over.

I plod downstairs to the kitchen to pour a large glass of wine. My phone vibrates as I'm getting settled on the sofa.

It's Nate. Again.

Every fibre of my being reaches towards him – not helped by the cute photo of us I made his icon yesterday morning, before things went south. My fingers inch closer to accept the call. By the third ring, he hasn't given up, and I rub hard over the hickey at the top of my neck, as if I can distract myself with pain. I can't speak to him yet. I haven't worked out what I want to do.

It should be a simple decision. If I like him as much as I think I do, it's worth trying. Visions of our future, how good it would be, flash through my head, but now the edges are tarnished with Mum's advice.

I mute the call and toss my phone to the side, sinking into the ensuing silence as deeply as I slump into my cushions.

The stupid thing is he would be the best person for me to talk this through with. I found telling him about Luke and Mike so easy. But it's not like I can return his call right now, is it?

Hey, Nate. Do you have five? I can't decide if I should break things off with you to protect Rory and keep my mum happy, and I was hoping you could help me. It's not me, or you, but my kid. I'm besotted with you. Promise.

Yeah, fucking right.

A double buzz indicates a text has been left for me and my body works on auto-pilot, my fingers scrabbling over the sofa without looking. I roll onto my back to read the message.

> **Boyfriend:** Hey. You're probably having too much fun to pay attention to your phone. I'm going to get an early night. You wore me out and I haven't caught up with my sleep yet. But I wanted to say goodnight and I miss you. See you tomorrow? Are you doing drop off or pick up? X

The kiss. Oh God, the kiss. It's only one syllable, small and insignificant to anyone else, but it adds to my dilemma. Nobody sends a kiss unless they mean it, especially not one bloke to another. Sure, me and Nate shared *a lot* of kisses this weekend. Kisses that were hungry and passionate, his tongue sweeping inside my mouth to taste every inch of me. Slower kisses where we poured every ounce of our souls into each other, more than only our lips touching. But that kiss at the end of his text has been sent to ruin my life.

I shiver, sniff, and reply.

> **Me:** rory has been an arsehole all evening talk to u tomorrow wont be at school

My thumb hovers over the x, debating whether to tag one onto the end of my reply. If I don't, he'll spend all night obsessing over what the missing kiss means. I know I would. But if I do add a kiss, I could be giving him false hope.

It takes me a whole ten minutes of agonising over it – during which Nate probably forgets he messaged me – but eventually, I chuck the x at the end of the message and press send. I switch my phone onto do-not-disturb, and my head flops into the cushions. If anyone else wants to speak to me, they can go fuck themselves.

My incredible sulk occupies the whole evening until I haul myself to bed at midnight, although by then I at least *think* I have my decision made. It doesn't stop the arguing voices, which sound like Nate and Mum, from raging around my head. I only get a couple of hours of sleep, and my bad mood rolls over to the next morning. Not even Rory creeping into my room, an hour before the alarm goes off, to cuddle up and say he's sorry helps to lift the dark clouds from my shoulders.

I suffer through the shift from hell, dropping two full plates of food and arguing with Simon when he has the audacity to ask if I'm okay. *Dick.* He banishes me to the office mid-afternoon, and I spend the rest of my day hammering angry emails into my keyboard, like it's the source of everything shit in my life. I don't hear from Nate, there's no good morning text, and I haven't sent anything to him. I'm worried that if I do, I'll spill all my thoughts and worries into the text. I at least owe him a face-to-face conversation.

By the time I key out, my shoulders are tight and a headache looms at my temples, throbbing with every step I take. I check the time on my watch. Half five. He must be home by now, preparing himself some sort of healthy meal. Then he'll want to settle down with a book. It's how he relaxes once he's done with his school work.

And here comes me to ruin his peace.

I'm not in control of my body. A puppet master leads me out to my car, not bothering to guide me around the puddles peppering the car park. The rain came out of the blue this morning, but it's stopped now, leaving low-lying, sinister-looking clouds to remind us British summers like to keep us on our toes. At least only my feet get wet. Lucky me.

Key in ignition. Car in gear. I don't bother to check the mirrors before I pull out of my parking spot and onto the main road.

Nate never told me where he lives, but he used my phone Saturday to order a taxi and I spent all of yesterday morning memorising it. It's borderline stalking, but it's not like I can message him and ask for it.

My SatNav guides me to my destination. Halfway there, I have to pull into a layby before a panic attack drives me off the road. What am I doing, turning up unannounced like this? He could have lovely evening plans that I'm about to ruin. Or a ton of marking he won't be able to concentrate on when I finally leave.

Deep breaths. Count to five. By the time I reach three, my fingers have released their vice-like grip on the steering wheel. *Be honest, that's all you can do. And if he's too busy to talk to you today, you can try tomorrow. You can't turn away now, you're already halfway there.* When I get to five, my vision stops pulsing and I can get back onto the road.

The rest of the journey is way too short, and I park outside the stack of flats before I'm ready for it. I check my appearance in the rear-view mirror. Heavy purple bags hang under my eyes, made brighter by my pale skin. I look like Rory did Saturday. Maybe I've caught what he had and I should stay away from Nate until I feel better. The hickey on the top of my neck is bright red and swollen from where I've pressed against it all day, and a spot that appeared under my nose this morning is the size of a beach ball from my picking at it.

I don't bother to tidy myself up. What's the point?

There are more puddles on my trudge across the road to the apartment block but this time, I manage to avoid them. There was once an old fire station here, and the village came out in force to protest its conversion. Money always wins, though. Fuck heritage and history. They're unimportant when rich people want to find more ways to grow their fortunes.

I follow a path through a green garden bursting with dahlias and daisies to the high-rise. Most of the fire station has been turned into a small shopping precinct, with a newsagent, a gym – *ah, that's how he does it* – as well as a pub. The waft of salt and vinegar from the chippy hits me as I draw nearer to the entrance, intensifying my bubbling nausea. I'd get even fatter if we moved in here. Not like that's going to happen now.

The front door is locked to visitors. On the left-hand side of the entranceway is a console with a list of flat numbers. Most of the slots are empty, but halfway down, next to 3A, Nate has written his name. The looping letters match the notes in his classroom and are so like him, especially next to the blank spaces of his neighbours.

Okay, Al, you can do this. It takes me three attempts to press the buzzer, my trembling hands preventing me from pushing that stupid button. The bell is abrasive, loud, and sets my nerves alight.

He could be out. Or he could have spied my rain-cloud-covered approach from his balcony and doesn't want to see me, doesn't want me to bring my mood his way. The lack of texts could have him in his own depression.

I wait, and wait a bit more, and only when I turn to hurry back to my car and pretend this bout of madness never happened, he answers.

"Hello?"

Say you've got the wrong flat. Run away.

"Alex. I can see you in the camera." *Dammit.* "What are you doing here?"

The rasp in his voice has me glued to the spot and my lips clamped shut. His gravelly tone reminds me of saying good morning to him while we lay naked in my bed. It's how he pounded into me when we were in the shower. It's the taste of him in my mouth. It's the utter devastation I'm about to cause.

We only had one night together, but all the talk of *more* gave me hope. Now, I'm about to throw it all away.

"I-is it okay for me to come up?"

"Uh. Yeah. Of course. I'll buzz you in now."

The flat is only on the third floor, but the climb of the too-white staircase brings heat to my cheeks. By the time I reach his landing, I'm out of breath and making promises to visit the gym. Not the one downstairs, though. Although I've fantasised about watching him throwing weights around and working up a sweat, I won't be able to face him after this talk.

"Is everything okay? Where's Rory?"

Nate is leaning on the door frame. I crest the last steps, and he holds his arms wide open for me. I don't have to think twice about stepping into them. He rubs my back, his cheek resting on top of my head. Immediately, the tension lifts. I focus only on drawing in breath, his scent, dragging whatever comfort I can pull from him. Footsteps come up the stairs behind me, a small snigger attempts to interrupt our peace, but I ignore it.

He's the first to pull away, leaning back in my arms, frowning. "What's up?"

"Ugh. I've had the worst day ever." I run a hand over my face.

"Is that anything to do with why you haven't texted me?"

"Well, you haven't—" *Shit.* I fumble my phone out of my pocket. It's still in do-not-disturb mode. I'm a fucking idiot. Ten texts and five calls from him. The family group chat has been renamed "Where is Alex?" and has 256 messages in it. I show Nate, grimacing. "Sorry."

His shoulders drop. "I thought— Sorry. I warned you I was too much."

"What? No. It's not you. Yesterday evening was hell, and I needed some thinking time. I guess I forgot to turn it off this morning." Jeez. If something happened to Rory, and I didn't pick up.

"I would have rung The Watering Hole." At my frown, he adds, "If anything had happened."

Of course, he would. Nate knows.

He continues, "How did you get my address, by the way? I mean, I'm not mad you're here, even if you look like a wraith right now. But I never gave it to you."

I mumble something about the taxi app and his eyebrows fly into his fringe. If this was a normal visit, he'd rib me about it, but my solemn mood must be seeping outwards, because he doesn't say anything else.

Time to get on with it. Stop dragging this out. All right, brain. I'm not sure why the git is being fucking impatient. It's not like this is going to be the nicest thing we do today.

"C-can we sit down? I need to talk to you."

"Sounds ominous." His arms flop from around me, worry passing through his eyes, but he doesn't say anything else. Instead, he closes the front door and leads me down the hallway.

His flat is the total opposite to my place. I follow him into the living room, hoping for a hint of *more* Nate, but find myself disappointed with the blank page. The walls are bare, aside from a large television, and painted in that awful generic magnolia landlords adore. A sofa sits opposite the TV, grey and L-shaped, but there are no indents in its cushions. It's unused, unnervingly fresh. The french doors lead to the tiny balcony he told me about, and there would be a lovely view of the village if it wasn't hiding behind raindrop-marked glass. Aside from a haphazard pile of exercise books, a novel that looks like it's a fantasy, and an empty mug stained with coffee – decaf, since it's well past midday – the place is too neat and tidy.

"It's all a bit new" – maybe he *can* read my mind? – "and I have a lot more furniture to buy. And a load of boxes in the spare room, waiting for me to have a day off to unpack. Who am I kidding? I can't summon the energy on a weekend, either. Most of my time is spent at school or doing work for school at home. Or with you now, it seems." He laughs, but it's a thin, nervous noise. "I'm hardly here to notice how sparse it is. If I could, this place would look like yours but—"

"I didn't say anything." I perch on the edge of a sofa cushion, too afraid of leaving a denim mark on his new upholstery.

"You don't have to. All of your thoughts, your feelings. You wear them on your face."

"I do not." I'm now painfully aware of my giant scowl.

He raises his eyebrows at me again. "So, are you going to tell me what's wrong? As much as I love having you here, you're acting...strange, and I don't like it."

I'm fidgeting more than usual and my eyes flit from his to the naked walls to the grey sofa and back. When he takes his seat, sinking into the cushions as if he's sat in the same spot for years, his thigh brushes along mine. The slight touch ignites my nerve endings, and I want to close my eyes, enjoy it for as long as I can. He might not want me this close after what I have to say.

"Yesterday was amazing—"

"Are you breaking up with me?"

"Nate, I—"

He jumps to his feet, his hands pulling through his hair as he paces the living room. "*I knew* I rang you too much and it annoyed you. That's why you didn't want to speak to me, right?"

"No. You did nothing wrong. You were perfect." My eyes keep on him, following his back-and-forth.

He scoffs, coming to a stop in front of me. "So perfect you've neither texted *or* called me back."

If only he knew how I wanted to call him to talk through my dilemma, how the only comfort I got was from the sheets still smelling of him, how I can't stop those damn fucking fantasies rampaging through my imagination.

"No. Me not replying has nothing to do with you."

Fuck, why is this going so badly? The damn guy won't let me get a word in edgeways. Of course, he was going to think it was something he did, especially after telling me all his other partners got fed up with him and his ways. *Especially* considering I've ignored his messages and calls all day. He chews his lip so hard that I worry he might draw blood. I sit on my own hands, not wanting to touch him yet. I don't deserve the comfort it gives me. I'm no fucking better than the rest of them.

"Listen, I—"

The words won't come. There's nothing I can say to salvage this. It's not been five minutes and I'm ruining everything. I get to my feet, slowly and unsteadily as if a sudden move will scare him away. His attention remains on me, his nostrils flared. *Fuck, fuck, fuck.*

Be honest, that's all you can do. I scrunch my eyes shut. My arms stay clamped at my sides. "Mum cornered me in the kitchen yesterday." *Okay, good start.* "She doesn't think I should be dating you because you're Rory's teacher. She suggested I call things off before we get too deep into this, before Rory gets involved. The reason I didn't answer your calls last night is because I wanted time to digest her advice. Think about it properly. I wanted to be sure I made the right decision."

"The fact you had to think about it hurts, Alex."

"I know. It's not what you want to hear, but I have to be honest with you."

"Why?"

"If it was only me, I wouldn't have any second thoughts. I haven't stopped thinking about you since the PTA meeting."

"But you have Rory to consider." The understanding in his voice sucks. "I'd never hurt him, Alex."

"I know. He's obsessed with you in the cutest way ever. I'm worried that if he gets used to having you around in and out of school and we break up, it will devastate him. It's not like you're some random bloke I met on an app. He'd be excited if he found out we were together. But what if we don't last?"

"But what if we *do* last, Alex, and it's the best thing for you *and* him? Good things are allowed to happen to you, too. It doesn't have to be all doom and gloom in your world."

I can't accept it. If I have something nice, I spoil it. I was close to Luke, he was my best friend, and look what *my* neglect did to him. Mike was my everything but I forced him to take on a small child and ruined what we had. Not that I'd change it, but I devoted my life to Rory two years ago. I knew what I was signing up to. I *have* to make things right for my family, to fill the massive gap Luke left behind. After all, it should have been me lying on that cold floor, bleeding out for fifty fucking quid.

"It would have been nice to have been with you for longer than a weekend. You would have made me happy."

"I still want to make you happy. But you have to stop being scared, stop letting your mum get in your head. I want you *and* Rory, and a life with the two of you. Eventually."

I pick at the hickey again. "This is confusing."

"It's not. Not really. The last message you sent me yesterday morning was talking about potential date ideas. What changed? What did your mum say?"

"That by wanting to see you I was being selfish. That Luke gave up finding someone else after Katie died because Rory's needs should come first. That I should do the same."

"For fuck's sake." A muscle in his jaw tics and he spends the longest time considering me. "Why does she have this hold on you?"

I've never looked that closely at it. My relationship with Mum is difficult, but it's not the worst by any stretch of the imagination. I wasn't abandoned by her, she doesn't favour my brothers over me, but...

"She was planning on going back to her career once Josh was out of nappies. She was the village GP, a tidy little job, not too demanding for someone with hundreds of kids. It was always the plan: four children, and back to being a working mum. She had loads of friends, was a member of the WI. She had a great life. Then I came along. I've been an inconvenience to her ever since. I arrived early, was ill for a long time, and she was in and out of the hospital with me. Add in how my blatant disregard to my responsibilities got my brother killed and..."

I lift my head to see tears shining in his eyes. He cups my face, his thumb grazing my cheek and I step closer to him. I reach out but stop myself before I touch his arm. I don't deserve any of this.

"Mostly I think she doesn't have a lot of faith in me. She wants me to be a better man. Heck, I want to be a better guy."

"It's not your fault you were premature, Alex. And the only person to blame for Luke's death is the criminal that stabbed him."

"She's only looking out for R—"

"By guilt-tripping you?" He scoffs. "You're her *son*. There are no rules about us dating, by the way. I asked my mentor yesterday because I was excited about us. If we decide things are going to carry on between us, I could help you tell Rory. You wouldn't be alone in this, Alex."

"I'm so so scared I'm giving up something brilliant, but I *have* to do this. I have to put Rory first. He's had enough upset in his life, and I—"

"You don't *have* to fill in any gaps your brother left behind. If Rory was acting up, or had development issues, then perhaps I'd understand your reasoning. But he's not. He's perfect. *You're* perfect, Alexander Webster, and you're a brilliant parent to Rory. You have sacrificed so much for him already, but you deserve happiness too."

My hand slides over his, pressing his palm against my face. The bridge of my nose burns, and when I blink, a sole tear escapes. His own fall freely down his cheeks, as if he knows what's coming next. I shake my head.

"I can't," I whisper, pressing a kiss against his palm before releasing my grip on him. "I'm sorry."

"What about the stall?"

The stall, of course. It's going to be rough as hell working with Nate on it, but I have to see this through. Luke wouldn't quit, even when things got tough.

"I– we still have to work on it. I guess we could still meet up tomorrow, like we planned?"

"Yeah. Sure." His tone tells me he would rather go days without the gym than spend any more time with me. I don't blame him.

"I should probably go."

I wait for a response, but he doesn't say anything else. Something glues me to my spot for a minute longer, and I drink in how he looks like it's the last time I'll be able to enjoy it. He's so fucking handsome. Eventually, though, I turn away from him, ignoring the voice in my head that shouts at me to stop, that I'm making one of the worst decisions of my life.

If I'd known last weekend was the only chance I'd have to spend with him, I would have dragged it out, made it last longer. I would have never let him go.

"See you tomorrow, then." With my shoulders hunched over, I leave the room.

"Alex."

The whisper of my name slips from his mouth, accompanied by the rapid pad of his feet over the carpet. Before I reach the front door, he slides his arms around my waist and buries his head against my back with a sob. I spin straight around, allowing myself to be swept up once again in his embrace. His shoulders tremble with every cry, so I slide one hand into his hair, tucking his head under my chin. It puts him at an awkward angle, but if it's bothering him, he doesn't say. I hold him as tightly as I can.

"I'm going to miss you," he mumbles against my skin.

"I'll miss you too. So much."

He pulls his head up to look at me, sliding two fingers across my jawline before tilting my head towards him, taking his time. His grey-green eyes burn into mine, and his hand scrubs up through my stubble, leaving a trail of heat in its wake until he's cupping my face again, his thumb rubbing against my cheek.

And then he kisses me, and I bask in the sensations that wash over me. I cling to him, as if the kiss is life-giving, and his arms are the only thing holding me up. I want this to last forever, even though I know the longer it carries on, the harder it's going to be to pull apart. Because despite what my mother thinks, I still need Nathaniel Jameson.

Yet, I'm the first to break away, my chest heaving with the effort as I fight to catch my breath. I open my mouth, determined to say *something*, but the chime of my phone brings me crashing back to reality.

I check it quickly. "It's my mum. I should go."

Nate steps away from me, his face flushed and his hands twisting around each other. "I'm sorry for grabbing you like that. I didn't want you to leave without one last kiss."

"I'm the one that's sorry, Nate." I step forward to take another kiss from him, then think better of it and move away.

"I'll see you tomorrow, Alex."

I nod, holding my head a little higher this time. Each step is heavy, but I continue moving away from him. As I walk out of his flat, I can't shake the feeling that I've just made the biggest mistake of my life.

Thirteen

I'M IN THE WORST mood the next morning, not helped by the text I wake up to.

> **Mr Jameson:** Can we reschedule this afternoon for another day, please? Something's come up.

Great. Not only have I thrown away what could have been the best thing in my life, but I've also ruined our chances of winning this summer fucking fête competition. There's no way I can pull this off by myself, and if he's refusing to work with me, I'm screwed.

I busy myself with getting Rory ready for school, and don't text Nate back until I'm on Josh's doorstep for the school run.

> **Me:** thursday?

> **Mr Jameson:** Sure. That's fine.

Sighing, I slide my phone into my pocket just as my brother opens the door.

"You all right?" he asks, a frown replacing his greeting smile. Behind him, Lottie and Ella are spread across the hallway, pulling on their shoes and coats with Aimee's help.

"Yeah. Fine. How about you lot?"

"Fine. Running late. How come Mum collected the kids yesterday? I thought you were doing it."

Oh. Here we go. "Something came up at work."

His frown grows deeper and I steel myself for his assault. My family is so fucking nosey. Tenner bet that as soon as Mum dropped off the girls yesterday, Josh was straight on the phone with Simon to find out why our plans changed. None of them are getting anything from me, though. I don't want them all up in my business.

I tighten my lips, shoving my hands in my pockets.

Josh eyes me for a moment longer, his mouth opening and closing as if he wants to throw further questions at me but can't work out what to start with. Luckily, Ella appears at his side, her arm twisting around his leg in a half-hug, putting a stop to his inquisition.

"I'm doing the school run this afternoon," he tells me instead. "Does Rory need picking up, too?"

Well, the plan was for the two of us to work on the stall with Nate, but now that's not fucking happening, I can at least grab some more hours in work. "Yeah. That would be great. I can work until six. Can you feed him?"

"Nah. I'll let him starve."

Josh shoves me off the doorstep. I lift my hand in a small wave, leading the girls towards the car. With a goodbye toot of the horn, we pull away from the house and I tune into the babble of the kids as I drive the short journey to the school.

I have to park two streets over since the roads are busy. I hold Rory and Lottie's hands and let them pull me towards the playground. I hate the school for having a stupid drop-off rule, and the kids not being old enough for me to abandon them on the pavement. I hate myself for not trying to persuade Josh to do this instead. I love dropping the kids off, usually, but the school yard is the last place I want to be. Nate is in charge, which means I get to see him a lot sooner than I had planned.

Fucking brilliant.

There he is, waiting in his usual spot next to the battered school doors. The light summer breeze lifts blond tendrils from his face and he turns more towards it, closing his eyes briefly to enjoy it. He looks tired, older than when I left him last night, with deep purple circles under his eyes. He had a bad night's sleep too, then. Despite the sun threatening to boil us in our own sweat, he's wearing a jumper, with adorable leather patches at the elbow. Over the weekend, I confessed that I thought he was a sexy librarian when we first met. If I hadn't just dumped him, I would have thought he was wearing it to wind me up. He *knows* I do the morning runs.

I could watch him all day, even though I'm not allowed to, even though the sight of him fills my head with confusing fucking thoughts. I made the decision not to be with him. I walked away. So why do I long to creep closer to him, to steal a kiss in front of all these damn kids? I lick my lips, as if preparing myself for it anyway. My body is a traitor.

A tug at my hand reminds me I'm here for a reason. Rory peers up at me. "Did Mysterio steal your thoughts?"

"What? No. Why would Mysterio be at your school?"

"Mysterio is everywhere," he whispers. Then he adds in a louder, more confident voice, "Don't worry, Alex. I'll get him for you."

With a slobbery kiss on my hand, the kid pulls out of my sweaty grip and is about to tear away to fight the bad guy when I notice he's wearing Thor's Helm.

"Not so fast." I yank him back, smiling briefly when he squeals, and remove the helmet. "Remember, no magic on the school yard, please."

"Yes, boss."

"Have a good day."

I get another kiss then he runs off after his cousins. My eyes connect with Nate's over the sea of kids, but he doesn't wave or even change the expression on his face. Instead, he allows me a brief second to watch him before turning his attention to a child by the door and his back to me. *Fuck.* We're never going to be able to work on this damn stall together now.

My misery follows me to work. When I pull up, there's no messages, no nice to see yous or wishes for me to have a nice day. Nate turning away from me was rough, but the lack of messages is even worse. They used to brighten my otherwise boring shifts, giving me enough of a boost to be cheery with the rudest of customers, and to complete the most mundane tasks while whistling. My lack of enthusiasm even extends to tending the pub's flower boxes, a job I usually enjoy. I water them because I *have* to, not because I want to tend them. All the fun has been sucked out of my life.

At least today is a stocktake day for me. The only other human interaction I get is Simon checking I'm okay once I'm in the office. He uses the exact same tone as Josh, confirming my suspicions that they've been chatting to each other about what I was up to yesterday. If they bothered to check in with Mum, I'm sure she would love to fill them in about why I asked her to have Rory yesterday. Whatever. Let them think what they want.

My phone rings when I'm on my lunch break, and I wrestle it out of my pocket as I take a reluctant bite of my toastie – boring ham and cheese. I haven't been hungry, but Simon was adamant I eat something before I fainted.

Only Mum rings in the middle of the day.

"Yeah?"

"Please may I speak to Mr Webster?"

Shit. It's Agnes bloody Palmer. I choke on the half-eaten clod of sandwich I've swallowed and I struggle to catch my breath. Jesus, she should come with a warning. She already thinks I'm an idiot, and now I'm slowly dying while she waits impatiently for me to confirm who I am. I can hear the tapping of her foot down the line and I take a swig of my water before I pass out from lack of oxygen.

"Mr Webster?"

"Y-yes, Agnes. I mean, Ms Palmer. It's me. Alex." I draw in breath after breath, wiping my watering eyes on the edge of my apron.

She doesn't check if I'm alive. "There's been an incident at the school. Rory is okay," she adds, as if she can sense my whole world has frozen. "But I think it's best if we have a discussion about it. Can you be here at ten past three?"

There goes my hope of earning some extra money today. I can go in, of course I can, but with her assurance that Rory isn't injured or sick, I hesitate. An incident, when said in her firm, no bullshit way, means he has misbehaved. Nate will be at the meeting. He is Rory's teacher, after all. Oh well, at least he can see for himself why we can never be together. I'll never be a member of the Perfect Parent Club, and he deserves someone who will. Ugh.

"Yeah, that's fine."

Agnes hangs up without giving me any more information, leaving me to spend the rest of my afternoon thinking about what Rory has done. Perhaps he finally managed to fulfil mine and Josh's legacy and stole the loo roll out of Ol' Mop Head's cupboard. I can't imagine Rory fighting any of the other kids. Although he loves a temper tantrum, he usually saves all his frustrations to take out on me, and he's never swung a punch. Not even when all his cousins overwhelm him.

Determined to impress Palmer, I leave work early. I reach the playground a couple of minutes before three to find the building still standing, and spot Josh chatting to the Perfect Parent Club. Of course, he's a member. The mums love him.

"Hey."

He jumps a mile. "What the fuck, man. What are you doing here? Did you forget it's my turn to do the pick up?"

"Nah. I got a summons from Palmer." The mums gasp and share knowing looks.

"That's what happens when there's not a mother in his life," one of them mumbles to the other. I bite back a swear. Rory is a nuisance, a naughty boy, a child that shouldn't mix with theirs. Fucking brilliant. I swallow every protest that he's a good kid. Can I call him that when for all I know, he set fire to his poop in the middle of assembly?

"Oh, shit. I got a call too. Ugh. They've been up to something, haven't they?"

The mums keep on mumbling their condemnation of my kid. Of course, they've forgotten all about Lottie's part in this. Nuclear families don't get the same judgement. I stand out, a sore thumb that doesn't fit into their quintessential, social media-ready village life.

"Fighting?" I ask Josh. The last thing I need is to brawl with these women on the school yard. That won't help mine or Rory's case.

"With each other or someone else?"

With Lottie, it could be anyone. That girl is as feisty as her mother. But I shrug. "Who knows?"

"Fuck's sake. It's only Tuesday, too. Work today was hell" – it's not true. He's a civil servant. Everyone knows they don't do proper work – "and now I have to deal with my brat."

He continues to complain about his shit day, but I'm distracted when the school doors open, and Nate slips out alone. The lines in his face are deeper than this morning, and he looks exhausted.

Great. Not only have I dumped him, but now my kid is making his life hell.

He glances my way, stares at me for a moment then beckons me over. I gesture towards Josh, but Nate shakes his head. He only wants to speak to me. *Fuck.* I dawdle over, my feet dragging on the tarmac. I don't want to be close to him. I'm not ready for this. My body still doesn't know what to do if I can't touch him. I'm not sure it can resist the urge. Just in case, I jam my hands into my pockets so I can't be tempted, and stop a full metre away from him.

"Hey." My words are shaky when they slide from my mouth.

Nate's hands stay fixed to his sides. He exhales hard. "I've left the teaching assistant to get the kids ready for home time. I wanted to pop out and speak to you before you get to Headmistress Palmer's office."

"What happened?"

"It was during break this morning. One of the other kids was bullying Rory. He's all right, I promise." He must spot the way my body stiffens because his hand shoots out and clamps over my shoulder, his fingers digging into my shirt. Warmth spreads from where he touches me, but it doesn't chase away the ice in my veins or the snarl yearning to break from me. "He and Lottie dealt with it, although not in the best way. I only caught the aftermath."

The beat of my heart rushes into my ears. *Bullying.* I've tried hard to avoid this, making sure Rory is a kid everyone will like. I've taken him to football, let him watch popular films, and gone without so he can wear clothes that fit him properly. I've done *everything* to stop him from being a target. He's dealt with enough in his little life.

Questions fight on the tip of my tongue, all of them desperate to get out. I gulp them down, though, not sure what I should say first. Nate tightens his grip on me, his thumb stroking the back of my shoulder. He shouldn't be touching me, not in front of the other parents and not after what I did to him yesterday, but I stare at his hand anyway.

He must notice, because he yanks it away as if I've burnt him. He casts his eyes down, chewing his lip, his cheeks bright pink.

"Why do I get the feeling you're hiding something from me?"

He stares at his feet for a moment longer before risking a glance at me. Finally, his shoulders lift and drop. "He called Rory an orphan."

I back away from him, my fists so tight my nails dig into my palms. It hurts, but I don't release the tension. Instead, I pace the small stretch of yard in front of Nate. I need air, space to get a grip on my anger before I become the Incredible Hulk. How the fuck dare they? The whole damn village knows about what happened to Luke, but who in their right mind teaches their child to pick on someone because they lost their parents? I bet it's someone from that group of bitches Josh loves chatting to. They've never liked me, so they must hate Rory too. Fucking bellends.

"Who?"

Nate takes a step towards me. "Ms Palmer will tell you more, Alex. Really, I shouldn't have mentioned anything, but—"

"Show me his parents."

"I don't know them."

"Of course you fucking do. If he's in your class, you would have met his parents. Tell me who they are."

"No." His hand is on my back but I shrug him off. So much for wanting to make me happy. He won't even help me with this. "Believe me, I would love to give them a piece of my mind about it. But this is my job, Alex, and it's not going to help Rory if you march across the yard and lamp someone. What kind of lesson would that teach him? I only told you because I didn't want Headmistress Palmer to blindside you in the meeting. It wouldn't be fair if you were unprepared. Are you okay?"

Who the fuck knows? My welfare is the least of my worries right now. "Is Rory okay?"

"He's a trooper. The words barely grazed him. Also, he thought it was hilarious that Lottie threw the first punch and only joined in because he wanted to have his cousin's back. Told me he doesn't care if he's an orphan, because he's more loved than anyone else in this school."

Shit. That kid, man.

"Of course he is." I release a shaky breath.

Even though I shouldn't, I step closer to Nate so that I can draw on some of the comfort he's so desperate to give me. But before I touch him, my brother saunters over. "Mr Jameson, what's going on? Why has Agnes called me and Alex in?"

The school doors fly open before Nate can tell Josh what happened, and children surge out. "Headmistress Palmer will explain. I can take you to her office."

Nate weaves his way expertly through the stream of kids flooding from their classrooms. Rory and Lottie perch on a bench outside the headmistress's office. His legs are swinging and he's humming to himself. A glance confirms there are no visible scratches on his body. When he sees me, he jumps from his seat and skips over to say hello. Maybe Nate was wrong. Rory hasn't been bullied. He looks like it's been the best day of his life.

"Hi, Alex. Hi, Joshy."

Nate raps his knuckles on the frosted glass. While he waits for an answer, he turns to the kids. "Can you two sit out here while we speak to Headmistress Palmer? I promise we won't be too long. If you can keep quiet, I'll add another gold star to your charts."

"Yes, Mr Jameson." Rory sings, not peeling his eyes off his teacher.

Palmer beckons us in. We step over the threshold and I take the seat furthest away from the door. All of a sudden, I'm thrust back to when I was six years old, and in trouble for fighting or bothering Mop Head. I wipe my sweat-slicked palms on my jeans.

"I've called you both here today because there was an incident on the playground during morning break. A child called Rory a name, and instead of going to tell his teacher, Rory and Lottie retaliated with their fists. This is a serious incident, gentlemen, and we have zero tolerance for this sort of behaviour. Nothing gives Charlotte and Rory the permission to dole out punishment as they see fit. The children are told that fighting is wrong, and that bullying should be reported to the nearest adult."

She folds her hands over her desk. "Fortunately, the parents of the child in question were understanding. On this occasion, they will not be taking the matter any further, and therefore, we will not be placing any sanctions on Rory or Charlotte. But if there is another fight, I will have no other choice but to suspend them. We do not reason with our fists in my school."

This is victim-blaming at its finest. "And the boy who bullied Rory? What *sanctions* does he get? Lottie only punched him to stand up for Rory. It's not fair if the bully gets away scot-free, especially if you have *zero tolerance* in your school."

"The child in question will be serving a week of detentions, beginning tomorrow at lunch time. Mr Jameson witnessed the incident, and was able to explain to me what happened, which is why I am choosing not to punish your children this time."

I'd forgotten Nate was in here with us, but when I lean back in my chair, his hand is there. His fingers twitch, as if to comfort me and I put pressure against them, even though I shouldn't.

"I promised the headmistress I'll keep a closer eye on what the children are saying to each other, and I'm going to plan some lessons on the diverse ways you can be in a family so that the whole class can learn something from this. Rory doesn't deserve to be bullied because he lives with his uncle."

The pressure between my shoulder blades increases and I release a long breath. Now I know Rory is safe, and won't be punished, I can relax a little. Although I can't completely kick back, not while Nate is touching me.

"Thank you, Mr Jameson." Agnes claps her hands together, signalling the end of our conversation. "Well, Alexander, Joshua, that's all I needed to discuss with you today. Please don't hesitate to call me if you have any further questions. The school secretary can arrange a meeting."

She rises to her feet and we follow Nate out of the office. Once the door is shut behind us, Josh sags against the wall.

"I have a whole other level of appreciation for Mum and Dad," he says, mock wiping his forehead. "Palmer is a whole lot scarier than when we were kids."

Rory giggles. "Were you naughty, Uncle Josh? Was Daddy too?"

"Your dad was the worst of us. Always in trouble. Uncle Simon used to tell him off all the time."

While Rory and Lottie fire more questions at Josh, I let Nate steal my attention. He lingers by the office. I wish I could pull him to me, kiss him until his lips are bruised and his hair is mussed and thank him for looking out for Rory, but I don't. I do step towards him, though.

"Thank you for today. Since we're here, and we've gotten over the initial awkwardness of seeing each other again, do you want to get on with the stall planning?"

He folds his arms, standing more upright. "I told you I can't. I have other plans this evening now."

Oh. Of course. Maybe that awkwardness is still there, then. As far as I'm aware, he doesn't have any friends here, so what is he doing that's so important? I yearn to ask, to get more knowledge about his life, but I only nod. I'm not entitled to find out more. "Oh, yes. Sure. Thursday then."

My eyes stay on him while I hold my hand out for Rory. Once his sticky little fingers are securely in mine, I give Nate a small nod, and follow the others out of the school. With every step, I grow sadder and fight not to look back at him, even when his gaze prickles my scalp.

I help fasten Rory into the car, and wait until I'm in the driver's seat before tapping out a quick text.

Me: Thank you for what you did today. looking after rory i mean

I don't get a reply.

FOURTEEN

BY THE TIME THURSDAY afternoon comes around, I'm a mess of nerves. I've barely slept a wink, plagued not only with nightmares about Rory being bullied, but of Luke's body lying on the floor, and of Nate not talking to me ever again. My hands shake as I work, I pick at my lunch, and every step I take is a fight with a body that never wants my shift to end so I can put off seeing Nate for as long as I can.

Sod's law kicks into force, though, and my shift is the fastest I've ever experienced, helped by the pre-summer holiday rush. Those without kids are getting away early before the beaches get rammed and the weather turns to shit. They visit our pub on their way to the seaside, excited to have a late breakfast before their day sunbathing; or pop in on their return, their bodies striped with pink like one of those drumstick lollies.

Me and Nate picked the library for our planning session because it's a neutral place and close enough to the school for him to walk Rory over after class. Despite visiting a hundred times before, I trip over the small step on my way into the building, jar my hip against the reception desk – earning myself a scathing look from the librarian – and knock over a stack of books waiting to be reshelved. I take a deep breath, puff it out upwards to force my fringe off my sweaty forehead, and smooth my hands along my jeans.

I can do this. Nate was kind to me, even after the fuck up of the parent-teacher conference, even on Tuesday after I dumped him. Friendship might be off the cards, but it's not like he's going to be a knob to me while we're working on the stall and while Rory is with us. I don't think Nate could ever be a knob. Even if he is, I need to get it together. There's still a few weeks of term left. I cannot fall apart every time I see him.

The foyer is empty, and Miss Tenfull's evil gaze follows me to the kids' section. I use the sound of Rory's laughing to locate him and Nate. They're standing in front of the children's fantasy shelves, books I usually deem way too old for Rory to read. He pulls one out, and Nate crouches to his level to see what it is. They flip to the back, discussing the content for a moment, before Nate takes it from Rory's grasp and adds it to a pile next to them. He says something else and Rory bursts out laughing.

God, this is torture.

Although I don't want to disturb their time together, the library shuts soon and we *have* to at least get a list of ingredients for me to order tomorrow.

I clear my throat and the pair look up.

"Alex!" Rory is the first to move, barrelling towards me and wrapping his arms around my legs with a vice-like grip, which I'm sure is only for show. I welcome it, stooping to kiss the top of his hot, sweaty head. Websters don't do well in the summer.

When we pull apart, Nate is watching us, his usual cheeriness completely gone. I wish things were different. I'd love to pull him into our embrace, twist my arms around the both of them and hold them close, but I can't. I made my decision. I have to live with the consequences.

"Hi." His greeting is a lot more subdued than Rory's. As Nate saunters closer, I notice he still looks tired, that there are still deep bags under his eyes. A loud yawn stretches his mouth, and he rubs at his eyes.

"Hey. How are you?"

He only shrugs at me. "Sorry about rescheduling, by the way."

"That's okay. We're here now."

The small talk is painful as fuck. As if working on auto-pilot, I step towards Nate, determined to push the stray lock of hair from his forehead, but Rory chooses that moment to plonk himself at the table, knocking over his stack of books. Like uncle, like child. When I drop to the floor to pick them all up, Nate stays where he is.

"We stole some supplies because Rory wanted another go at his sign. I said if he does a good job at it, I could get it laminated tomorrow ready for us to use."

"Great idea." I add the last book back to the pile then watch Nate retrieve the large sheets of paper and crayons, spreading them across Rory's table.

Rory gets to work straight away, his tongue poking out of the corner of his mouth. Since there's no space for me and Nate, I nod towards the next table over. We settle at it together, our backs to Rory. The tiny table forces our knees to touch, and I try my best to rearrange my body so that they don't. Mostly to spare me from getting worked up from the basic contact Nate is allowing me. Getting a stiffy in the kids' section isn't appropriate.

I miss you, I long to tell him, but instead, I take another look at his pale face. I don't get a chance to check in on him, though, because he says, "Did you say we have to get the ingredients sorted today?"

Business only then. Fine. "Yeah. They need to be ordered tomorrow so that they come to the pub on time since it's extra to our usual orders."

He busies himself with his notepad and pen, flipping to a new page. I rub my hand across my jaw before deciding to get on with it for now. There's no way I'm going to let him leave this afternoon before I check he's okay, though. I know I don't have that right anymore, that I was the one who dumped him and am probably the cause of his sleepless nights, but I still care about him. I still want to make sure he's all right.

Our close proximity is torture, but it helps me study him. A thick line of stubble graces his usually clean-shaved jawline and his glasses are dirty, his hair messed up. During a brief pause in our planning, while I take a sip from the bottle of water he placed on the table, he almost falls asleep. When he talks, his usual sunny tone is forced, and it's like every move is a hard task for him. I don't need to ask if he's been to the gym today. He must have been too exhausted.

He lets out his fifth yawn. I drop my pencil on my sheet of paper, pivoting my body more towards him. My knees yearn to slide against his, but I bend my legs to the side so that I don't touch him.

"Late night?" I quip. Maybe if I keep the tone light, I can show him we can still be friends, that he can still talk to me.

"Something like that," he mumbles.

"What's going on? It's okay to talk to me, you know. Just because we're not— y'know. Doesn't mean I don't care."

The look he shoots me, eyebrows raised and cynicism threaded through his frown tells me he doesn't believe me. He stays quiet, though, pulling another piece of paper off the pile to add more notes.

"Is it—is it about Monday night?"

"Not everything is about you."

The snap hurts, but I keep on pushing. Even if I'm only adding to the amount he must hate me right now, I can't shut up. I'm fucking worried about him. "What, then?"

He sighs and it rattles through me. Setting down his blue crayon, he says, "I'm only on a temporary contract and it finishes in three weeks. On Monday, Agnes told me that they're looking to extend my contract to a permanent one, but I'll need some of my lessons assessed and they want to interview me during the last week of term. I don't get to know which classes they'll be coming to, only that they'll just show up when it's time. So I've been on the edge all week. And if I don't get the job...well, it's a whole load of upheaval, and I'm not sure I want to go through all of that *again*. I don't want to leave East Beechmill. I guess all of that on top of Monday *and* the PTA stuff is getting a bit too much for me."

Fuck. I don't want him to leave, either. I can't imagine living a life without him in it, even if it's only seeing him in the mornings at drop-off. It's selfish, I know, but I can't help the way I feel.

"You don't have to help me with the stall," I offer.

"I want to."

His face has softened somewhat, and he stares at me with the same intensity he did in the bedroom. It tells me that he can't imagine living a life without *me* in it, even if he only sees me at drop-off. Maybe there's hope for our friendship, even if we can no longer be *together* together.

I reach out and rest my hand on his lower arm. The touch is feather-soft, and almost not there. I don't squeeze his arm, or let my fingers stroke over his skin, but the minor contact is still enough to set my pulse racing.

I keep my voice low, so that Rory doesn't overhear us. "You're an excellent teacher, Nate." The words burn their way up my throat. "Your class loves you. There's no way the old bat would let you go. She's not stupid. And she must have some say over it, right? You're like her protégé."

"Do you think winning this competition will help my case?"

"Oh, absolutely. With the money we're going to bring in, she'll be able to build a whole new school. How could she fire you? But," I add, straightening my face into a serious look. I don't want him thinking I always deflect with humour. I can be comforting and understanding and serious when I need to be. "We're not going to deliver a good stall if you're not sleeping, Nate. You're going to need energy to survive the next few weeks. Have you eaten today?"

He pulls out of my grip and pushes his hair out of his face, sitting straighter. The gap he creates between us is barely two inches, but it feels cavernous and wide and it's like I'm experiencing the loss of our breakup all over again.

He shakes his head. "I don't have the appetite."

"Ah, you're one of those people who don't eat when they're stressed. Me too. You need to start eating, though. If you need me to text you to remind you, I can. It's important, and I should know. It's how I make a living."

"I don't need the texts, thank you." The gap grows even wider. "But I promise I'll try and look after myself a bit more."

"Three square meals *and* snacks?"

"I'm not sure about the snacks..."

"But—"

"Alex."

Fine, I've overstepped my mark. My cheeks burn, and I slide my paper back to me. "Sorry. I just—"

But I don't get a chance to tell him that I care.

"All done!" The tension breaks as Rory shoves himself between us, pushing his paper onto the table. "Look at this."

Although I reply, I cannot muster the same energy he has. I keep my eyes on Nate as I say, "That's fine."

At least our meeting is a success.

With the help of Rory, me and Nate plan out a menu, make a note of everything else we might need and finalise our arrangements for the stall. All that's left is for me to order the food and ensure the equipment is ready for setting up. My gut twists at the thought that I won't have an excuse to see Nate until the fête – aside from the glimpses I may steal from him at the school – but maybe that's for the best. Perhaps the distance will help make this easier on us, allowing him to concentrate on bagging that contract.

Despite our misfire with me pestering him too much, working with Nate and Rory was fun, and I'm in a good mood when we leave the library. We say goodbye at the car, and, not wanting to go home yet, I take Rory to The Watering Hole for dinner.

When our food is in front of us, I bring up the bullying incident. Our schedules have been busy over the last couple of days, and there's not been a chance for me to sit and discuss it properly with him. Of course, I've checked in with him – I'm not a completely neglectful parent – and he seems unbothered by it all, but I have to make sure there aren't any lingering bad feelings.

"Has everything been okay in school?"

He takes a bite of his tuna and cheese pizza. Once he's swallowed, he says, "Being an orphan doesn't make me sad."

"So why did you fight the boy? You know, you don't always have to do what Lottie says."

"Lottie is the boss and we didn't want him to pick on anyone else."

"Who?" I haven't been able to get the name of the bully and I haven't spotted any kids wandering around the yard with a black eye. It's frustrating as fuck. It's not like I'm going to do anything bad, but I'm entitled to have a stern word with his parents, to make sure it doesn't happen again. "It's okay to tell me. I promise I won't go and punch his dad."

He laughs, but his face turns serious quickly. "Mr Jameson said he's going to look after me."

"That he will. If anyone says another word, I want you to go straight to him, okay? And stop fighting, even if Lottie thinks it's a good idea. Sometimes, I think your brain is a sieve, and you forget all the advice I give you."

"I remember. You said only idiots fight."

Okay, it's a little hypocritical considering I wanted to punch the lights out of the parent who turned their kid into a bully, but I'm a protective papa – or uncle, I guess – bear. I have to look after Rory. But kids should never fight.

"That's right," I reply. "I don't want people thinking you're a thug. I've brought you up better than that."

He chews for a moment, away with the fairies. I recognise the look well – glassy eyes, a tiny bit of drool slipping from his mouth. Sometimes, being in a fantasy world is much better than reality. I don't blame him.

"Alex," he finally says after demolishing half of his pizza. "Why don't you have a boyfriend?"

The question takes me by surprise. Although I try to be as open as I can about my life, the conversation of dating and relationships has never come up. Perhaps because he's only six. I find myself stuck for a moment on how to respond. Should I lie and say I'm not interested in having one when, in fact, there's nothing I want more? Or should I tell him that I almost had one, but decided to focus on him instead?

"Why do you ask?"

"Aunt Aimee and Uncle Josh said you needed one and that getting some action might make you happy. What type of action? Like a car chase or a shoot out?"

I choke on a sip of water, loving his damn innocence. Kids are fucking brilliant. "I should remind them that small ears are *always* listening, shouldn't I?" I play with the chips on my plate. "My last boyfriend didn't work out too well for us."

"He wasn't very nice. He didn't like me."

Mike did, at least at the start he did. But it soon turned sour as life got more stressful. "I'm not sure he liked me all that much either, buddy. Sometimes, adults pick the wrong people. When I find my next boyfriend, he has to be extra special. He has to love both of us, not only me, because we come as a package. But honestly, I'm happy with it being just me and you right now."

"We're stuck together forever."

"Ugh. Not forever. But at least until you're eighteen and I can chuck you out of my house."

The enormity of those years used to wake me in the middle of the night, terrified of what they meant. The thought of someone relying on me for everything for that long was petrifying. Now, I'm not sure I'll ever be ready for them to end. But maybe Nate and I will still be single in our mid forties and can finally get together when Rory goes to university. I bet Nate would be the hottest silver fox.

I continue, "I guess I haven't found the right person yet."

It's a blatant lie. Nate's face is already at the forefront of my mind, despite my best efforts to push the thought aside.

"I like Mr Jameson."

Maybe Rory is only talking about him because we spent the afternoon together, or perhaps it's because Nate is Rory's favourite teacher and it's wishful thinking. But the kid's wide open eyes, the way the left side of his mouth curls upwards, filling his cheeks with pink tells me it's deeper.

Shame I fucked things up, then. "I know you do, kid. So do I."

"He's almost as nice as Nanny Gail."

It takes every ounce of effort I have to keep chewing on my pizza and swallow without bursting out laughing at his comment.

It's great that Rory only sees the nice side of my mother, and hasn't picked up on any of the tension, especially from Sunday, but she is nowhere near as nice as Nathaniel is to me.

"The problem is, though," I tell him around another bite of food, "if I had a boyfriend, it might mean me and you will have less time to spend together. I'd have to go on dates and stuff."

"I could come too. I like dates and I'm a good egg."

I laugh. "How many dates have you been on, buddy?"

"None. But on the TV they always go for food. And Iron Man buys Pepper lots of presents. I like presents. And food."

Sometimes, I wish I thought the same way he does. It's all black and white when you're a child. I also wish we'd had this conversation earlier. Getting his perspective on things has added another million thoughts to my already in-turmoil head. Of course, I knew that Rory loved Nate, but have I been too hasty in throwing things away? Instead of blowing him off completely, perhaps I could have asked to slow things down. It's mental that after only a couple of weeks talking to each other, we felt the way we did. We were already calling each other boyfriend, for fuck's sake. Dragging it out longer, using the summer holiday to *really* get to know each other might have been the better option.

For fuck's sake. I've really screwed up, haven't I?

Remembering that Rory was talking to me, I shake my head and focus back on him. "Oh, man. I wish dating was as easy as going for food. Maybe you can be my wingman, though. Nice men can't resist cute kids like you. Now, finish the last of your pizza off before I eat it. We need to get home and finish your homework before bed. We're going to have to stay in Mr Jameson's good books so you survive the rest of term."

With a full belly, it'll be easy to get Rory bathed and to bed, once he's done his maths. And I can have a proper think about what this conversation means for me and Nate, and how I can potentially fix things between us.

FIFTEEN

IT DOESN'T TAKE LONG for me and Nate to text each other again.

I send the first message, although I wait four whole days before I crack. I'm quite proud of myself, actually. It's only a short one – a quick text to wish him good luck with his assessments in school – but it's enough to break the silence between us. Soon enough, we're back to our normal flow.

Talking with him again is great even if most of our conversation is about the fête. The temptation to flirt with him is still there, but I resist it for now. At least some of my resolve lingers, however thin it might be. I have a lot of hard work to put in before I can tell him I made a mistake. I need him to forgive me first.

The Saturday of Beechmill Primary's summer fête finally comes around. Over the past week, an enthusiastic buzz has settled over the village, and everywhere I turn, people are talking about it. In a small place like this, not much else happens, and a school event is the height of the social calendar for most who live here.

Fresh out of the shower and dressed, I wander across the hallway and push open Rory's door, leaning against the frame to watch him. He's out of bed and wearing the shocking green T-shirt I had printed for anyone helping us on the stall today. He's paired it with his white football shorts and neon orange socks. His school bag lies open on the bed, and he roams the room, collecting items and stuffing them in.

"Good morning. Watcha doing?"

He doesn't pause in his mission, talking into the drawer where he keeps his crayons. "Packing."

"Yeah? Where're you going?"

"To the summer feet. Nanny Gail says you should always be prepared."

"All right. But we have everything we need packed into Uncle Simon's van. You can bring whatever else you think you might need but not too much, okay? You have to carry that bag yourself. And we have to leave now. Mr Jameson won't be happy if we're late."

I'm determined to be on time today. I want to prove to Nate I can be a good person, worthy of his time.

"I'm ready." Rory shoves Thor's helmet on his head, zips his bag up and heaves it onto his back, staggering with the weight of it all. "Wait. What about bacon?"

"I've made us rolls to eat in the car, you hungry caterpillar. Now mush."

I keep my hand on his bag to support him down the stairs. Our stall won't be a success if I have to spend the day in the Minor Injuries unit with him.

"Hey, Alex. We're matching today. Isn't that cool?"

This child will never stop being adorable. His enthusiasm makes me glad that I invested a little bit of my own cash to buy us a uniform if it makes him feel a part of the team. Although, I have refrained from the brightly coloured socks and white shorts that he has on, the effect is still the same – we look like we belong. He's going to lose his shit when he spots Nate wearing the same top.

Simon is already unloading crates from a white transit van emblazoned with the pub's name in massive green and pink letters when we get to the school playground. Rory runs off when he spots Nate, throwing his arms around his teacher's hips in an over-the-top greeting.

"We have the same top," he says with a squeal, his head buried against Nate's stomach.

"Yes, we do, Rory." Nate does his best to prise himself from Rory's grasp, though, he can't hide his smile. "So does everyone else working on the stall."

"Hi," I breathe out as I stop next to him, forgetting about keeping my distance. I can't help it. He's picked up a bit of a tan from all the time he's spent outside with his pupils recently. Instead of the green top washing him out, he looks like he belongs at the beach. And with Rory now clinging onto his hand, I find myself regretting every decision I made last week. How could I be such an idiot?

Think of the bigger picture, Alex. Right, Rory is my priority. Which means I *have* to focus on the stall today and not my grief over my lost relationship with the most perfect man ever.

"Mum's here," Simon warns me as he draws closer. "Take this."

He shoves the box at me, forcing me to step away from Rory and his teacher. Nate catches my eye, and I can't stop the grin from spreading over my face, too. He leads Rory over to Aimee, who has the first babysitting shift of the day. The box is heavy and strains in my arms as I watch him chat away to Rory, helping him to unpack his bag. It's a natural action, as if Nate has been parenting all his life, and I fall for him a little bit more.

I shake the thoughts of him out of my head. I can't just pounce on him straight away. Anyway, all our focus needs to be on the stall, but perhaps I can talk to him later.

Two rows of mis-matched tables – plastic formica from the school, picnic benches from people's homes and even the odd pasting table – form an aisle that leads to the pitch at the bottom of the playground, where the rest of my family are setting up. I greet members of the PTA as I pass them, and delight in the way most of them say hello back. Some of them even know my name. The only people that don't are the members of the Perfect Parent Club. That's fine. I still don't want to be a part of their cult.

I weave around deck chairs and excited kids, the flap of rainbow streamers and banners distracting my attention. Once I've abandoned the box with the others, I help Dad unfold a dusty gazebo. Mum takes command in the centre of our pitch, bossing the army of Websters into getting the stall set up and running. I want to argue that it's *my* project, that I should be in charge but I let it slide. I don't want anything to ruin today's good mood.

I next see Nate chatting to Henry as they stack takeaway boxes into piles. It doesn't seem awkward from where I'm standing, tacking the rota onto a leg of the shelter. Either Henry has forgotten the fact he saw Nate's dick a fortnight ago, or is trying his best to move past it. I haven't told him we broke things off. It's none of his business. But it does make me irrationally happy to see them getting on so well.

I grab a pack of shocking pink tablecloths and wander over to our picnic tables. Luke loved clashing colours, and always wanted the pub's brand to be bright and garish, so that people would remember us. By taking inspiration from a pack of highlighters, we've done him proud today.

"I'm not sure about all the colours." Nate sidles up to me. He takes one corner of the cloth I'm unfolding, and helps me spread it over the table. "Everyone else has gone for rainbows or pastels. You know, proper summer colours."

"Then yes, we picked the right colours. We want to lure every-one in with the crazy decorations, and make them stay with our delicious food."

A clink of glass and a swear disturbs us. On the table next door, Josh is adding the last few bottles to his stand. Heatherton, his assigned teacher-partner, is already snoozing in a deck chair. I wave at my brother, and he flips a finger at me in return.

"I spotted a bric-a-brac, a name the teddy stall and a garden sale," I tell Nate. "We're on to a winner."

"Yeah, I reckon so."

I lean in closer, using the staple gun to attach his end of the cloth to the table. All of a sudden I want to apologise for breaking up with him. Forget waiting until the day is over, or having some sort of self-control. The moment is kind of perfect. Nobody is paying us any attention, distracted by their own jobs. We're alone. Rory is off bothering his cousins. I could apologise without anyone butting in, explain why I made the decision I did. Then we could enjoy the day together properly.

"Hey, Nate. I was wondering if we could—"

"Please could all PTA members join me at the stage."

Bugger. Of course, Palmer had to be the one to interrupt my moment. Annoying old bat. I rub my jaw, and follow Nate to the school entrance, locating a spot amongst all the others to listen to what she has to say. Agnes strolls onto the stage, looking out of place in her usual headmistress attire – a long, straight skirt, a starched blouse and her hair pulled into a tight bun. Everyone else is dressed as casually and in as little as they can without being offensive to ward off the heat. It's going to be a hot day, but not for Agnes Palmer. A top-tier teacher like her doesn't sweat, or tremble in the face of relentless humidity.

The music that's been filling the yard for the past hour fades into a soft thrum, and her strong voice carries over the group without a microphone.

"It's almost time to open the gates. Before we do, I wanted to say thank you for all your hard work. It's no mean feat, putting together all of this in such a short time. Whatever the final amount raised, you can be proud of what you've achieved. This should be the best school fête to date.

"As always, if you need anything, I'll be stationed at the school doors with the nurse. We have plenty of water and suncream on hand. Pop by whenever you need a top-up. It's a hot day. Stay hydrated and take plenty of breaks. But most importantly, have fun."

She steps off the stage to a round of applause. It's easy to get swept up in the excitement. The atmosphere buzzes over my skin and I shiver. Why didn't I join the PTA when Rory started at the school? I've been missing out. I've already agreed to chaperone the school disco next week, and committed to staying on next year. Not only has having a task to focus on helped me and Rory grow closer, but there's the added benefit that I can spend more time with Nate. Even if we're only friends moving forward.

But hopefully, eventually, we can work together as more.

A tug at my elbow pulls me out of my musings, and when I spin towards it, I'm greeted by Nate's handsome face.

"I've got a missed call," he tells me. "I'm going to pop into my classroom to take it, but I'll be back before it gets busy, okay?"

The exhilaration of the event almost has me leaning in to kiss him, but I stop myself. That would ruin any chances with him. "Sure. Whatever you need."

I stroll back to the stall with Josh.

"Feeling confident?" he asks.

"Yep. We've got this in the bag."

"I'm fucked. Are you sure I can't attach my stall to yours and come and help you instead? It's not like Heatherton will notice I'm gone. We can offer a bottle of pop with every burger sold."

"Nope. You need to learn that you can't win every time. Anyway, I don't have any more tops."

"You bought the whole family one apart from me?"

I shrug. "Should have given up sooner."

"Wanker. Talking of winning, are you seeing Mr Jameson?"

The question catches me off guard. How does he know something has happened between us? Okay, so we weren't exactly discreet, but there's not been any hint of it in the family chat. I told Mum I'd finished with Nate after the fact, and she's been shooting me and him looks every time we get close to each other all morning. Maybe Josh has worked it out for himself? Or Henry finally snitched.

I study my brother closely. We've confided in each other about everything since we were little. I was the first person to learn about Aimee, to find out she was pregnant with James. Josh stayed by my side when I was racked with guilt over Luke, he was the brother I went to when Mike broke my heart. Surely, I can share what happened with him. It's not like it matters if the rest of my family finds out now.

"We slept together a couple of weekends ago."

Josh fist-punches the air. "I fucking knew it!"

"What do you mean, you knew it?"

"You were strutting around the farmhouse like you owned it the other Sunday. Henry and Simon tried teasing you about the Beechmill scores, and you didn't bite. At the meeting with Palmer last week, he couldn't keep his hands off you, although he was trying to be discreet. You forget, baby brother, I know you better than anyone else."

"Well done for working it out *after* I broke up with him."

"Wait....what? Are you a fucking idiot?"

"I think so. Mum got in my head and—"

"You let her talk you out of being with him." My brother practically face-palms himself. "Mr Jameson is perfect for you. For a start, he's probably the only other gay man in the village." Josh clearly hasn't downloaded Grindr recently. "Plus, he's great with kids and just an all-round nice guy. Don't be stupid, Al."

"I know, I know. I'm going to try and put things right with him, I promise. Especially because Rory has been asking why I don't have a boyfriend. Apparently, *someone* has been saying I need more action. He wanted to know if you meant car chases or shoot outs."

"Which one would you prefer?"

"A car chase. I'm a rubbish shot."

"Look, if you don't want your kid hearing things he shouldn't, then you need to stop him being nosey." Josh doesn't have the decency to blush or look shameful. "And you do deserve more action. I know you have this big complex about wanting to do the right thing for Rory, and it's all heroic and shit, but I promise you'll be a more relaxed dad if you're getting boned more regularly."

"You're always so good at advice, Josh."

"Thank you. Let me know if there's anything I can do to help."

"Thanks, bro."

We part ways at our stalls, and he joins Heatherton, who is still fast asleep. I do feel sorry for my brother, for a small moment, but shake it off as Simon beckons me over. We already have our first customer.

I position myself behind the cash box, shifting the desk fan to point directly at me. Nate returns as I write down the order.

"Nice of you to join us again," I tease, my eyes remaining on him until he's at my side.

He scoffs. "I wasn't gone long."

"Everything all right?"

"Yeah, all good."

If it was *all good* then why did he have to take the call in his classroom? I don't get a chance to question him further, though. A queue is already forming at our stall. I take payment for the order and pass the slip to Simon.

He eyes it closely, his face lighting up. "Beef burger with banana and mayonnaise? Brilliant. Might be one to add to our permanent menu if it tastes good."

"You're not allowed to sample *everything*," Jaya argues.

I leave them to it and return to Nate, who's already taking the next order. I place my hand on his hips to squeeze past him to reach the cutlery, my groin brushing against his backside. It's tight confines in the stall. Not that I'm complaining. Rory was supposed to be acting as a messenger as it's easier for him to move around the tiny space, but the lazy kid hasn't shown up for his shift yet.

"It was my mum, if you must know." Nate eventually offers, even though I kept my mouth shut. "She wanted to wish us luck for today. Give us some advice, since she runs her own cafe back home."

I grab a wooden fork and knife from the pile and rest them next to the waiting takeaway box. One of Nate's terms for the stall was that it had to be sustainable. Everything is compostable or reusable.

"Oh is she like our mum?" Simon butts in. "Has an opinion on everything we do? I'm probably the only one who listens to her."

"Because you're a suck-up and her favourite." I share a knowing glance with Nate, who fights back a laugh.

"Must be a parent thing," he suggests with a small shrug.

"Oh, god," I reply, "I hope not. My main goal is to not be like Mum where Rory is concerned."

We laugh then turn our attention back to the growing queue of customers. As Rory predicted, the stall is a roaring success. Business starts slow, but soon picks up as we barrel towards lunchtime. He's not allowed any of the glory for it, though, since he's barely here. Every so often, he zips over to shout words of encouragement at us before running back to whoever is in charge of looking after him for that shift.

The lunch rush tapers off, and the babble of excitement dissipates, making it easier to hear the music blasting over the yard. I'm topping up the cutlery when "It's Electric" bursts from the speakers, followed by a cheery whistle. I drop what I'm doing and spin to face Nate.

"I fucking love this song."

I grab his hand, pulling him out from behind our work table and to the space in front of our stall. The waiting customers turn to watch as I move in time with the music, but he stands there, blinking at me.

"Don't tell me you never learned the Electric Slide?" I stop.

"We were never a dancing family."

"Come here. It's the easiest one to learn."

If there's one thing my parents did right, it was to make us join in at every party and disco they took us to, every kids' club and playscheme they could afford. I guess you need all the rest you can get when there's a hundred children to look after.

"Oh, no, Alex. I'm not sure if I should—"

I yank him closer, waiting for the right time in the music. "Grapevine left, and right. Two steps back. Step touch, brush your foot as you turn to face the next direction. Then, you start again."

He's as graceful as a giraffe on roller skates, but he soon gets the hang of it. The crowds, the stall, my family, all fade away as we dance together, laughing when one of us gets the moves wrong. It's like I'm a child again, not caring what other people think because I'm too fixated on having fun. I touch him every chance I get, even when the kids from his class join in. Half of the fête dances with us, but I'm not paying attention to any of them. All I can focus on is the man next to me, and his clumsy, flailing limbs. I don't even care when he steps on my toes.

The song eventually finishes, and I'm gutted when we're forced back behind the table, our chests heaving.

"I know all of the classics," I explain. "We were Butlins kids. Cheap and cheerful holidays were all Mum and Dad could afford, and they forced us to the kids' clubs so they could have a break."

Nate laughs, pushing his fringe off his sweaty forehead. "I kind of wish we had holidays like that. We used to go skiing or abroad, and my parents focused more on getting out and exploring."

"I'm not entirely sure a Butlins holiday is up your street, anyway."

I poke him in the ribs, taking the moment to admire how flushed he is. A cough from the customer waiting drags my attention back to the stall, and I get back to taking orders, Nate still at my side.

The stall is too fucking busy all day – which is a good thing, I promise – but it means we get no more time alone until we're packing away. It hasn't stopped us slipping into old territory as the afternoon passes. The dancing broke the remaining tendrils of frostiness between us, and we've been flirting like I never dumped him.

All it's done is make me want him more. Every time Rory comes over, Nate speaks to him like he's his own. He gets on well with my family, and even Mum is warming to him by the time the gates close on the school yard.

I finish stacking the dirty pots and pans, tucking them into the van before wandering over to where Nate is wrapping leftover ingredients, ready for their journey back to the restaurant. He's sweaty, dirty and tired-looking, and it makes me wish more than anything that we were heading home together so we can bask in the glory of a job well done. Perhaps celebrate like we did in my dream.

When his head turns at my approaching footsteps, he flashes me a huge, but weary smile. At that moment, with the sun still painting everything in bright gold, I decide to do something for myself. Rory will be okay. Mum will get over it eventually.

Wherever Luke is, I bet he's cheering me on. I know he'd want nothing more than his kid to have a chance at a proper family, a chance to be loved and enjoyed by even more people.

I'm going to ask Nate back out. I'll need to grovel like fuck first, but it'll be worth it.

"We did well today." Nerves hijack my mouth and I resort to small talk so I don't say anything stupid. I don't want to assault him straight away with an apology.

"Yeah, I think so, too. But was it enough to win?" He wriggles his eyebrows at me, and I giggle. *Giggle.* Like a little girl. *Come on, Alex. Pull your shit together.*

"We better have or Rory will never forgive me."

"Well, at least we'll have beaten Josh. That's one of our goals met."

We side-eye my brother's table. He's packing his bottles away, his movements slow, his eyes focusing on his task even though Aimee is talking to him. Poor Josh. Although people stopped at his stall on their way to ours, only a few walked away with something.

"See, I was right. Any type of sale was a bad idea. Nobody wants the shit you don't want."

"Yeah, yeah. I should have listened to you from the start." Nate nudges my shoulder, his touch lingering against me for a moment longer than it probably should.

A comfortable silence settles between us, and I help him pack the last of the food. I take every opportunity to touch him, grazing my fingers over his, resting my hip against him, slipping my hand over his side. Once it's all tucked into the boxes, we share another knowing look. This one makes me giddy. It's like I've stepped off the waltzers at the village fair, my head light from all the spinning. This is the moment I've been waiting for. He's not once stepped away from my attempts to get closer, and I'm certain he wants me back too.

I scratch at the stubble on my chin, keeping my voice low. "So, Nate, listen. I've been hoping to talk to you this afternoon."

"Oh?" Panic flashes in his eyes, but he leans on the table, turning his back to the rest of the world. He draws his lower lip between his teeth. "What's up?"

"It's not bad. I was just— I thought that maybe we—"

A teenager approaches, her thumbs hooked into the straps of a bright pink rucksack and a bright smile on her face.

"Sorry, kid. You missed all the food. The fête ended half an hour ago."

"Oh, I don't want anything but—"

Nate spins around, his face as grey as the takeaway boxes.

"Chloe? What are you doing here? I thought you missed your train and I was going to meet you in an hour or so?"

Wait, what?

"I wanted to see your stall, Dad. I managed to grab my connection, and..."

Her words fade out. No matter which way I digest what she said, I cannot make sense of it. Nate is a dad. I can't put the two things together. He's never— He hasn't— I shake my head, hoping a good rattle will help me get my thoughts in order, but it's no good. They're all over the place.

There's no way he has a kid. The girl standing in front of us must be fourteen, maybe older if she's travelling around by herself. Surely, there's no way he could—

I'm wrong, of course. He's only a year younger than me. More than old enough to be the dad of a teenager. She's a carbon copy of him, too, although she wears her blonde hair in a straight sheet down her back and it's pulled off her face by a flowery headband. She even fucking smiles like him.

I'm going to be sick. I'm giddy again, but this time it's violent, distorting the edges of my vision. The world tilts and twists, but there's nothing for me to reach out for, to steady myself. Nate is too close to the table, and if I touch him, I may react in a way I don't want him, her, my family or Rory to see.

Take a step. Then another. Get away. My legs collide with the table behind us, silent protests popping like bubbles from my mouth. *No, no, no.*

"You're— she— what?" are the only words I manage to voice as I retain the tiniest grip on reality. But it's too late. He's already yanked the rug out from under my feet, and the perfect world I'd imagined for us is spinning from my grasp.

"Chloe, you mind giving us a minute?" Nate asks.

"But, I—" She glances my way, her eyebrow arched. He's told her all about me, if her growing grin is anything to go by. I expect her to argue back – she looks desperate to meet me properly – but she turns and takes a few steps from us, her hair swishing as she moves. She perches on the trestle table next to Rory, who looks like he might be digging for worms. The tiger face he had painted on earlier has melted in the sun, the colours mixing into a murky brown and collecting in patches on his skin. It makes him look like some sort of foreboding spectre, albeit a tiny one, and I shudder.

Nate's hand shakes as he reaches for me. "Alex, I can explain."

I scooch along the table, shaking my head. I chose to trust one man, put all my hope into our future together, but he never had the decency to return the favour. We spent an entire night together, whispering our greatest fears to each other. We talked about the struggles I had with Rory, how worried I was that his past was going to affect his future. Sure, we had a setback, but I was about to make that right again.

My only wish these past two years was to help my family get over Luke, to fill the massive gaping holes he's left in our lives. I've worked hard to keep Rory healthy and happy, I've picked up every extra shift I can so that Simon can still see his family. I've played the dedicated son, joined the fucking PTA. Did everything by the god-damn book. And the one moment I chose to let that slip, to go against Mum's advice and do something for myself, *this* happens.

I *know* I shouldn't feel this betrayed. That Nate never owed me his history. But it doesn't stop the news of Chloe hurting. Every secret I've told him, the tidbits of my life I've given him flash through my head, and my heart sinks further. At least now it's in the mud, it'll be easier for him to stomp all over it. I'm fucking delusional. Why would he want to be *my* boyfriend when he can't tell me he has a daughter?

"Don't." I keep my hands clamped at my sides. "I can't."

"But—"

"No!"

My shout echoes over the remnants of the fête, drawing the attention of Chloe, Rory, the last few Websters helping us to pack up, and lingering members of the Perfect Parent Club. Josh abandons whatever he was packing away to step closer to us, but I don't have the energy to tell him to fuck off. I don't need him interfering right now.

I push my hand through my hair. When I speak, my voice is more quiet, subdued.

"I can't believe you kept something this big from me after everything I told you. I asked you to tell me more about you, to share your secrets. I have given you countless chances to tell me you have a *teenage* daughter, but you chose to keep her from me. Do you not trust me? Even after I assured you nothing would change what I thought of you, you still kept quiet about her."

I pace the tiny space I'm occupying, being careful to stay away from Nate. "I'm a fucking idiot. I was besotted with you. All day, I've been working up the courage to apologise to you, tell you how much of a mistake I've made and *beg* you to take me back. Why didn't you tell me about her?"

He draws his lip through his teeth. "I wasn't sure I would be staying here."

"So, what? You were going to hide her from me all summer until you fucked off to somewhere else?"

"No. I was going to tell you on our date. I thought it would be cute, give us something to talk about. But it never happened and—"

"Oh. It's all my fault?"

"No. Alex. That's not what I meant. Since we broke up, I figured I could bring her here and then she could meet everyone. If I get the job, she might stay here so it'll be good for her to have friends."

He takes another step towards me and I keep on backing away until I'm out of the suppressive air under the gazebo. I can't breathe. I have to get out of here. My head swivels left and right, searching for the quickest exit.

There. The gate is open, my car waiting only a few steps away.

"I trusted you, and you let me down." I pick at the now-faded hickey on my neck, as if causing myself pain can stop the last tendrils of composure from slipping out of my grip. "I have to go."

I march towards Josh, each step purposeful, my head held high.

"Alex. Please talk to me. Don't walk out on me like this. It wasn't intentional. I got excited about making a big deal of her being here. This is the last thing I wanted." Nate follows me, his feet brushing over the grass. I ignore him. I *can't* look at him, or I might break.

Josh stands alert next to his table, his arms folded over his chest. His gaze is wary and flits between me and Nate. He heard everything, then. "Most of the packing is done, yeah? Leave Rory with me and go sort yourself out, okay? I'll take him to the pub with the others."

"Yeah. Thanks."

Rory walks over, but I can't bring myself to say goodbye to him. He'll have questions, he'll want to know why I'm arguing with Nate, but I don't have any answers. I can't even explain why I've reacted the way I have. After all, Nate owes me nothing, especially after the way I treated him.

I fish my car keys out of my pocket, and walk away.

SIXTEEN

THE WALK TO MY car is torturous. With every step, visions of Nate and Chloe tease me. How identical they look. One glimpse was enough to tell me he's a good dad.

So good he kept her a secret.

How could he do that to me? No matter how hard I rack my brain, there's no logical reason behind it. Although I *should* have stayed at the school to hear him out, even if only to put my mind at rest, there's no way I can turn back to ask him. My skin is still warm from the aftermath of being betrayed in front of my family. All I'll be faced with now is a look from Mum that says "I told you so" and all those stupid sympathetic glances that wind me up.

No thanks.

So instead, made-up reasons why Nate couldn't tell me zip through my head. He was never into me. He never intended to be in a relationship. Even if he gets the permanent post, he wants to move away from the village and cut off ties from me. He doesn't trust me with Chloe.

I don't blame him. I'm barely keeping Rory alive. And I freaking dumped Nate because Mum got into my head. Not setting a great example there, am I?

By the time I reach my car, I've whipped myself into a frenzy. I'm so distracted, I fumble to unlock it. When I hurl myself in and slam the door shut, a loud thunk tells me another chunk of rust has detached itself from the chassis. *Fucking brilliant.* Another thing I need to replace. Like everything else in my life, the car is a piece of shit too.

"Fuck!" I yell as loud as I can, dragging out the word until I run out of breath. I pound my fists on the steering wheel, short beeps adding a staccato melody to my tantrum. Movement catches the corner of my eye. A member of the Perfect Parent Club ushers her kids past, her ponytail swinging brightly behind her, mocking me. Her gaze is fixed on me, cautious and wary. "What the fuck are you looking at?"

She hurries away and I slump against the wheel, squeezing my eyes shut. Only, that's no good. Because those damned visions of Chloe and Nate are more vivid. It's almost like they're here in the car with me. *Why* didn't he tell me? Am I really that awful a person? *Don't answer that, brain.* Nate has a lever arch folder full of evidence to prove how vile I am, and we've only known each other for a few weeks. Then there's everything else. Luke died because of me. Mike left me. My own mum doesn't trust me enough to look after a six-year-old.

I am the worst.

I stir out of my depressive thoughts when someone else walks past the car, arms full of boxes. Packing up must be almost finished. Josh *and* Mum and Dad's cars are parked close to mine and the last thing I need is to be caught like this, especially when I'm not in the mood for answering any questions. I wipe my nose on my arm and turn the key in the ignition before pulling away from the curb. My downward spiral consumes my attention, and

I drive on autopilot, taking lefts and rights at random and letting the flow of the traffic dictate where I go.

After twenty minutes of driving, my self pity has drained into numbness and I switch my brain on long enough to pull into a parking spot at the seaside. I'm greeted by salty air when I step out of the car and I pull in as much of it as my lungs can take. It seeps through the murkiness of my brain, blowing away the toxic thoughts and taking with them some of the tension. I release the breath in one hard cathartic puff and my body relaxes a little.

It's quiet here. The shops are already shutting up, leaving me with the whole seafront to myself. I shove my hands in my pockets and amble to the pebble beach.

This is one of my favourite places in the world – not that I've seen much of it yet. All the brochures describe it as the entrance to the Jurassic Coast, and it sure deserves the title. Tall red cliffs flank either side of the beach, towering over its visitors and protecting the land behind it. Mum and Dad would often bring me and my brothers here to let off steam, and we'd pretend dinosaurs could surface from the choppy tides, or were peeping over the ridges of the high rock faces. This is where Dad taught us how to fish, and we spent hours scurrying over the rockpools, collecting a zoo of strange little creatures. We would skim stones into the water, competing for the most skips before we lost our prized pebbles to the English Channel. I was the smallest, the weakest, never managing more than two or three jumps and I always lost. My booby prize was to carry everyone's buckets of shells, squirming sea slugs, and squat lobsters to the car. Then Mum would order me back to the rocks to release the beasties so we could go home.

I need to bring Rory here and teach him everything Dad showed me. Luke would have already had him hunting down fossils and ensnaring crabs, I bet. God, I suck at making the kid's life fun.

The tide is coming in, but there's still enough space for me to walk along the pebbles that click and clatter under my feet. Every so often, I stoop low to find a flat stone, then skim it into the sea. I continue this way until I've reached the other end of the shoreline.

Why can't I have an easy life?

The thought catches me as suddenly as the cold water seeping into my trainers. I retreat from the water's edge and plonk myself down on a large, flat rock, avoiding blobs of seagull poop and baked-on melted ice cream. My phone has been vibrating against my leg since I left the school so I pull it out to check on whatever chaos I abandoned. The list of missed calls is long, and I scroll my thumb over it. Josh, Mum, Nate, Simon, Henry, Josh, Nate, Nate, Nate, Nate...

They're only ringing because they care, but I can't face speaking to any of them. Not yet. My little grey rain cloud from last week is back, hovering over me and blocking out the sunshine of what was otherwise a fantastic day. I don't know what to do now. Part of me wants to stay here until the sky goes dark then light again, moping over the shit hands life keeps on dealing. But I have Rory, and I should pick him up at some point this evening. It's not fair to abandon him. The kid hasn't done anything wrong.

I switch apps, speeding past the photos of me and Nate, ignoring the acid crawling up my throat whenever I catch him beaming at the camera. It doesn't take me long to reach the hundreds of snaps I have of Rory. Okay, he's only six, but he's always been there for me with a shit joke, or the latest bug he's dug out of the garden, or his best impression of Thanos. Once, he tried clicking his fingers to get rid of the broccoli on his plate. It didn't work. It only wiped out half of the portion.

The corners of my mouth twitch as picture after picture of Rory's gappy grin fills my screen. He's happy. Why do I need more? We were doing fine without Nathaniel Jameson in our lives, and we'll carry on being fine after him.

But Nate makes you smile in ways Rory can't.

Shut up.

I return to the list of missed calls until I find Josh's name. It takes him four rings to pick up. "Heya, mate. How's it going?"

His friendly, familiar tone reminds me of late nights, crawling into his bed when I was little and had a nightmare, of getting drunk with him and the others and sharing all our dark secrets. It makes me miss Luke more than ever. He'd know what to do. But so will Josh.

"Not too bad," I reply, "all things considered. Is Rory okay?"

"Not gonna lie, he was upset when you left without him. But I told him you had to save the world and now he's zooming around the pub, pretending to be you. He and Lottie have capes, though fuck knows where they got them from. I think they're table cloths. One second." He fumbles the phone and there's a couple of footsteps on the creaking wooden floor of The Watering Hole. "Lottie, no. I told you to stay away from the dessert fridge…I don't care if Rory *needs* it. He's not sad now…No, he can wait, just like everyone else."

The chaos in the background brings a watery smile to my face. Some things never change.

He returns to the call. "Sorry about that. Our kids are brats. I think Simon is close to locking them in the store cupboard."

"Sounds like they deserve it." I attempt a laugh, but it's more of a dried huff. "Did it take long to finish packing up?"

"Nah. I was already done, and Nate and the girl he was with helped the family finish tidying your stall. Rory, too. Wouldn't leave Nate's side."

"Chloe. Nate's daughter." Saying it out loud doesn't make it feel any better. Her name drags like barbed wire over my tongue.

"Oh, is that who she was?"

I scoff. "I know you were listening. Stop pussying around."

There's a pause. A door shuts, and the rumble of background noise disappears.

"How are you feeling?"

"Like shit. I know we weren't together, but—"

"Because you told him about Luke and Rory, you feel he owes you his whole life story? Or is it because you shagged and now you're imagining your lives together?"

My cheeks heat. "Well, not exactly, but—"

"Mate, I love you, but the two of you only spent one night together. See, this is your problem. You always dive headfirst into anything that takes your interest, but some people don't move at the same pace you do."

"It's not like I was going to ask him to marry me."

"No? Bet you thought about it though."

Well, it would have been nice. Eventually.

He takes my silence as an admission and laughs. "Oh, Alex. You're in deep, aren't you?"

"Absolutely not."

"Sure. So what are you going to do?"

"I don't know. I wanted to ask him back out today. I thought he felt the same way. Clearly not."

"Bullshit. He wants you as much as you want him. Every time I looked over, I could see the two of you flirting. You couldn't keep your hands off each other. It was reciprocal."

"What do *you* think I should do?"

He sighs. "I can't decide that for you, mate. But perhaps you should talk to him. He's worried about you."

"I can't see him. Not yet."

"You know the longer you leave it, the harder it's going to get."

"I dunno. He's with Chloe right now, so it doesn't seem fair. He doesn't get to see a lot of her." Or at least, I don't think he does. The fact I have no idea only deepens my shame.

"All right. Well, when you're ready, meet us at the pub. Simon put dinner aside for you."

"Thanks. See ya later."

I hang up and stare at my phone. Nate's name is next on the list, almost pulsing for my attention. I can't speak to him. Not yet. Instead, I shove the device back into my pocket and go for a walk.

I wander the beach for another hour, the sea slowly stealing the strip of pebbles away from me. I resist the urge to throw more of the stones into the water. It's not like it's going to help me decide whether to speak to him or not.

The wind picks up so I settle on a bench near the car, shivering. I'm still in my stupid T-shirt, and the early summer nights aren't warm enough to be outside without a jumper. Especially on the coast. It's okay, though. I'll be back in the car soon. There's one more thing I need to do first.

I call Nate, but it rings and rings. A brief moment of relief flushes through me. He must have abandoned his phone to spend more time with Chloe. Good. I should hang up, leave him to it, but something keeps me hanging on. When he *finally* answers, just as I'm about to give up, my anxiety comes rushing back.

"Oh, thank God you called," he says without a hello. "I was getting worried about you. Where are you? We walked over to the house, but nobody was there. Where's Rory?"

"I drove to the seaside."

I didn't want to tell him where I was hiding. He doesn't deserve to know the secret spots I retreat to during my low moments. I fucking hate that I let it slip anyway. Now it's one more thing he knows about me, when he'll never be willing to share back.

"A-are you okay?"

"No. This sucks."

"I'm sorry. I had every intention of telling you. I thought it would be cute if I saved it for our date. I—I didn't want to put you off. When I said that people find me too much, this is ex—"

My eyes burn and I blink it away. I'm not ready for this. I can't listen to him. "Nate. Please. Don't."

He breathes out hard, like I punched him in the gut. It sounds like a swear is longing to escape but he's biting it back. For fuck's sake. I want him to swear it out. Maybe if he'd lose his shit with me, I'd feel better about walking away. It's like he never gets annoyed. I dumped him and he kissed me. Why isn't he angry?

"When then?" he asks after a moment of silence. "When can I explain myself? Try to make things better? Why are you calling me if you're not going to give me a chance?"

"I'm not sure why I called you."

"Perhaps because you *know* it's the right thing to do, Alex. Earlier, before Chloe showed up, I thought that we— I thought that maybe—" He sighs. "I would like a chance to explain about Chloe. About what happened between me and her mum. *Please* let me come and talk to you. I can get a taxi and meet you at the house and—"

"Where is she?"

He doesn't answer straight away and I can picture his forehead scrunching, him drawing his lip between his teeth. "She's in her room."

I rasp my fingers through the stubble on my jaw. He clearly doesn't see a lot of her, and I immediately feel guilty for stealing some of that time away from him. But I can't sleep on this. I need to hear him out.

"Can I come to yours?"

"Yeah. Chloe won't interrupt us."

"I'll be there in half an hour."

I hang up and rest on the bench a minute longer, watching the darkening clouds fly past. This day has been far too long already, and my bones ache in a way I'm not sure has anything to do with how tired I am. It's like I weigh five hundred pounds as I haul myself to my feet and drag them towards the car.

At least the drive to Beechmill will give me time to prepare what I'm going to say to Nate. I don't want us to fight, yet there's definitely some shit we need to get out so we can move past this all.

Fuck. This might be the worst conversation of my life.

Seventeen

I **SNEAK INTO THE** apartment block as someone leaves and drag myself up the three flights of stairs to knock on Nate's door. The traffic on my return drive from the seaside was non-existent, and I couldn't find any reason to delay my visit. So here I am, waiting for him to answer, while my feet fight to run away.

No. You can do this. You want to talk to him. You have to talk to him.

I take off my glasses to give me something to do. I clean them and slide them back onto my face yet he still hasn't opened the door. Sure, it's only been five seconds, but I huff. For someone super keen to speak to me, Nate isn't in a hurry to let me in.

I'm about to turn around, give up and put this down to a momentary lapse of sanity, when the door flies open.

My heart *plummets* out of my chest, past my stomach and bounces down three flights of stairs until it hits the dusty pavement outside the entranceway. Nate is a mess. His hair is pulled in every direction, his uniform for the stall is crumpled and...is that a food stain over his right pec? Red rings of sunburn poke out from the edge of the sleeves and a thick line of pink crosses his nose. I stare at him, obsessed with the light freckles now showing on his face, fighting the urge to run my fingers over them, count them and draw pictures in them.

It seems like I've only been getting a fine-tuned version of this man, a careful image that he's created to lure me in. This is the real Nate and I've found someone who's just as messy as me, just as fucked up.

Now he's revealed himself, I don't want to run away.

I pause on the doormat, aware of his lips moving but not registering what he's saying to me. The revelation that he's human, just like everyone else, has me hypnotised.

It makes me desperate to learn more about him, find out about *his* past. This feeling tells me that I've really ballsed things up with him, being so selfish with him and his time. If I'd stopped blathering on about myself and my worries, and took the time to ask *more* about him, I might have broken down some of those barriers sooner.

The urge to peel away more of his perfectness, layer by layer, itches the tips of my fingers. It's fucking frightening, and the cowardly part of me wants to scarper. And quick. But I keep my feet firmly planted on the welcome mat. I can do this.

"Alex? I invited you in."

"Oh. Yes. Of course. That's why I'm here." Awkwardness stretches my laugh way too thin, making it sound almost maniacal. *Pull yourself together.* I take a deep breath, spotting the battered pink Nikes next to Nate's Converse as I slip off my own trainers. "Where's Chloe?"

He nods towards a closed door. "In her room. Her airpods will be glued to her ears all night."

"Does she know I'm here?"

"Yes."

I'm not sure why I asked. Why wouldn't he have told her? Even if he didn't, the flat is tiny and she can probably hear everything we say. Sweat trickles down my spine.

I follow him along the hallway and into the living room, only relaxing when he closes the door. It's only been a few hours, but the impact of Chloe on Nate's perfect, tidy flat is noticeable. It's like a pink glitter bomb has gone off. A selection of bracelets sit on the side, a jumper hangs over the back of the loveseat and there's an empty pizza box on the floor.

"Oh, I meant to pick that up." He scoops the box off the floor and takes it into the kitchen. When he returns, he has a bottle of red in his hands. Two glasses already sit on the coffee table, next to a stack of teen dystopian novels. He perches on the edge of the sofa. "Do you want a glass?"

I shake my head and remain standing, worried that if I relax, I may find it too easy to slip into acting normal with him. I don't want anything to get in the way of us clearing the air. "No, thanks."

"Oh. Okay."

He fills the glass almost to the top and takes a long drink. Once it's back on the table, he stares at me, waiting, expecting. There's never been this awkward kind of silence between us before. Since the PTA meeting, we've been close, filling the gaps in planning for the fête with conversation about everything and anything. We always sat side by side, almost touching, even before we slept together. Now, there's a ton of unasked questions sitting in that space. Now, I feel worlds away.

"We should talk," I blurt out at the exact same time he says, "I guess I should explain."

Quiet follows, broken only by the pad of soft feet as Chloe moves around her room. She's *too* close and I take a step towards the balcony to create more distance. I can't deal with her *and* Nate tonight.

"You go first," I offer after I gather my thoughts and shove away all the insecurity taunting me.

Instead of talking, he plays with his glass, takes another mouthful of wine and swallows. It's like now I'm offering him the chance, all his words won't come. I want to scream at him to get on with it, to explain what the fuck happened earlier. But he remains silent.

"Nate." I wince at the impatience in my voice.

He sighs and slides his glass onto the table. "Chloe is fifteen. I married her mother, Rachel, when we were young, and Chloe came along soon after. We had a nice little life just the three of us and—"

"So what happened?" I ask, the question out of my mouth before I realise I'm interrupting him. For a guy keen to hear Nate out, I'm sure getting in the way.

"I discovered I had feelings for a male colleague."

"Oh."

"Yeah. It developed into crushes on other men, celebrities, that sort of thing. I didn't even consider that I was bisexual until, after a few too many pints, I confessed everything to a friend and they talked me through it. It took me two more months to tell Rachel. Turns out I was worried for a reason. She kicked me out."

"Oh, Nate." His confession makes me long to move to him and wrap my arms around him. I want to protect him from all the people who have been so shitty about his sexuality. His own fucking wife kicked him out. Chloe drops something in the other room and I stay where I am, my fingers looped around the handle of the balcony door as if I can keep myself tethered there.

"I moved to my parents', and we tried to find a way to make things work. She couldn't move past the fact I fancied guys, though. It's like she thought I was cheating, even though *nothing* happened. I would never. After a year of trying, we called it a day and got a divorce. It's really hard to be with someone who won't accept me for who I am."

He cradles his head in his hands, a hard breath escaping from his lips.

"Chloe was mad about it for the longest time," he eventually continues, his words hard to hear since they're spoken into his lap. "My moving away didn't help."

"Why did you, then?" This is the one part I just can't understand. I try not to sound accusatory, but I can't help it. "Luke didn't get a chance to stay with his kid. There's no way I could leave Rory in the next village over, let alone in another county. I don't see how—"

"Things went from bad to worse after leaving the house." He lifts his head, making eye contact with me. "I couldn't stay at Mum and Dad's long-term, but I couldn't afford my own place in London. Then there were my friends. I can count on one hand the ones that supported me. The rest? Well, they blamed me for the breakdown of the marriage. I lost my job, the divorce was messy. The custody battle was something I *never* want to go through again. There was no way the judge was going to side with me because I was living with my parents and unemployed. So Chloe got to stay with Rachel, and my life fell apart. I tried dating, but nobody wants to date a homeless guy who can't even look after his kid.

"I needed a change, to get as far away from London and Buckinghamshire as I could. When I saw the advert for the job in Beechmill Primary, I jumped at the chance. It's so hard to be away from her, though."

He pauses to take another sip of his wine, and I use the break to ask, "Why East Beechmill, though? Most people are desperate to leave. They don't usually come here out of choice."

"I liked the idea of living in a small village. Nobody would know me and I could start afresh. Be myself. It took some negotiating, but we finally agreed that she would spend the summer holidays with me here to try it out. Then it's up to her where she lives permanently. And although I desperately hope she picks me, I worry every day about how hard it will be being miles away from her mum, her grandparents, her friends. We have a plan for if she does decide to stay here, though. We went on a tour of King's School when I first moved here and she sat the entrance exams a couple of months ago. She passed, of course, and the school offered her a full scholarship. She has until August to accept."

I let out a low whistle. "Kings is a tough school to get into. Simon got a place, and his girls, but Mum and Dad didn't bother with the rest of us." It was pointless, given how thick we all are.

Nate smiles. "I'm so proud of her."

"Why keep her a secret, then?"

"I didn't keep her a secret from you. Not intentionally. I just didn't get the opportunity to tell you."

Unease settles on my shoulders. I never asked. Never once bothered to question him about his family, even though he knew everything about mine.

"I didn't give you the opportunity, you mean?"

He sighs. "A little bit. But also, given how things went with Rachel, I was scared you were going to judge me. It doesn't look great when you're talking about how dedicated you are to your *adopted* child and I moved hundreds of miles away from mine. In your eyes, I'm probably as bad as Mike."

"I'm not perfect." I'm surprised at how quiet my words are. I expected an argument with him, but this openness is more cathartic somehow.

"You are to me. You stepped in to look after Rory while I ruined my marriage with my bi-awakening. And you were so into me. I couldn't believe my luck. I guess, I didn't want your opinion of me to change. I didn't want to scare you off."

"Scare me off?" I scoff. "Did you think I'd abandon you without giving you a chance to explain?"

His eyebrows fly into his fringe as he mumbles, "You *did* abandon me, though."

Before I learned about his divorce or his child. I sink onto the floor, my back pressed against the glass and my head falling against my folded arms.

"You *know* why I had to, though," I reason, hating how whiny I sound. That's the people-pleaser in me. "I had to protect Rory."

"Your *mother* thought you had to protect Rory. When have I ever given you reason to believe he's at risk with me?" I flinch at the sharpness in his voice.

"I was confused. I had all these big feelings for you after spending one fucking night with you. It was too soon and Mum was the devil in my ear. And I'm the idiot who listened to her." I sigh and raise my head. "These past few weeks have been torture. Trying to squash down my feelings for you, trying to treat you like only my kid's teacher. Standing so close to you at the fête, but not being able to kiss you. I wanted to grab you, wrap you in my arms, tell the whole fucking school how much I l–like you. Because I do."

The words fight to get out of my mouth. It's been weeks of pent-up frustration, and now I've opened the floodgates, there's no stopping me. During my babbling, Nate has moved to kneel on the floor in front of me, staring at me with an intensity that would usually scare me off. Instead, I sit up straight to meet his gaze. I crane my neck in defiance, not letting the hand he ghosts over my knee put me off.

"It's fucking crazy. I've only known you for a few months, yet you consume my thoughts. You're in my dreams. My fantasies. I *hate* what you did to me today, but I can't hate *you*. Because it's all my fault. I never gave you a chance to talk. No wonder you don't trust me."

"Alex." He reaches out to stroke my cheek with his spare hand. "I do trust you. I'm just...a bit set in my ways. I was adamant that our date would be the right time to tell you about Chloe. When that was off the cards, I thought telling you today was the better alternative. I still wanted you to know. Then the trains got messed up and she was delayed and then— Well, you know the rest."

"I shouldn't have reacted the way I did."

His chuckle is soft and vibrates all the way to my cheek. "I mean, I don't blame you. To be fair, you took it better than when I've broken news to other people. At least I didn't need to get stitches. I didn't like it when you walked away from me. It–it scared me."

That's what I've always been like, though. I guess I learned more from Mike than I thought.

"When I called you earlier, I wasn't even sure if I wanted to hear you out. But as soon as I heard your voice, I knew I had to. That if I didn't, that could be the end of whatever this is between us."

"I'm glad you came, Alex."

He shifts nearer to me so I part my legs, giving him space to kneel between them. The fact he wants to be this close after everything means a fucking lot. I rest my head against his hand and sigh. "I'm sorry."

"Me too."

This time, the quiet isn't filled with tension or awkwardness. A silent conversation passes between us, thrashing out the last of this mess. We sit in the moment for a while, until a loud clatter from the spare room forces us apart. Huffing, he lets go of me and sits back on his haunches.

"What happens now?" I ask as the feel of his fingers slipping from mine fills my entire body with cold water. This can't be the end.

He rubs his forehead. "It's the end of term and I have Chloe to think about, as well as my interview and final assessments. But how about we get back together for another talk after the disco? Maybe some space will help us to decide what we want."

I want you. I bite the words back, in case it's not what he wants. I would have been more certain about it this morning but too much has passed over the last twelve hours. "I can probably get someone to sit for me."

If I'm honest with my family about why I need them, then someone is bound to step up, right? And if they don't? Fuck it. I'll dump Rory at the neighbours or drag him along with me. I'm not going to let anything else get in the way of my second chance with Nate.

"Well, if not, there's always Chloe."

Of course, she's old enough. "If it's not going to be too much for her. I could always pay her, or..."

"She'll be fine. She's already been telling me about *some kid* that wouldn't leave her alone this afternoon."

"I need to teach him better people skills."

With his hands in his pockets, Nate chuffs another attempt at a laugh then leads me out of the room. It's quiet behind Chloe's door, but I try not to think too much into it. She's probably already abandoned her unpacking and has fallen down a social media rabbit hole. Doom scrolling is the best distraction when you're bored, or when your estranged Dad is having a deep and meaningful conversation with his almost boyfriend.

Fuck. Doing any of this with a teen around is going to be hard, isn't it?

When we reach the door, Nate leans against the door jamb, watching me put my trainers back on. It heightens my self consciousness. I overthink every loop of my lace and it takes me three attempts to get both shoes fastened. I'm really going to win him over at this rate.

When I'm finally standing upright he gives me a small smile. "Will I see you at drop off tomorrow?"

"Not this week." I'm really mad at the fact I have to work, despite needing the money. "It's busy in the pub and I've had to shift my hours around to get Wednesday afternoon off."

"I'll see you Wednesday, then."

"Yeah, see you Wednesday."

I should walk straight past him and back down the stairs to my car, but I can't leave like this. It'll be too hard to pass him, especially when he folds his arms across his chest and his muscles bulge against his tight T-shirt.

"Get some aloe vera on that burn," I say, stopping on the threshold. I graze my fingers over one of his arms lightly then lean in to give him a soft kiss on the cheek. The corners of my mouth threaten to twitch up at his surprise.

"I will. Night, Alex."

"Goodnight."

I squeeze his lower arm then force myself away from him. *Fuck.* It's going to be a long wait until Wednesday.

EIGHTEEN

I **WAKE THE NEXT** morning with an elbow embedded in my cheek.

I keep my eyes closed for a moment, allowing myself to believe that yesterday didn't happen. That it was all a weird dream, and me and Nate are back together. There were no hidden daughters, and instead of me walking out, we celebrated a successful stall with some glorious sex.

Please, please, please, please.

When I open my eyes, I'm greeted by Rory, not Nate. The kid wriggles, as if he knows I'm watching him, and his breathing morphs from the calm, steady rhythm that lulled me to sleep last night, to something deeper and sharper. He grumbles, stretches, and almost punches me in the face.

"Oy! Watch it, you."

If he wasn't six, he might see through the synthetic joy I force into my tone. I *have* to shake myself out of this mood. I don't want everything to affect him or ruin his day. Although Nate and I left things on an okay note last night, I still can't stop the feeling that I've fucked things up forever.

Okay, I can do this. I puff out a breath then shift to my side and grab him, tickling all over his body. Playing with him always cheers me up. Although, I tickle-fought with Nate in this bed, too. *Shut up, stupid brain.*

"No! No!" Rory tries to squirm away from me. "Stop it."

"Nope. You fidgeted all night long. It's time for payback, buster."

His infectious giggles are the balm I need. He kicks out, determined to get away from my waggling fingers, but I'm bigger, and eventually, he succumbs to the attack.

We playfight, rolling over the bed until we're both panting for breath. I make sure Rory gets a chance to retaliate, so it's not all one sided. I'm well aware I'm a lot stronger than him. My feet end up on the pillows, and his head rests on my calf.

"I won," he declares.

"How'd you work that out?"

"It's the rules. I'm the boss, sooo I say I win."

I could argue with him, tell him I'm the one with the money which makes me the one in charge, but I let him have this one. I make a mental note to not be so lenient on him next time. Once our breaths have returned to normal, he scurries down the bed, getting close enough for our noses to touch. *Personal space? What's that?*

"Chloe is my new friend."

"Is she?" I ignore the way her name pops the tiny bubble of happiness protecting me and Rory from the rest of the miserable world.

"I like her. Did you know Mr Jameson is her dad?"

"Nope." My voice breaks and I swallow the frog that's all of a sudden stuck in my throat. Is it too much to ask for some space from it all? "He didn't tell me until yesterday."

"She's cool. She's sooo funny and knows good jokes. Hey, Alex. Why can't Elsa have a balloon? Because she'll—"

"Drop it, kid." I wince at Rory's pout. *Fuck. Fuck. Fuck.* Alarm bells ring in my ear as I panic for a way to make things better. Wait, I know. Food. "Do you want a champion's breakfast?"

"Yeah!"

"Go and get yourself dressed. I'll meet you in the kitchen."

Once we've devoured breakfast and tidied up, I make the most of Rory's energy and walk him to Mum and Dad's. It's drizzling, and the temperature has taken a massive nose dive since yesterday, but that won't bother us. With our wellies and raincoats on, we set off from the house and head through the village, ignoring the clouds shrouding the whole place in grey. The rain at least makes the place look pretty. The trees are more green, and the grass is perking up after being so parched. Even the flowers lift their heads towards the sky as if to drink from the clouds.

We pass the old fire station, with the scent of coffee and chips trying to lure us over. I risk a glance at the third floor, although I'm not sure what I'm expecting. It's not like Nate and Chloe will be sitting on the tiny balcony in this weather, but I hunger for a glimpse of him. Bloody feelings and emotions and brains. The world would be a much better place without them.

The balcony is empty, so I return my focus to Rory.

His pace slows when we get into the countryside, the fields and crops stealing his attention. He stops at every gate to count grazing cows, or watch tractors as they move between fields and outbuildings.

"What's in here?" He climbs to the highest rung of the last gate, his wellies squeaking on the metal, and I steady him with a hand on his back. Just in case.

"Corn."

"Like what we have for dinner?"

"Yeah. This is where Nanny and Gramps get it from. Though, sometimes, Farmer Cole grows other things, like runner beans, or cauliflowers."

"Why?"

I don't fucking know. I dig out my phone and flick to the browser, grateful for the telecom companies invading our stunning green fields with their monstrous 5G towers. "Plants release different nutrients," I recite. "So swapping the crops makes the soil better." *Thanks, Google.*

"I see," Rory replies although with his eyebrows still furled, I don't think he really understands. Not that he has to get agriculture. There's a while before he needs to pick a career.

Thunder rumbles in the distance, although it doesn't come with lightning yet. I pull Rory off the gate and hoist him onto my shoulders so we can horse trot the rest of the way to the farmhouse before it pisses down. The clouds grow darker during our approach, and the first fat raindrops hit my hood. I stoop so Rory can slide off me, and he runs ahead, a bright yellow flash racing through the chickens, sending them squawking and fleeing from his roar. He doesn't bother to knock, and barges into the house like the worst guest ever.

"We're here," I shout out, hanging up the coat he abandoned and tidying away his wellies. I add my own to the haphazard pile. Roast lamb wafts through from the kitchen, and I follow my nose, letting it lead me to Mum. Although it's only been a few hours since breakfast, my stomach rumbles. There's nothing better in the world than Mum's cooking, even if it often comes with a dollop of unsolicited advice on the side.

I kiss her cheek, ignoring the way her gaze rakes over me, assessing how I am. Before she asks any annoying questions, I hustle to Dad, peering over his shoulder at the latest headlines. "Anything exciting going on in the world of East Beechmill?"

"Nope. It's all boring, just as we like it. They've done a nice write-up of the fête. You can have a read once I'm done browsing the classifieds. Did you bring your car?"

"Nope. I can't be your mule today, Dad."

"Good. He can't fit anything else into his workshop," Mum butts in.

Now he's retired, Dad has taken to collecting broken household items to repurpose as plant pots. I got my love of gardening from him. The backyard is full of old TVs, bathtubs, and cabinets, now sprouting with flowers and bushes. Creative is one word for it, and luckily, I've managed to avoid having some of his creations in my garden. It's not the look that I'm going for. He's going to run out of space here soon, though, and I'm going to run out of excuses.

"Who else is over today?"

"Only us." Henry and Sophie blow in with the wind, rain running in rivulets off their coats. "The kids didn't want to come. Said it was too awful out to leave."

"Lucky you having children you can just abandon."

Mum gasps. "You'd never abandon Rory."

Sometimes I'd love to. While I comfort her by trying to explain my joke, I assess the pros and cons of a quiet family dinner but can't come to a conclusion. Should I stick it out or run away? On one hand, it's a blessing not to have all of my brothers and their wives here, all as hungry for gossip about my life as they are Mum's roast dinner. But without the buffer of the rest of the family, there's nobody to hide behind. And just how long will it take for her to strike?

Once he's out of his coat, Henry crosses the kitchen and pulls two bottles of beer out of the fridge. Pointing them in my direction, he asks, "Treehouse?"

Wait, is this part of some big plan? He's never usually one for deep and personal chats, so the others must have put him up to it and made themselves scarce so they don't have to suffer my misery. I glance between him and Mum, who is already settling with Sophie and Dad at the kitchen table with a mug of tea.

I shrug then sigh. At least with Henry it'll be short. "Okay."

We slide our feet back into our wellies and run through the soggy grass and mud, our heads ducked low against the rain. Our feet slip on the wet wood but soon we're under the small amount of shelter the treehouse gives us.

Dad owns a construction company – well, he used to – and he built the treehouse before I was born. Back then, the wood was dark, and the tree was still young. Over the years, the limbs have grown around it, and, during the spring and summer, it's shrouded by leaves, making it a fantastic hideaway from the British heat. The elements have faded the grain of the wood, smoothing it down as they batter the structure. I'm glad it's stood the test of time, though, and the next generation of the Websters are getting a chance to enjoy it.

It's a squeeze to get two fully-grown adults in, but eventually, we settle with our backs against the furthest wall. My feet dangle out the door, catching the drops from the massive oak leaves. The confinement means we're sitting hip to hip, with elbows invading each other's personal space. It's cosy, though, and shields us from the violent weather outside.

Henry pops the caps on the bottles. I take a deep breath as I wait for mine, letting the scent of wet wood take me back to when I was twelve, and Simon and Luke gave me my first taste of booze. They'd snuck a bottle of whiskey out of Dad's cupboard one Halloween. It was a bad idea for my first try of alcohol and before the bottle was half-empty, I was dizzy. I almost fell out of the tree in my attempt to get to the house.

I didn't make it, and spewed all over the patio. Although I used the hosepipe to wash away the evidence, I left amber stains on Mum's lovely flagstones and it didn't take her long to work out what happened. I was grounded for a fortnight, a massive injustice. The twins stole the booze but managed to hide the bottle so they didn't get punished. I was merely in the wrong place at the wrong time.

"So, how much did we make in the end yesterday?" I ask Henry before taking a swig of my beer.

Drinking straight out the bottle and putting the world to rights is the perfect way to spend a summer afternoon, especially one as dreary as today. I've thrashed out so many issues and problems over the years like this, although it used to be with Josh or Luke. Never Henry. He was out of the house before we could have real problems to chat about.

"A good amount. The fête overall was a huge success. Agnes looked chuffed."

"Ah, man. Did she make a big speech?"

"Yeah. It's a shame you missed it. Of course, she has to tally all of the takings, but the way she was gushing about our stall, we've won."

"Dammit. I would have enjoyed basking in some of that glory. I hate that Nate got to enjoy it and I didn't."

"He didn't, though. Left before Headmistress Palmer closed the thing officially. Anyway, she's announcing the results at the school disco Wednesday afternoon. Are you still paired with Mr Jameson to chaperone?"

"Yep."

The treehouse goes quiet, and I play with the label on my bottle, debating how much I'm going to let slip to my brother. Out of the corner of my eye, Henry opens his mouth then closes it again, his eyebrows scrunching as if he's thinking of how to broach the subject.

"Spit it out," I growl.

"Mr Jameson has a kid, huh? Was she the one talking to Rory?"

"Yep." I pop the P.

"And he never said anything to you about her?"

"Nope."

"Have you worked out what you're going to do?"

I shrug. Do I tell him that we spent the evening talking, but when I got home, the silence from my phone was almost too deafening. Or do I pretend I'm having nothing to do with Nate, walking away from him just like Mum wanted me to.

Which would get me in the least amount of trouble?

"We spoke last night." Good. Nice and vague.

"And?"

Christ, what's with the twenty questions. I didn't sign up to play Mastermind today, and there's no way I'd pick the love life of Alexander Webster as my specialist topic.

"It's tricky. Sure, we weren't together officially, and only spent that one night together, but he encouraged all this openness from me. I'm not sure whether I should be mad at him for not returning that, or annoyed with myself for not creating a safe space so Nate could share with me. Although we both apologised to each other, something just doesn't feel right."

Okay, not so vague. That's the problem with me. Once I open my mouth, *everything* comes spilling out.

"I think you're being too hard on yourself."

"Am I? I dumped the guy after Mum got in my head. And even before we had sex, we spent all that time texting and talking on the phone, building up to something. But it was always about me. Oh woe is Alex for having a six-year-old to look after or moaning about something Mum said, that probably wasn't even that bad. I never really asked about him so it's no wonder he didn't tell me. Not exactly the perfect boyfriend, am I?"

"Did he explain why he kept Chloe a secret?"

"He was waiting for our date."

"Funny thing to bring up on a date."

"Is it?"

"I guess if you'd had the date *after* you had sex, it might not have been." Henry scratches his head. "But first dates are about impressing someone. 'Oh, by the way I have a kid I hardly see,' isn't all that impressive."

"It wouldn't have bothered me. It got...complicated between him and his ex-wife."

Henry clears his throat, probably stopping me from telling all about Nate's life too. "I hope you can make things work, Alex. It's clear Nate is good for the both of you. Rory wouldn't stop following him around yesterday."

"Mum thinks I'm being selfish, wanting a relationship with Rory's teacher."

"Fuck off. You know that's bullshit, right?" If he could stand up, Henry would be on his feet right now. His spine straightens and he clutches the bottle so hard, I worry he might smash the glass.

"Is it? When she found out about me and Nate, Mum kept on banging on about how I was being selfish, putting my needs first, and that Luke would never have dreamed of having a partner while he was looking after Rory."

For the first time in what feels like a million years, Henry laughs. He throws his head back and it bangs against the wall of the treehouse. "Having Rory never stopped Luke from dating. In fact, he was really enjoying the scene."

I freeze, my insides turning cold. "He what?"

"Sure, it took him a while to get over Katie. Her death was so traumatic for him. Then Rory was so small that it was tricky grabbing five minutes sleep, let alone finding time for dinner and a shag. After a year or so, though, he was looking more relaxed. He started letting us help with overnight stays, and could barely be contacted when he was out. He said he was drinking with pals but there was a look on his face that he didn't get at the bottom of a bottle. There was a definite change in him."

"Was that after Rory's first birthday? It was like a switch had been flicked and he was back to his usual smarmy self."

"Yep. I cornered him at the party. In this very same treehouse. It didn't take me long to get the truth out of him. He made me swear to take it to the grave. Which, ironically, turned out to be his."

We clink our bottles together in a small tribute to our brother, but my mind isn't focusing on his death. Luke was never one to be secretive. Simon? Yes. Henry? Abso-fucking-lutely. But me, Josh, and Luke were like the three amigos. I can't believe he kept something as simple as going on dates from the rest of us. It's a good job we're in the treehouse, or my jaw would be in a muddy puddle by now.

"Why all the secrecy?"

Henry shrugs. "Guess he thought that he was doing Katie's memory a disservice. He didn't believe me when I said that no-body cared."

"Of course we didn't. All we wanted was for him to be happy."

"Exactly! And if being with Nate makes *you* happy, Alex, then you should do it. Fuck what anyone else thinks."

Mum chooses that moment to call us to the house for dinner.

"I don't think she knows," Henry adds with a glance out of the treehouse, "so maybe just keep what I told you between us, yeah? She's very old school, and it would only upset her if she found out."

Does that mean I'd have to keep me and Nate a secret? I'm not sure I could handle that. What's the point in being happy if I can't tell the world about it or if I can't enjoy it with the rest of my family? Would Mum ever approve of us?

Every inch of me trembles as I roll over and shuffle down the ladder, and it's nothing to do with the weather. A million thoughts rampage through my head, all of them fueling an anger I didn't know I had. I keep my head ducked against the rain, but my steps are slow, as if the mud and wet grass are holding me back. I'm not sure I can stay quiet over lunch. Perhaps I should go home to avoid any drama before it happens. If Mum mentions what happened with me and Nate yesterday, I might explode. I don't have to head in through the bifolds. I could detour around the side of the house, abandon Rory again and run home. Well, walk home. I'm sure I could find something in the house to eat. But my feet continue their trudge to the kitchen door.

Traitorous bastards.

Sunday lunch is quieter than normal since there's only a few of us. We all fit around the kitchen table. Our conversation is surface level – what the kids will be doing in their last few days of school and how it compares to when we were small. Holiday plans come next. I need to remember to book something for me and Rory, soon. It'll do us good to get away from East Beechmill, and everyone else. Perhaps we can go to Scotland, get us some real distance. Or abroad, if I can find enough money. The chat comes around to yesterday's success. The taste of lunch sours as the family analyses each stall, trying to determine who might have won. Rory adds his own input, but I can't raise a laugh. Not when Mum's gaze burns into me from across the table, her mouth flapping open and closed in her search for a moment to interject her questions.

So I keep the conversation going, skirting around our stall and asking inane questions about the other stands. Eventually, though, I run out of options, and the talk reaches The Watering Hole. They shower me and Nate with praise, although nobody mentions him by name, until the conversation runs dry.

Then Mum strikes.

"Well, I enjoyed my shift at the stall. It was a lot of fun. Colourful." *Wait. What?* I lift my head from the potatoes I've been picking at. She opens her mouth again, ruining the lovely façade she was creating, the false sense of security she lulled me into. "I especially enjoyed it when Mr Jameson's daughter showed up. Did you know he has a child, Alex? Because I have to say it was a surprise when Rory introduced the girl to me. You didn't mention this *Chloe* when we spoke the other weekend."

"That's because I didn't know."

Her frown is way too over the top to be genuine and my cheeks burn. "Why didn't he tell you?"

"I don't know." I move from torturing the potatoes to pushing my green beans around the plate.

"Odd for him not to say. I suppose she doesn't live with him?" She doesn't wait for me to confirm or deny it. "Guess he'll be moving back to wherever he came from then to be near to her. Probably for the best."

A glance across the table shows Rory's face drop and his lower lip wobble. *Fucking thanks, Mum.* "We don't know that for sure yet, Mum. He's applied for a permanent job at the school. We're hopeful that he'll get it."

"We are, are we?"

"Yeah...well...*I'm* hopeful." This is not the conversation I want to have in front of my entire family. To their credit, everyone's attention is on their plates, apart from Rory's, but they're all listening. There's no way they're not. Sophie is probably taking notes to share with Aimee later.

"I thought you finished things with him the other week?"

I don't see how it's any of your business. But I swallow the snark, though my hands shake as I cut another piece of meat. I'm no longer hungry. The mouthful of lamb I take is chewy, dry, and tastes of copper.

"I did," I say around my food.

"Oh. Well, like I said. It's better you put Rory's needs first. He's going through a big time moving up a year, and Luke would ne—"

Something inside of me snaps. I swallow the lump of meat, wincing as it drags down my throat, sticking like her words. *Luke would never do that. Luke only thought of Rory. Luke sacrificed his happiness.* Clearly fucking not. Luke knew it was important to have a life outside of his kid, but he couldn't share any of that, not even with his brothers. Probably because he was so scared of upsetting Mum. Now, she gets to pull out the 'your dead brother was a saint' card to get her way. And there's no way I'd meet her expectations. It's unachievable. I can never bloody win.

The guilt she's put me through wasn't a small trip, but a two-year journey. Yes, I know it was my fault he died. I've owned my mistakes. But I'm never going to be allowed to move on from it. Not until Rory is out of the house and living his own life. Even then, I'll probably be held to some level of responsibility for what I did.

I *can't* let this become my status quo. I refuse to be alone any longer and miss out on a chance of something amazing because of something I did two freaking years ago.

"Did you know Luke was dating, Mum?"

Henry kicks me under the table but I don't flinch. I just continue to stare at Mum as the rest of the room fades into nothing around me.

"I don't know what you're talking about, Alexander, but—"

"Luke was dating regularly. He just didn't want any of us to know because he thought we'd judge him for it. It's a shame he felt like he had to hide it, really."

Henry curses when Mum drops her cutlery to the table. I'm in deep shit with my oldest brother but I don't care.

"He wasn't...He didn't..."

Her face turns pale, her eyes drawing into tiny, thin slits. She's trying not to cry in front of us. But her reaction doesn't stop my rampage. I'm past the point of no return. Is it fair for me to talk about my brother like this? Absolutely not. Especially when he can't defend himself from the urn on Mum's mantelpiece. But the way she's been treating me is completely undeserved.

"I don't want to have to hide things from you, Mum. Especially who I'm seeing and other things that make me happy."

"I just think if it's something that affects Rory, you have to be more consid—"

The deep breaths I've been taking are not working, and my grip tightens on my knife and fork. If I was stronger, if I worked out more, I would be bending the metal right now, but instead it just digs into my palms.

I scoff. "Like I don't think about him every damn minute of every day. Rory is *always* my first priority."

"I think you're being unfair to your mother, Alexander," Dad chimes in.

"No, I'm not." I don't slam my hands on the table. Rory doesn't need to see me flip out like that. But the sentiment is clear in the sharpness of my voice. "What is unfair is Mum trying to control my life. It's like she has no faith in me. She assumed I would just jump into a relationship with Nate without considering all of the eventualities.

"Rory adores Nate. Not because he's his teacher, but because Nate loves Rory, too. He cares for him, looks after him, reads with him. Even outside of school, when he doesn't have to. Do you know how rare it is to find a guy who likes other men, who accepts the fact that I have a child and doesn't even blink about the rest of my fucked-up past? Chloe would have been the icing on the cake. How great would it have been for Rory to get a ready-made family? With two dads who love each other?"

"I think—"

I cut Mum off. "Is it because Nate is Rory's teacher or because he's gay or is it just because I've found someone? Because Luke was dating a bunch of randoms, but you still thought he was Parent of the Year."

"Don't you dare speak about your brother like that." She's released the tears now and her face is bright red, but I won't back down. I won't let Luke get in the way of what I want anymore.

"Why not? It's the truth."

"It's not. I would have known—"

"Henry told me. He knew." I glare at my brother, but he stays quiet. *Git.* "I will never be Luke, Mum. I can't fill the gap he left even though I really wish I could. Especially if it helps you. I have to find my own way to make up for the mistakes I made. All I want is to be a good dad and a good brother and son, but sometimes it feels like you don't care what *I* want. What I need."

"Rory's had a tough life. I'm just trying to—"

"Protect him? So am I. But I don't think it'll damage him if Nate and I make a go of things. But that's for me to decide, not you or anyone else in this family. The only other people who get a say in it are Nate, Rory and Chloe."

Everyone at the table must be able to hear the pounding of my heart. Who'd have thought joining the PTA would lead to my most rebellious phase – sticking up for myself? I would never have dared to speak to her like this before. I'm not sure I'd ever do it again. So much is at risk. She could throw me out of the house, and refuse to help me again with Rory. I could be disowned.

I don't want that. I normally love being a part of this family. This is the only time I've ever spoken up. The rest of the time, I'm a doormat for her. Or I used to be. I continue to glare across the table at Mum, unwavering, and daring her to carry on arguing with me or defending Luke. I will not be the first person to back down, not this time. After what feels like forever, she finally shifts her attention to her dinner plate.

"Charles, love. Pass me the gravy, please?"

She takes the offered boat, her hands shaking, but she remains quiet. Is this a win? It doesn't feel like it. The tension builds on me as she slowly pours the gravy over her meat then tries to take a bite out of her lunch, though even her chewing is at a snail's pace. Mascara lines paint under her eyes and the meagre amount of food I've managed to eat threatens to make a reappearance. All I've done is smush her into the ground and now everything feels like shit. It reminds me of how Mike used to be with me – walking away when he'd had enough. It's how I treated Nate yesterday. Well, no more. That's not how I want my future to be with anyone, and especially not Mum.

Well done, Alex. Your list of people you're upsetting keeps growing and growing. I went too far, but we both need space before I fix things.

My shoulders droop as awkwardness descends over the table, and she continues to pick at her lunch. I fill my fork with more food, even though I'm no longer hungry.

"So, Henry. This disco on Wednesday. What can I expect? Is it going to be awful like when we were kids? Or have they finally splashed out on a good DJ? Are you helping with the buffet, Mum?"

"Uhm. No. There's not going to be one this time."

Even with me and Henry reliving the most awful of our school parties, the tension doesn't shift. We eat the last of our dinner around stilted conversation and once everyone has finished, I offer to tidy up.

Mum disappears, and as soon as I put the last plate on the draining board, I seek her out. It doesn't take me long. She's down at the bottom of the garden, where Luke's tree is. I find an umbrella and hurry down to her, opening it up over her already wet head.

"I'm sorry for what I said about Luke, Mum."

She lifts her head and my nose burns at the sight of her red eyes and blotchy face. God, I'm an absolute twat.

"I really didn't know. And even if he wasn't...doing what you said he was doing, I've still been treating you unfairly."

"You just want the best for Rory. I get it."

"For you, too, though, love. I saw how Mike hurt you. I don't want you to have to go through that again."

I sigh. "I don't think you can protect us from everything. Especially when there are so many of us. You'd be too busy to enjoy retirement."

This stirs a laugh from her, although it's weak. I shift my umbrella to my other hand and pull her to my side, trying to embrace her the best I can.

"I never wanted you to take Luke's place," she murmurs into my side. "I don't blame you for what happened, either."

"I messed up, Mum. You don't have to protect me from that. I live with that every day. He's gone because I ignored my responsibilities. But I can't let that mistake stop me from living the rest of my life. Nate will be good for me *and* Rory, if he'll have me back. We have the chance to build something special."

"And what if he doesn't get the permanent job and decides to move away?"

"I don't think he will. He's a brilliant teacher, Mum. Really cares about the kids. And he likes East Beechmill."

"But what about Chloe? Surely he wants to be where she is?"

I sigh. "I had the same thought. But he's going to make it work."

"It'll be hard. Being in an established relationship with children is difficult enough. I wouldn't want to try courting someone when you've both got a child around."

"It's worth a try, though, right?"

She stares at Luke's tree for a moment longer, so I stay quiet, giving her time to digest everything. It's been a big weekend for all of us.

Eventually, though, she looks up at me. Her eyes are still red. In a small voice, she asks, "You really like him, don't you?"

"I do." My cheeks burn but I nod. We don't usually do this sort of talking. Not since Luke left us. "I know it hasn't been long but he's just....phenomenal."

"What are you going to do about him?"

"We agreed last night to take some time after the disco to talk."

"Is that it?"

I frown. "What do you mean, is that it?"

She loosens her grip on me, shaking her head. "I thought I brought you up better than this. If you want a boyfriend, Alexander Webster, then you need to woo him."

"Woo him?"

"Yes. Flowers and presents and whatever else it takes."

What the actual fuck? "But it's a Sunday evening, Mum. Nowhere's open. And I doubt you'll allow me to send garage flowers."

"Sweetheart, we have a whole garden of blooms here. Come on. I'll share my secrets with you."

In the most bizarre twist, she loops her arm into mine, forcing the umbrella mostly over her head as she drags me around the garden. She continues to natter my ear off as we gather a small collection of blooms and then she pulls me inside to put them together.

Looks like Nate is getting a present tomorrow, then. I just hope it's not too little too late.

NINETEEN

I SEND RORY TO school the next morning with a bouquet of hand-picked flowers for Nate. Not just any flowers, either. All of them were chosen by me and Mum from her garden. I make sure to tell him this on the note, too, so that he knows the work I'm putting in.

Rory doesn't ask why he has a job to do first thing on a Monday morning, but there's a stupidly wide grin on his face that tells me he knows exactly what the bouquet is for. The tiny git was probably listening to every word at the table yesterday.

I haven't had a chat with him about it all yet. He hasn't mentioned it, and there were no awkward questions or nightmares once we were home from the farmhouse. It's tricky, navigating deep family shit like this with a child who bursts into tears if I hand him the wrong pyjamas. The last thing I want him to think is that me and Mum were arguing because of him, that he was at fault somehow. Who knows how his teeny little brain works.

Still, if he's not brought it up, it might be better to let it lie. Christ. Parenting is fucking hard.

Josh calls me after drop off, when I'm already on my way to the pub. Over the car's Bluetooth, he tells me how Rory shoved the flowers into Nate's face while he was chatting with a parent, bellowed "these are from Alex" at him so loud, the whole village probably heard then ran away, giggling with Lottie.

Fuck. Maybe it was a bad idea to deliver the present in such a public way? I could have taken them to his flat later, or arranged for a delivery of a proper bouquet from one of those big posh places online. Rory isn't exactly discreet.

Thoughts like this continue to taunt me until my phone pings while I'm watering the window boxes at the pub.

> **Mr Jameson:** A small person delivered a beautiful bunch of flowers to me this morning. From your mum's garden?

> **Me:** yeah she helped

> **Me:** did rory embarrass you or get you in trouble

> **Mr Jameson:** Luckily, I waited until I got into my classroom to read the note. I was too busy swooning over the thoughtful gift that I didn't notice Elsa trying to paint George in blue glitter. I got to them before she got it up his nose, though.

> **Me:** lucky george

> **Mr Jameson:** Still can't believe that your mother let you pick flowers from her garden to give to me. Did she know they were for me? Has she had too much sun?

> **Me:** it was her idea

Mr Jameson: Well, they're lovely. But why? I don't deserve flowers from you.

Me: you deserve flowers every day

Me: good luck with the interview i really want you to stay in beechmill nate

Mr Jameson: I really want to stay here too x

It feels so good to be messaging again, even if it's only a small conversation. The kiss seems a nice place to leave it; I don't want to push my luck with him or scare him off by being too keen. Mum said I need to let the small gestures do the talking. For once, I'm really listening to her advice, especially as it's already working so well and has got us texting again.

So even though my fingers itch to ask how the rest of the assessments are going or if he thinks he's in with a chance, I tuck my phone back into my pocket. God, it would be so easy to slip into texting him constantly again, to fill that need of having some sort of contact with him all the time. But I want to do things differently this time. Show him I care about him and it's not all about me.

Plus, distance makes the heart grow fonder, right? And while I wait, I plan to woo the socks off Mr Jameson, just like Mum told me to do.

East Beechmill Primary School has deemed Tuesday as *Gift Your Teacher* day. Well, that's what it said in the newsletter, anyway. *If you have any thank you gifts or cards for the staff, please bring them in* **THE DAY BEFORE** *the end of term to make it easier for them to be taken from classrooms.* I guess everyone will be busy with the disco on Wednesday, and Palmer will want no distractions.

"Why did you decide to get all romantic when I'm doing drop offs?" Josh asks, as he yet again calls me while we're both on the way to work. "That hamper weighed a fuckton."

This gift was all my idea. Instead of the traditional candles or plaques or best teacher mugs, I found a wicker basket in Dad's shed, cleaned it up, then stuffed it full of things that remind me of Nate.

Two bottles of the wine that I can now only drink with him, because its dark cherry scent reminds me of how good he tastes when I kiss him. The treats he admitted he allows himself after a workout – flavoured peanuts, yuck. I also managed to find the next book in the fantasy series he's been reading, thank fuck for the supermarket. It was a pain in the ass dragging Rory around the shops when all he wanted to do was go home and watch *Iron Man 3* after dinner at his Nan's. It's surprising how few treats I can bribe the kid with.

When Nate texts me to say thank you, this time on his lunch break, our messages stretch out a little bit longer, until I'm wishing him good night at gone 11. We intentionally avoid talking about *us*, instead focusing on what we've been up to, how his interview went, our plans for the summer holidays. Sure, the messaging is slower than it used to be, both of us creeping towards some sense of normalcy. But it feels good, like I might be able to win him back.

There are no presents for him on Wednesday, so I reach for my phone as soon as I'm awake enough to be coherent.

> **Me:** good morning it's the final day of school well done on surviving it

Grey light bleeds through the edges of my curtain. I throw my phone to the duvet then stretch and yawn. Although I'm keen to be quiet, perhaps engage in a quick morning chat with Nate, my peace doesn't last. My small yawn sets off a rumble of footsteps over the landing that grow louder with every second. I brace myself. Rory barges into my room and throws himself onto my bed.

"It's the last day of school!"

"No it isn't." I fight to keep a straight face. "Didn't you read the letter from Headmistress Palmer? There's one week left. The party is *next* Wednesday."

He straddles my legs. "No. You said three more days and" – he counts on his fingers – "today is number three."

"That's great counting, buddy. Well done on surviving your first *real* year in school. With two separate teachers, too. How do you feel? More clever?"

He relaxes, flopping onto me and resting his head on my stomach. I stroke his hair. "Ah-mazing. I learned all the things ever. My brain is going to explode."

"Ouch. That might hurt. Perhaps keep your brain intact, yeah? I need you to get a good career, earn loads of money so that I can quit my job and you can look after me."

"I can't work. I'm only six."

"Sure you can. Gramps was down the mines at your age. Can you see in the dark? If you can't then we're going to have to switch your diet to only carrots."

He watches me with a cold, assessing stare. "I'm going to ask Mr Jameson about the work."

"Ask away, kid, but he'll back me up."

"Do we have a present for him today?"

"Nah. Figured us being at the disco would be enough of a gift. Are you excited about the party?"

"I dunno. It's my first one."

"Oh. Could have sworn you were a party animal."

"James says you have to dance with girls." He shudders.

"Don't you want to?"

"No. Dancing is boring."

"Well, nobody can make you do anything boring, mate. Go and have fun. I don't think I'll bother dancing with anyone either."

"Won't you dance with Mr Jameson?"

"I'm not sure he'll have me." His stomach rumbles and I laugh. "Let's get breakfast. I'm starving, too."

In contrast to the dawdling start to my week, today's shift goes way too fast. The restaurant is busy all day, and in between waiting tables, I focus on cleaning out the grotto so we can expand our outdoor space. It's been my project for a week or so now and I think I'm close to finishing. By the time Lee, the duty manager, comes to take over, I'm a sweaty mess and close to running late.

At least I remembered to bring a change of clothes with me so I don't have to rush home. I also arranged for Rory to stay behind once school finishes to save on faff. Well done, past me. With only moments to spare, I rush to the office to clean up. Simon is at his desk, finishing a pile of paperwork, and he wolf-whistles as I swap my uniform for the Hawaiian-print shirt I treated myself to yesterday. For some reason, there's an overbearing need for me to look my best this afternoon that has nothing to do with the kids or my role in the PTA. I've even stopped caring about the Perfect Parent Club. Not that I was ever bothered by them, of course.

I use the small mirror hanging on the back of the door to tidy my hair, wishing I'd remembered to shave this morning. It's no good. I'm a mess. Hobo chic will have to do.

"What are you making all this effort for?" Simon teases.

I shrug. "I want to stay on the PTA next year. Having a project to share with Rory has helped us to bond."

"That's good. I suppose working with Mr Jameson is a bonus, right?"

Nate made such a good impression on most of my family Saturday that everyone asks about him. It's never how's Alex, only how's Mr Jameson? It's a good job I'm not desperate to forget him. "Nice to see none of you know how to let a topic go."

"It's my job as your older brother to be curious about your love life. How are things with him, by the way?"

Henry told everyone what happened Sunday. It was easier to let him than having the same conversation over and over again.

"We've texted a little the past few days, but I haven't seen him since Saturday. Is everything sorted for later, by the way?"

"Yep. We've got the big table booked for everyone. The plan is in place."

"Perfect."

"You're lucky I could extend my shift. I wouldn't want any of the others in charge of this."

"I know, and I'm eternally grateful." I'll have to make it up to him by covering some of his double shifts over the holidays, but the extra money will help. Maybe I'll be able to afford to take Rory away for a proper holiday. Has the kid got a passport? "I'll text you when we get the result of the competition. I know it'll be hard to wait."

"Good. Even though in my head, we've already won. Business is booming, and the extra publicity from the fête must be behind it. Unless it's food-related, or tickets to see Taylor Swift, you and Nate can share the prize. A trip to a posh spa might be what you two need to rekindle your—"

"Cheers, mate." I cross the office to fist-bump him. "Do I look okay?"

"Like a dream."

"Thanks. Talk to you later."

I take one final glance at my reflection then leave the office. I collect the boxes of snacks I put away earlier and weave around the wait staff with practised ease. It would suck if someone spilled food over me now. I want Nate to swoon as soon as he lays eyes on me. Just like I'll be doing over him.

The school is a ghost town. The disco doesn't start until five and most of the kids have gone home to get ready. I grab a parking spot close to the gates for once, and load up on the boxes and Rory's party outfit before strolling towards the building.

Grey clouds have kept the summer weather away all week. Usually, I'd moan about the lack of sun but we don't need it today. It's not raining, and that's all that matters. The hall will be stuffy as hell with hundreds of kids throwing themselves around, but the cooler air will stop them from overheating. Which means less pukes and traumas to deal with. Fingers crossed.

I nudge the doors open with my hip and make my way along the corridor. A rabble of noise greets me as I approach Nate's classroom, and I quicken my pace, keen to see him and Rory again. My eyes widen and my pulse blooms when I reach the threshold, stopping dead at the sight greeting me. Nate and Rory sit together at a small, round table, joined by Lottie, Ella and Chloe. Someone has emptied out a box of crayons and the surface is covered with paper. All five of them scribble away, chattering about their plans for the summer. The ease with which Nate fits in steals the breath from my lungs.

It's all I've ever wanted. Someone for me and Rory to come home to, who fits in with all the madness of our lives. Who can get on with the kid, maybe eventually treat him like one of his own.

I stare at them for a while longer, unnoticed. I'm only shaken out of my stupor when Nate tells a joke and the rest of the table laughs, and it's my desperation to be a part of the group that pushes me into the room.

"I'm sorry to interrupt arts and crafts, but I have food," I declare.

It's a good job that I brought more than we needed. Josh forgot to warn me that his two were staying behind as well. *Wanker.* I hang Rory's outfit on the nearest coat hook before setting out the boxes on an empty table. It's all finger food – stuff leftover from the lunchtime wake we hosted – but it'll give us all enough energy to survive the party until we can get a proper dinner later.

Nate is the first to abandon his drawing. Although he's only a few metres away from me, his journey across the room takes forever. As he walks, his hips swing as if he's purposely trying to catch my attention with them. It works. I'm fucking entranced. I lick my lips.

I have a whole plan for us this evening, but the way he holds my gaze empties out my head, and all I can think of is how good it would be to tumble back to bed with him. There's a script of things I want to say to him, but in my memory, he didn't look *this* fucking tantalising or distracting. How am I supposed to have a serious conversation with him today when he looks this handsome?

My palms slick with sweat, and I wipe them on my jeans, all the while trying to ignore how disarming he is.

"This is amazing, Alex. Thank you."

Oh, the view up close is even better. He looks even more handsome than usual. Relaxed, even. He's wearing a shirt similar to mine, and has swapped his usual chinos for a pair of light denim jeans that are so tight, it's a wonder he can breathe. And his hair is wavy, exactly how I like it. His sunburn from the weekend has faded but the freckles remain. Yet again, I have the urge to trace my fingers over them. I hold on tighter to the trays of food instead.

"There were loads of leftovers, and I thought..." I trail off as he stops next to me. Although our arms don't touch, electricity zips between us, warming my body and stirring up all the ways I've missed him these past few days.

Fuck. I'm ruined. Done for. This man now owns my soul, and we've not even made it to the making-up part yet.

We're still holding each other's gaze and I take a step towards him, forgetting where we are, forgetting who is in the room with us. It's only us, and I'm like a predator desperate for my prey. All I need to do is lean forward a little, touch my mouth to his and—

"Thanks, Alex. I'm starrrving."

Rory wriggles between us, oblivious to what he's interrupting. Nate's eyes flick to the kid then back at me, now full of disappointment. *Yeah, me too.* I need to have a word with Rory about being a cockblock. Dating when you have kids is hard enough without them being a space thief.

I don't get a chance to get close to Nate again. The rest of the group joins us, only widening the gap between us. The fuckers.

Nate helps me lay the food out, and it takes asking the kids five times before they sit down to eat. Once the trays are emptied and everyone is cleaned up, we get to work helping the rest of the PTA in decorating the hall. A member of the Perfect Parent Club hands me a list of tasks, and every time I gravitate towards Nate, she comes up with more jobs, or more excuses to pull me away.

"Oh, Alex. We need you to hang the bunting." "Alex, help us move this table."

For an hour, her commands keep me away from him, and by the time we've finished, a flood of children fill every inch of the parquet flooring and the disco is in full swing. Multi-coloured lights swish around the room in time to the steady beat of the latest pop songs, most of which I don't recognise.

If I thought looking after Rory and his cousins was hard work, this is warfare. Drinks are spilled, kids get upset, and I use every plaster in the small first-aid box. I don't last an hour before I'm desperate for a break, my head already pounding from the suppressive air in the hall, the constant thump-thump of the music, and the smell of stale farts and cheesy toes. Maybe I'm getting too old for this shit?

After checking Palmer doesn't have her beady eyes on me, I slip into Nate's empty classroom to catch my breath. The plan is to take five minutes and use the quiet to check my messages, but when I open my phone, an alert from my football app distracts me, and I'm soon pulled into yesterday's results.

"What are you watching?"

I drop my phone, wincing as it clatters on the hard wooden floor. "Fuck!"

Chloe stoops to pick it up, inspecting the screen before handing it back to me. "Not smashed. Phew."

"I was checking the scores," I mumble, like I'm fifteen again and been caught watching porn – which happened more times than I'm comfortable to admit. Not that I have to explain myself to a teen. She frowns, and I kick myself for being aloof. She's a fucking kid and I'm a grown up. I can do better.

"We watched the Millwall game last night. Such a shame." She shifts to lean against the table I'm sitting on. "I thought they'd do better this season."

"You like football?"

"I *play* football. Arsenal Ladies Juniors."

"Fuck off?" *Shit.* Do I need to be more careful with my language around her? Sure, she's like 14 or something, but Nate might get annoyed with me. He only curses when he's mad, or during—

"Yeah. Centre forward."

"You're fucking brilliant, kid. You play for one of the best teams out there *and* you got into King's School." Never mind Rory's claim, Chloe is now *my* new best friend. Is that weird? I don't care.

"Thanks."

"So, what else are you into?" If I'm going to fix things with Nate, I need to make an effort with Chloe, show I can accept her in my life as willingly as he's accepted Rory.

Pink floods her cheeks and she draws her lower lip between her teeth the same way Nate does.

"I kind of like fashion and make-up. Taylor Swift. Reading."

"Well, I'm no good with most of that. Aside from Taylor Swift. I bet I know more of her songs than you."

This ignites an energetic back-and-forth in which we discuss what our favourite songs are, the mad theories in the fandom, and when she's *finally* going to drop her latest album. I lose track of time until the conversation comes to its natural end. Then we sit in silence for a moment, giving me a chance to marvel at how well we get on.

It's like I've always known the kid. Perhaps it's the practice I've had with my brothers' teens, but I could easily pull up a million other things to talk to her about. But we enjoy this moment without any awkwardness, her legs swinging back and forth from where they dangle off the table.

The quiet doesn't last for long, though.

"Do you still like my dad?" she blurts out, the pink on her face growing to a deep red.

The question should startle me, especially in the blunt, rushed way she's asking it, but her openness is admirable. Me and Nate could learn a few things from her.

"Yeah. He's the best thing that's ever happened to me. Apart from Rory, of course."

Play it cool, Al.

"Does that mean you're going to ask him out? He told me what happened between you. We text a lot, me and Dad." So that's who he was always on the phone with. "He likes you. You make him happy. But me and him are a pair. I promise I'm not a brat, though. I didn't mean to interrupt the two of you at the fête. It was bad timing and I—" She puffs out a hard breath and pushes her hair out of her eyes. "Now he's got the permanent post, he'll have time to properly tell you all about his life, and about me."

"Wait? He got the permanent job?"

She clamps her hand over her mouth. "I'm sorry. I thought he texted you. Please don't tell him I told you."

I barely hear her over the rush of my heart in my ears. He's staying here. It's the best news I've had all week, the most perfect thing I need ahead of tonight. Not only that, but with Chloe saying she thought we were texting, it means he's talked about getting in touch with me. Me and Nate are a pair of fucking idiots. Why didn't I kiss him earlier and get things rolling sooner?

Although my feet are desperate to race to him, to declare my love to him, I give myself another minute with Chloe first. There's a plan in place, and it'll be perfect if I can pull it off. And perhaps I could do with her help.

"Thank you for coming to talk to me. I'm sorry if I was rude the other day. It was all a big surprise and I don't do well with surprises."

"Yeah. I told him off. I'm, like, dedicated to getting the two of you back together now. Dad seemed so much happier those weeks you were talking, and I know that's because of you. He didn't moan about how he only goes to the gym and work. He had plans, someone to spend his time with."

"Well, I'm glad you think that, Chloe. Because I think I need your help."

I don't get time to expand further because she lets out a small squeak and bounces in place. "Yes. I'm in. Rory and I are a hundred percent team Alex."

"Okay. Do you think you can persuade him to come to the pub after the disco later?"

It's the missing part of my puzzle. Everything else has been set up. Simon is making sure we have plenty of our favourite wine in and my last gift is waiting for Nate at the pub. But I haven't worked out how to get him there yet so that I can surprise him. I guess I hoped the thrill of winning the competition would give me an opportunity. With Chloe on my side, it should be easy-peasy.

"Yes. Of course I can. If you win then I can go on about wanting to celebrate or something. Plus he keeps on talking about me getting to meet more people around the village." She releases me, beaming widely. It fills me with confidence. After all, they talk about *everything* according to her, and if she's this sure that things will go my way, then I must be doing something right.

I want to tell her about my plan, make sure it's the right thing to win him over, but the music quietens and Chloe frowns. "Shit." Well there's the answer to whether I'm allowed to swear around her. "I saw you come in here and wanted to grab you because I overheard Palmer saying she'll be announcing the winners soon."

"We better get going then. I don't want to miss it."

Telling her the plan can wait. It'll be obvious when they turn up at The Watering Hole, anyway, and she comes across as a clever girl. I'm sure she'll piece it together by herself.

I follow her out of the classroom, tucking my phone into my pocket. Rory is in a corner of the hall with five other boys, no trainers, and using his white socks to slide over the polished floor. The marks on his jeans shows he's upgraded his moves to using his knees, too. Great. I leave him there and sidle up to Nate, who is supervising a vigorous-looking game of Stuck in the Mud.

"Hey," I start but then the music dies completely and there's a tap on the microphone. Palmer is on the stage. Nate throws a quick smile at me before we turn our attention to her. The lights come up at the same time his fingers graze against mine. Feeling bold after my conversation with Chloe, I wrap my hand around his and squeeze. When he tightens his grip on me, I swear I could float right up to the sky with how happy it makes me. Inside, I'm fucking dancing, but I only allow a smirk to slip out while the rest of me remains aloof as I concentrate on the stage.

"Good evening, everyone," Palmer says. Josh steps close to me and Nate, his phone held high so Aimee can watch the announcement. "I won't keep you long as your parents are waiting to take you home. It has been a fantastic year for us at Beechmill Primary, and the summer fête was the icing on the cake. I have tallied the totals from the weekend, and I am pleased to tell you we raised over two thousand pounds, beating last year's record. We can now start work on the playground, and we are already going out for bids for the contract."

Applause breaks out around the hall, the kids shouting and screaming along. "Of course, this is all down to the hard work of the PTA. Every year, you find interesting ways to keep the crowds coming in. This year's prize has been donated by a group of local businesses, and is a family day-pass to Thorpe Park. The stall that raised the most money is—"

She's interrupted by a synthetic drumroll. The DJ ignores her barbed look, letting the percussion build up to a trumpet fanfare. The kids love it, pounding along with their little fists against their knees and stamping their feet. The tension grows and the hairs on my arms stand to attention, my breath coming in short, shallow gasps. Although I'm positive we've won – there's no way anyone else raised more than us, we were busy all day – the longer we wait, the more doubt creeps into my head.

The noise breaks, and Palmer declares, "The Watering Hole."

Nate grabs me, twining his arms around my waist and burying his head against my neck. His swear vibrates on my skin and I almost lose it. Adrenaline courses through my bloodstream, and I rock him back and forth on the spot, my hand drifting up his back to pull him closer. I am the luckiest fucking guy in the world. Not only did we go and do a fucking win, but now the man of my dreams is back in my arms, our chests, hips – *bloody hell* – even our feet are touching.

It doesn't get better than this. Well, until Chloe and Rory join us, forcing their way into the tiniest of gaps to get in on the action. *Now* this is the best thing ever.

"I can't believe it," I sputter out when Nate and the kids pull away. Behind us, Josh and Aimee whoop and holler. The applause eventually dwindles, the crowd dispersing to waiting parents, but my gaze is fixed on Nate, Rory and Chloe as they perform a celebration dance, none of them keeping in time to the goodbye song blasting through the speakers.

I'm close to swooning over the view in front of me. A perfect, ready-made family unit. It's all I ever wanted. All right, we're not official yet, and there's going to be a lot of talking later to get to a point where we can be together again. But we can make it work. I'm determined.

Okay. I blow my fringe out of my face and right my glasses. *Time to get the plan in motion.* I glance at Josh who gives me a nod and hangs up on Aimee. Once his phone is tucked away, he throws himself at me and Nate, looping his arms over both of our shoulders.

"Well fucking done, you guys," Josh shouts over the music. "Aimee is raising the troops, getting the family to The Watering Hole to celebrate properly. You joining us, Mr Jameson?"

Nate's shoulders slump and a frown crosses his eyebrows. He keeps his eyes on me, silently questioning my plans. So I feel extra bad when I say, "Yeah, come on, Nate. It'll be fun."

"Dad. I want to go," Chloe joins in, catching on straight away. She's brilliant. She pulls at his arm. "I want to meet everyone else."

He sighs. "I guess we could for a bit."

"Great. We'll clean up and then sort out lifts," Josh says, still tapping messages into his phone. "I'll come find you when I'm ready."

It takes a lot of effort to keep my grin at bay as Josh disappears again and Nate turns to me. "I thought we were going to—"

"We will."

And then I do something I never thought I'd be able to. I turn and walk away from him, swinging my arms and trying my best to look nonchalant about it all. Whoever was bossing us around earlier gives me her orders for the strike down – rubbish collection. But drawing the grossest job card doesn't spoil my mood and I attack my tasks enthusiastically. The sooner I get it done, the sooner I can whisk Rory over to the pub and get the real celebrations rolling.

And hopefully, Nate will still want to talk after all of this.

Twenty

NATE IS IN MY car. *Nate is in my car.*

Alex, breathe. I've got this. It's not like it's the first time he's been there and hopefully, it won't be the last. I can't go losing my shit every time he's in the passenger seat.

My internal panic isn't helped by the dreary weather, which forced our windows up. The lack of ventilation means his earthy scent fills every inch of the car. Can you get high from huffing someone's aftershave? If so, I'm well on my way.

I'm not sure how, but I get us to The Watering Hole in one piece. We don't pull over and kick the kids out so that I can declare my undying love to Nate. Neither do we crash. He keeps stealing glances at me, which makes me grip the steering wheel so hard the leather creaks. It's all I can do to keep my hands to myself, to not reach over and rest my palm on his thigh. My eyes stay firmly fixed on the road.

The kids keep the conversation going. Which is great, be-cause my lips are glued shut. Rory fires questions at Chloe about

Thorpe Park, since he's never been, and she gives him animated reenactments of her favourite rides, pushing his car seat a little to mimic the rock of a rollercoaster, or pretend to swoop and fall like a death drop. The scene keeps the dopiest smile on my face. I'm all fucking heart-eyes and sparkle emojis and I don't freaking care who sees. My brothers could throw their worst at me, and I'll still skip around the place tonight.

"You're lucky you booked the big table out." Simon hurries past us as we enter the pub, his hair stuck to his head in a sweaty mess and his face beetroot red. Looks like his late shift has turned into more than sitting in the office, barking commands at everyone and he's actually had to get stuck in. Sucks to be him. There's no way I'd want to wait on our family. We're feral.

"Congratulations, Alex, Nate," I say in a shit imitation of Simon's no-nonsense tone. "Really glad you won. Thanks for texting me."

We loiter in the doorway to avoid the hurricane that is my second-eldest brother, who doesn't notice my teasing and continues to set place settings on the huge table that takes up all of our conservatory. Once that's done, he goes hunting for more chairs. I could help him, but I have more important tasks to take care of. Mainly making sure Nate is sitting near me, and nowhere near Mum. Despite our Sunday chat, I don't want her scaring him off and Josh called to warn me that she and Dad were on their way, keen to get involved in the celebrations.

Why the fuck not? We do everything else together.

Speaking of, my brother crashes into the back of me. "What the fuck are you doing standing around in the doorway like a lemon? Why aren't you sitting already?"

"I was waiting for Simon to finish so he didn't rope me in. Fuck off am I doing unpaid work for him."

Although I follow Josh to the table, I'm laser-focused on Nate. He sidles around the long oak table, sliding between the chairs and the wall with Rory and Chloe in tow. When he plonks himself in the middle with the kids either side of him, I push Josh out of the way to grab the seat opposite Nate. I'm nothing if not subtle. Nate flashes me a look that's somewhere between a grimace and a grin. *Fuck.* I didn't think about how nerve-wracking this is for him. Sure, he met my family at the fête, but that was before, well, Chloe, and it's not like he got a chance to sit down and chat to them properly. Perhaps I should have asked him first if he was up for it, instead of bullying him here.

He flicks through the menu. "I ate way too much leftovers, and I'm really not hungry, but that lemon and chilli meringue sounds amazing."

"I've been living off it for the past week." I rub my tummy. "You should order one. On the house."

"Nope." Simon steps in, an order pad ready for us. "No freebies here. Not for you, Alex, or any guy you're trying to impress."

If only he knew about the free food I've already given Nate. My cheeks heat up, especially as Simon timed his comment with the rest of my family piling into the empty chairs around the table. He's rarely funny, but they all laugh at him anyway. *Great.* Here goes another evening I spend squirming in my seat.

I should expect it. They all know my intentions with Nate, so they're not going to give me an easy night. Of course not. Why would they let me do my thing in peace?

"I can pay," Nate says. "It's not a problem. Alex doesn't have to buy me dessert to win me over."

The world stops, and a pink fuzziness blurs the edges of my vision. Or are those tears or the constant flow of love hearts that appear every time I look at him? If we were alone, or only with the kids, I could forget about talking with him and rush over to kiss him. Fuck being formal about it. If I snog him to death, there'll be no problem understanding what I want from him. But his comment only fuels more laughter from my family and I shrink lower in my seat.

It's going to be a long night.

My family's attention soon switches to the stall – the entire reason we're here. We pull it apart, analysing everything we did and how it helped us win, before tearing down everyone else's offer. The Perfect Parent Club doesn't have shit on us. Then we move onto the prize, the family trip to Thorpe Park. For once, it's my brothers' turn to be jealous of me.

"Perhaps we could all come with you?" Josh suggests, his gaze a little too eager for my liking.

Mum tuts. She's been quiet for the most part, keeping her thoughts to herself, but more than once, her gaze has shifted between me and Nate. Her face gives nothing away.

"Normally, I would agree with you. It would be nice to have a family trip somewhere fun like that. But perhaps Alex and Nate want to go by themselves. With the kids, of course. It's not fair for us to throw ourselves at them and spoil their lovely break. Especially without an invite."

No. Fucking. Way. I stare at her, the last of my chewed pie almost falling out of my mouth as I search for the hidden meaning in her words. But her smile is warm and genuine, and when Nate presses his foot against mine under the table, I close my mouth and give her a nod. She's definitely on our side.

She might change her mind, however, if she could feel how Nate's foot is now rubbing the bottom of my leg. Somehow, he's managed to push my jeans up so his foot is making contact with my skin. When did he take his shoe off?

I swallow and take a moment to compose myself. Turning to my brother, I say, "Yeah, exactly. We wouldn't all fit in the hotel, anyway. It's like the size of a storage container."

Yep. The prize came with an overnight stay, too. Me, Nate *and* the kids will be squishing ourselves into the tiniest space possible. A great way to get to know each other and ever so romantic.

The evening zips by, as if the dawdling week stole all of the extra hours from today. After using up most of his energy at the disco, it doesn't take long for Rory to crash. He slides onto my lap without any coaxing and tucks his head against my chest. Despite his best efforts to stay awake, he drops off pretty quickly, his thumb in his mouth, just like when I first got him. He'll be out for the night now. Mjölnir could crash into the table and it wouldn't wake him.

I've been working my way around the table all evening, taking advantage of trips to the toilet and people moving to talk to others to try to get closer to Nate. I have to lure him outside to chat. The sky is fading from its light grey to oranges and reds, telling us we're going to have a good day tomorrow. But I don't want to have to wait until the morning to speak to him. I *cannot* have another night's sleep without knowing he's mine. Properly.

The more he gets on with my family, though, the more they welcome him into their folds. Every time I shift closer around the table, a brother or a child gets in between us. Finally, there's only one seat separating us, but I'm pinned in it by my over-sized lump.

Nate is in a full-blown conversation with Henry about books, and when that finishes, he turns to the rest of the table and declares, "We should probably head off. Chloe must be getting tired."

Wait. No. It's the worst news ever, and I watch, helpless, as he gets to his feet, rousing Chloe from her phone. She hasn't long rejoined us, having been away from the table most of the evening with the older children. She throws her dad a frown, showing no sign of the fatigue he's alluding to.

He pulls on his denim jacket, oblivious to my internal panic. I try to get up, but Rory mumbles something about Thanos in his sleep. My arms are dead from his weight. *Fuck. Fuck. Fuck.*

Mum watches me like a hawk, her gaze burning into the side of my face. Before I can warn off her nosey questions, she shifts over a couple of seats and holds her hands out. "Here. It's been ages since I've had a little one sleep on my lap. Let me have him for a bit."

What has she been drinking? When I imagine my fairy godmother, she wears a ton of glitter and sequins and is probably a drag queen. There's no way I'd picture my mum's frizzy hair, and body that's not unlike mine. But since I'm desperate, I slide Rory onto her lap. Like a baby koala, he curls up to her, his thumb slipping out of his mouth the only sign we've disturbed him. I run a quick hand over his sweaty forehead before getting to my feet.

"Nate, before you go, can we—" I don't finish my sentence, but as soon as his attention is on me, I nod away from the table.

He tilts his head in silent acknowledgement. My brothers are watching us closely now, but to their credit, they don't jeer or jest. As soon as we're gone, they'll probably put bets on us. Good luck to them. I hope Henry wins.

Nate stays close to me and we weave around empty tables and restaurant staff until we reach the fire exit. It's not alarmed – we still need to fix the system – and when I hit the escape bar, it's a little too hard. He laughs at my eagerness and his hand finds its way to the small of my back. I shudder, but I'm not sure if it's from the cool evening air or the sound of his chuckles.

"You didn't bring a coat with you."

His breath is hot on the back of my neck, warming me enough for now. I spin around and end up toe-to-toe with him, our noses almost touching. All it would take is for me to lean in and we could kiss, but I can't give into that want yet. We *have* to talk, make sure we're both on the same page. Then we can address the mounting tension between us.

I keep my eyes on him as I take his hand and pull him more into the space. The gasp he releases fills me with pride and I don't let go of him as he takes in my handiwork.

Lavender bushes surround the secluded spot, filling the air with their powdery scent. Hydrangeas bob in the light breeze. In the middle of it all, underneath a sky crossed with fairy lights,

waits a small, tall table that neither of us can sit at. Earlier, I threw
a linen cloth over it so it could host the gift box and bottle of wine
I'd found. I can get proper furniture for the space later.

"Did you do this yourself?"

"Yeah," I breathe out. "One day, I might want to revisit my
dreams of being a gardener, and stuff like this will help me build
a portfolio."

"I'd hire you for sure."

"Were you really going to leave without talking to me?"

"Honestly, Al? I was getting a bit fed up. I thought perhaps you
didn't want to speak to me after Saturday."

"I've been trying to get to you all night. But you keep on talking
to my brothers, so—"

"It's not my fault they like me more than you."

"Oy!" I nudge him but instead of moving away, I release a deep
sigh and drop my head onto his shoulder. "Thank you for coming
tonight."

His body relaxes, almost immediately, and his chin finds the
spot where it belongs, right on my crown.

"Thank you for inviting me. It's been lovely getting to know
people. Chloe fits right in."

Silence drifts between us. I'm sure we both have loads to say
to each other. My speech has been written and rewritten over
and over in my head. But now that we're here together, words
don't seem enough.

It doesn't matter. I'm happy to enjoy this moment with him,
soak in the closeness I've been missing the past few weeks.

Eventually, though, he breaks the quiet. "Alex, I—" He shifts
and our gazes meet. I'm bowled over by the lightning strikes of
grey in his eyes. They're so much brighter than how I remembered them. "I'm sorry about keeping Chloe from you. It was a
stupid mistake."

I rub my jaw. "You're not the only person to blame. I never
once asked you about your family, or if you even had one. I didn't

show interest in your history. But I mean what I said, Nate, I want to know all about you. Every tiny thing, even if you think it's insignificant. I want a whole fucking encyclopedia of you. I'm such a dickhead for making you think that I don't care, that I would run away from your truth."

"We're both dickheads, then."

"I think so. And there'll probably be a lot more dickish moments too. Neither of us are perfect. But we have a chance to move in the right direction now, don't we? Get the fresh start you came here for."

"We might as well, since I got the permanent job."

My voice is low but strong. "Chloe let that slip earlier. Nate, I'm so proud of you. I wish you would have called me so that I could celebrate with you, or at least get you a card."

"Well, we were texting, but I wasn't sure if you'd want to hear my voice."

"I always want to hear your voice."

"Good. Because I've missed talking to you these past few weeks. I–I'm head over heels for you *and* Rory. I can't help it and I'm fed up with keeping it all in. This whole "it's too quick, it's too soon." By whose standards? Some random magazine columnist who says you can't develop feelings before x amount of weeks? It's a load of tosh. Who cares if it's been four weeks or four months. It's fast, but that feels so very us."

"I think so, too." I stroke his cheek with two fingers. "How could it not, when you're so brilliant? You make it easy to forget about how shit the rest of my life was, the mistakes we've both made. Instead, you force me to focus on feeling good, and getting what I want. You scare away all my self-doubt, erase all the shit advice my family gives me. You empower me to work on *me*. And I'm ready to stop trying to fill the gap Luke left in our family, and do something that'll make *me* happy."

He's beaming at me, his smile so blinding it's like the sun catching in the ripples of a pond. It tears me away from The

Watering Hole, from East Beechmill, from the whole of fucking Devon and it's only me and him in the world.

"You fucking deserve it, Alex."

Oh God. That's it. I'm done. Him swearing is my aphrodisiac. Who needs oysters and asparagus when he's sneaking out curse words like he's telling his students a story? I almost, *almost*, spew out that I love him, but swallow the words down. When I tell him, it'll be even more romantic than this little spot. Like in bed, or on holiday, or when the kids can hear it. And not inspired by my straight-laced hunk of a man using the f-bomb.

I slide my fingers from his cheek, tracing the sharpness of his jawline as if the angles of him aren't already ingrained in my mind. He sighs and closes his eyes. I tilt his head more towards mine and press my lips to his in the gentlest of kisses. Our noses graze and our glasses bump together when we deepen the kiss, and he slides one hand into my hair to hold me to him.

Every inch of my body fills with warmth. This is home for me. I no longer have to hide us and I can kiss this Adonis whenever I want to, wherever I want to. To celebrate, and to lay my claim on him, I part my lips and run my tongue along the seam of his mouth, groaning as he grants me access straight away.

"Alex," he moans into the kisses in a way that makes me want to drag him into the car and back to my cottage, kids be damned. They can find their own way home.

I break up the long, hard kiss with smaller ones, getting a glimpse of his blissed-out look – eyes closed, a pink flush across his cheeks – before I press lazy pecks against his jaw. When I reach his mouth again, I give him one final kiss then press my forehead to his.

"Can we take things slower this time?" he asks. He releases my hair, only to take my hand and rest our linked fingers on my thigh. "I mean, the kisses are great, but perhaps we could get that date first before we jump into bed with each other."

The blush remains on his face, deepening as he squirms where he's stood. He's gone all shy on me. It's not the Nate I know, but it's freaking adorable. And I'm more than happy to oblige. Slow will be good. I can wait a small while until my pillow smells of him again.

"You mean, this isn't enough for a date?" I laugh when he opens his mouth to argue back. "Of course I can wait. But I have something important to ask you first."

"Oh, do you?"

The corners of his mouth twitch as if he's fighting back a smile, like he's trying to be serious. I untangle myself from him, grab the box from the table before dropping to the floor on one knee.

"Wait, Alex. This isn't sl—"

"Oh, shush. I'm not proposing to you, you goof." I pull a glass paperweight out of the box and hold it out to him. "You've turned my world upside down, Mr Jameson. I didn't know I could be as happy as you make me. I know that I come with a lot of mess, chaos and noise, as well as a six-year old, but I promise that me and Rory will make your life worth it. Even if you'll never have a moment's peace again."

"Ask the question, Alex."

"Will you be my boyfriend?"

His mouth tightens into a straight line, and his eyelids grow heavy. He sighs. "It's just that—"

"What?" I fight to get up off the floor. Dammit, why am I so old and decrepit? He never struggles to lug himself to his feet. Perhaps I *should* go to the gym with him.

He puts a hand on my shoulder, pushing me back down and joining me on the floor. Pebbles embed themselves in our knees and I feel like I'll be picking stones out of my skin for the next year, but it'll be worth it.

"I wanted to be the one to ask you."

"Oh, for fuck's sake."

I throw myself at the man, mostly in relief. He wants me to be *his* boyfriend.

He laughs into my neck. "Is that a yes?"

"Yes. Yes. Of course it's a yes. It's the best offer I've had in a long time. I fucking adore you, Nate, and me and Chloe get on so well. I can't wait for all of us to be a family. She came looking for me earlier, and I think she was being a wing-person for you."

"I put her up to it."

A grin fills my face and my cheeks ache in a way that I never want to stop. I find his mouth easily, giving him short kisses, drawing in the scent of him between gulped breaths. I want to keep him in my arms forever.

When we pull away, he helps me to my feet then folds his hands over the paperweight. "Is this for me?"

I'd almost forgotten about it, even though it lies heavy on my palm. "Yes," I reply, offering it to him. "So you can work outside on your balcony again without the wind interfering."

It's only then that his eyes fill with tears as he takes it and I have to look away, my nose burning. It takes us both a moment, and he says thank you with a kiss.

"Should we go and tell the kids?"

I'd absolutely love to update them with our news. Yet there's a small tug inside my belly that says *not yet*.

"Can we wait until we've had at least one date?"

Nate raises his eyebrows at me. "Why? Are you worried about what your mum will think? Still?"

"No. No," I rush to placate him. "I want to wait until we've had that date. We can tell everyone else: Mum, Dad, my brothers, the school, the fucking Perfect Parent Club—"

"The Perfect Parent what?"

"It doesn't matter. I just want to be able to tell Rory when he's a little more conscious and not grumpy because I've just woken him up. I want to do it when we can sit him down and talk to him properly."

Nate's blinding smile is back again, smiling so bright I could power the entire pub from it. "That sounds perfect actually." This time, he kisses me first. "But we better head inside before they send a search party for us and inadvertently wake him up. Plus, Chloe must be wondering where I am."

"Do you want me to take you two home?"

There's a moment of silence before he shakes his head. "No. Not tonight. If I get you anywhere near my flat, then I might not let you go. I'll order a taxi."

"As long as you're sure *and* you text me when you get back."

"I'll go one better and phone you once Chloe has gone to bed. Maybe we can make up for the lack of contact we've had this week. Texting small talk is fine, but it doesn't replace the proper conversations we have. It's frustrating not being able to talk to you."

"You're telling me. I haven't had a chance to tell you about the *chat* me and Mum had on Sunday."

"You know, I thought there was something different about her tonight." He squeezes my hand. "Will you tell me about it later?"

"Yes. Absolutely."

We head down the path towards the pub and it's like I'm back to walking on the springy summer grass, like mayflowers are floating around us. The little dark rain cloud has gone and I only went and got what I wanted.

And it's pretty fucking perfect.

TWENTY-ONE

THE FOLLOWING THREE WEEKS pass in a blur of work, dates and time spent with Rory. July melts into August, like an ice-cream in the sun, and it doesn't take long for me to reach my coveted last shift before my annual leave. First stop, the theme park with Nate and Chloe, and then we're going camping.

Yeah, I was sceptical about sleeping in a tent, but he can be persuasive when he wants something.

It takes me half an hour to get home from The Watering Hole, thanks to the tourists flocking to the village, stuffing our quiet slice of heaven full of strangers, piling into our cute little bed and breakfasts and blocking all the roads. I fucking hate summer in a seaside county.

At least I have Nate to look forward to this evening. He's been in France all week with Chloe, and got home late last night. The plan was for me to grab the two of them on my way home, but he texted me earlier to let me know he's making his own way to the cottage. Probably so that I have time to grab a shower first. Shift work in this heat is a recipe for a stinky Alex.

I unbutton the collar on my uniform as I enter the house, desperate to get out of the soaking shirt. Today was so hot, it broke Simon into *finally* ordering us air conditioning. It's a miracle none of us have died of heatstroke yet. My legs are tired from running around tables and the millions of patrons pouring into the pub, driven inside by the burning sun.

I stop at the bottom of the stairs, shirt half-open and use the newel post to bear my weight to remove my shoes. A draft catches my curls, lifting them off my sweaty neck, and I freeze.

On Mum's advice, I've been closing all the windows and curtains before I leave in the hope of keeping the place cool. The house should be empty. Rory is with Henry until later. After the last time, my brother would have messaged if he'd brought the kid home early. Not that there's anything for him to interrupt. Me and Nate have only kissed since the night of the school disco, although after a week apart, I'm hoping for more once the kids are in bed.

I grab the golf umbrella from the stand next to the door and pad softly towards the kitchen. While I move, I check to see if anything is out of place, but the house is as I left it – messy, because I haven't had a chance to do any housework.

The French doors are wide open – *huh* – and the lyrical back-and-forth of a saw sounds from the garden. Something metallic clatters to the floor, and there's a sharp intake of air. Whoever has broken into my house cries, "Fudge!"

Wait. Burglars don't break in to do DIY. That voice raises the hair on my arms. But why the fuck would—

Abandoning the umbrella, I race out to the garden in time to catch Nate clamping his lips around a finger.

"What the hell are you doing here?" I didn't know woodwork was his jam.

He stands amongst the piles of off-cuts, my dad's old work-bench in front of him. His face shines with sweat and he sucks on his finger, his head tilted. Over the patio stands a half-built contraption that looks like it might fall over with the smallest gust of wind and now I know who built the bookshelves in his classroom. There's no real shape to the pile of wood, but it is as tall as the doors I'm frozen at.

A small jagged cut is revealed when he rips his fingers out of his mouth and examines it. "Quite frankly, I'm not sure. Your dad was here. He said he'd come over tomorrow to help me, but I wanted to get it finished before you got home. It's supposed to be beautiful for the rest of the month, so I thought once we got back from our holiday, we could have somewhere nice to hang out. Only, I don't know how to build these things, and I'm afraid I'm making a bit of a mess."

I raise an eyebrow at him, at the wood dust streaking yellow highlights through his hair. "I can tell that. But what is this" – I gesture to the contraption – "supposed to be?"

"It's a pergola," he mumbles.

I didn't hear him properly. There's no way this man has spent his first day back in the country building *me* something. Sure, the evidence is all over the garden, but the image isn't computing in my head.

"A pergola? Why?"

He shrugs. "You said you wanted one. The first time we were out here you said it would be nice for you and Rory to have one. To protect him from the sun. I wanted to start sooner, but we were too busy going on dates and then I had my holiday."

"You're building me a pergola because I said something one time?"

"Well, I'm being romantic and I..." he trails off, his shoulders dropping. "Didn't Mike do things like this for you?"

"Build a garden feature for me?" I scoff, stepping more to-wards Nate. "No. He barely remembered my birthday. Mum used to remind him. It was me who did all the romantic stuff. Organised dates, bought flowers, cooked. But when did you plan all of this? You never mentioned it to me and we didn't get off the phone until gone eleven last night."

We meet at the edge of the pergola. "It's how surprises work, Alex," he tells me. "I got in touch with Josh and he helped me organise it all. I wanted to do something nice for you."

I wanted to do something nice for you.

Although he hasn't got a clue what he's doing, he's *trying* and that's more than anyone else has done. Mike and I got together so young that making an effort meant I got an ice-cream for dessert when we went for fast food. By the time we were in our own place, he was only doing the bare minimum.

But Nate has gone all out. He's as hot and sweaty as me, and there are plasters on at least two of his fingers. There's dust on his knees, on his jean shorts, over his wide, strong chest.

"Is Chloe here?" is all I manage to squeak out.

His smile grows, sending those grey lines shooting through his eyes, marking his joy. "No. She's with Henry, too. Getting to know his girls since they're the same age."

"Wait. Are all of my brothers involved in this?"

"Even your mum. She was here earlier, making sure me and your dad were fed and watered while we worked. I asked Simon to keep you in work for as long as he could."

I *knew* I'd restocked the dishwasher detergent and refilled the sauce bottles the other day. What a git.

An overwhelming urge to wrap myself around Nate steals the rest of my thoughts and this time, I don't ignore it. Placing my hands on his arms, I push him back, steering him around the workbench and shoving him into a rattan chair.

"Alex, what are you doing?"

I quiet his questions with a searing kiss, giving him a taste of what my mouth can offer him before moving to his jaw and neck.

He throws his head back against the seat straight away, giving me the best access to the column of his neck.

Although he's not fighting me off, he still moans his complaint. "But I've been working all day. I stink."

"I don't care. You're fucking delicious." Salt lingers on his skin and I run my tongue along him, delighting in the noise it draws. I don't spend too long there, though. I've waited far too long to get his cock in my mouth, and it's my only goal. Turns out, having people do nice things for me is another of my kinks.

I drop to my knees, one hand pushing his T-shirt up so I can admire the hard planes of his stomach while the other pulls at the buttons of his fly. He runs a thumb over my bottom lip, dipping it inside and I take the initiative, sucking on it.

"Alex, fuck." He shudders as I pull his semi-hard dick from his pants. If I play this right, I'll be able to get my own out soon enough, experience what it's like to get fucked in the sun, but for now, my attention is only on making him feel good.

As soon as Nate's thumb is out of my mouth and clasping the arm of the chair, I tease his tip with my tongue. God, I love his cock.

"Please."

And there's the begging.

I waste no time and take his swollen dick inside the wet heat of my mouth, keeping it shallow to start, to tease him. He reacts instantly, lifting his hips to reach me and I grin around him before pulling him out with a soft pop.

"Take it slow, babe," I warn him. "We have all evening."

The next time I take him deeper, bumping his dick against the back of my throat. Up and down, I move in time with his thrusts, groaning when he tangles his hands in my hair, yanking in a way that creates just enough pain. Fuck, I need to palm myself. My cock aches for him, but I'll wait, be patient. If I'm coming this afternoon, it's because of him, not my hand.

It doesn't take long for Nate to squirm in his seat. His eyes scrunch up, a sure sign he's getting close so I take him deeper, harder.

"That's it, Alex. More."

The front door slams and I almost choke on him. He's lucky I don't bite him in surprise. Footsteps stampede through the house, like his whole class has come to visit.

Fuck. Fuck. Fuck.

I'm barely back on my feet, letting Nate tuck himself away as I stand in front of him, willing myself to deflate and quickly.

"Alex? Nate? Are you here?"

Oh *shit*. This cannot be happening.

"Not-a-fucking-gain!" Henry catches the last of us tidying up, his hands covering Rory's eyes while he turns his own gaze up to the sky. "You have three bedrooms in this house. Why aren't you using one of them?"

Chloe waits on the other side of my brother on the doorstep and I catch a glimpse of her green face before she spins around to stare back into the house. *Great.* Her reaction is enough to drive the last of my horniness from my body. That's it. I'm a volunteer celibate from now on. I can't do anything sexual when a teen is in the house.

Henry doesn't creep closer, but as soon as Nate is on his feet again, my brother throws us a wicked grin. "This *is* the time we agreed, isn't it?"

We must have lost track. A glance at my watch confirms Henry is perfectly on time. We're idiots.

"Yeah. To the second." I grimace.

"Great. Enjoy having the kids back. They're both starving. I'm never coming here again."

His phone is already out of his pocket as he turns to leave. *Fucking brilliant.* The front door slams. Nate's face is as red as mine feels.

"Later," he tells me and gives me a quick peck, not caring that Chloe is now staring at us like we made her watch our Only Fans channel. I'd love to shove my tongue down his throat, let him taste the precome that still lingers there. Huh. Seems like not all the horniness is gone. "We'll tell them about camping, tire them out with a takeaway and I can have you to myself." He lowers his voice, his lips far too close to my ear. "Then, it'll be your cock in *my* mouth."

Chloe makes puking faces at us as we link fingers and saunter towards them. When we reach her, I throw a hand over her shoulder and pull her into my side.

"So tell me about your holiday, kid."

She rabbits away as we head back into the house side by side. It feels so natural, so normal that it's like she's always been here. With Rory trailing after us, asking inane questions about eating snails and speaking French, our perfect little family is finally all home.

And I can't wait to spend the rest of our lives together.

ACKNOWLEDGEMENTS

A story has to start somewhere, and this one wouldn't even existed if it wasn't for the HPRomione Discord server, and HSP200 in particular, for giving me the original idea, and encouraging me to write it. It started its life as a fanfic, so of course, I have to thank my wonderful Circle Chat friends — Annie, Paige, Amanda, and Laura — for being my OG beta readers, for encouraging me, and being the most perfect support group. Even though we don't talk much anymore, I still love you so much and one day, I will travel to your side of the pond to meet you all in real life (and to sign your books).

Although I always had dreams of getting this book into readers' hands, it wasn't until my wonderful writer friend Vee invited me to her new writing server that it finally became a reality. Vee, Esme and Heidi, I'm sorry for all the meltdowns, the second-guessings, the whining when things haven't gone my way and for sharing your sometimes brutal opinions. Alex and Nate would not be who they are today without your generous feedback. To Jen, my fellow queen of romance, especially for hopping on video chat and talking me down off a ledge (and helping me with the sex scenes), and everyone else for being just really great friends.

To Marin and Lara, my child and grandchild. Thank you for enabling me and sending me books to keep me sane.

To my family and friends, my Brawler teammates and my colleagues — thank you for your enthusiasm, for understanding when I cancel on you because I have "book stuff" to do. For offering to read, for being my biggest cheerleaders, and for not judging me when I told you what I was up to. Your love and support means the world to me.

Last, but certainly not least, to my wonderful bookstagram street team. amsjadee.reads, along_the_tale, ymdash.reads, m organe.bookshelf, jayjaymite_reads, jen.lifeinbooks, booklover.k ez, readwithlaraa, fmc.reads, marnis.bookshelf, robertas_book-stagram_xo, throughthepages735 and coffee_book_catz. Thank you for helping me promote this book and sharing your thoughts and feelings, for the absolute bonkers comments, and for sharing all my posts.

Keep your eyes peeled for more Alex and Nate, coming Christmas 2025.

Printed in Great Britain
by Amazon